FROM BITTER TO SWEET

COMING HOME TRILOGY BOOK 3

THE WAY TO A WOMAN'S HEART SERIES

SHERIDAN JEANE

First published in Medina, Ohio, United States by Flowers & Fullerton.
FROM BITTER TO SWEET

www.FlowersAndFullerton.com
Medina, Ohio
Library of Congress: 2023907440
ISBN-13: 978-1-63303-026-8 (trade paperback)

First edition: 2023

To my dearest Tom Roberts, my partner in crime, my music man, my yinzer coach, and the Heinz ketchup to my fries. Your unwavering love and support have been the rhythm to my melody and the harmony to my chords. Thank you for always being there for me, through the snow and the slush, and for dancing through life with me, even when we stumble.

I'm grateful for every moment we've spent together, from listening to Jelly Roll Morton's sweet tunes to the way you hold me tight when the music fades. You make my heart sing, and I cherish every note of our love song. Thank you for being the vinyl to my turntable (or the shellac to my Victrola), and for making every moment feel like a swingin' good time.

BOOKS BY SHERIDAN JEANE

Contemporary Romances

The Way to a Woman's Heart series - the **Coming Home** trilogy

Slow Simmer
Here's the Scoop
From Bitter to Sweet

Coming in 2024
The Way to a Woman's Heart series - the **Destination Wedding** trilogy

Too Much On My Plate
Say Cheese!
Turkish Delight

Historical Romances

Gambling On a Scoundrel

§

Secrets and Seduction series:
Lady Cecilia Is Cordially Disinvited for Christmas
(A prequel only available through my VIP club)
It Takes a Spy…
Lady Catherine's Secret
Once Upon a Spy
My Lady, My Spy
Along Came a Spy

COOKING CLASS

Kincaid

My phone chimed with a text just as I slid my truck into a spot outside the Not A Yacht Club—my brother's restaurant—for my Monday night cooking class. I climbed out of my Ford into the April sunset. A pleasant wash of heat rolled off the parking lot.

I leaned against the door of my truck as I checked the message. It was from John Murphy, a potential new client.

> John: I forgot to mention Chrissy wants the master bathroom to have one of those all-in-one bidet toilets.

> Me: Sure thing. I'll include one in the bid.

I updated my notes for the Murphy bid using my smartphone. Adding a bidet meant I'd need to put an electrical tie-in near the toilet. Not a big deal since they wanted me to gut the room and start from bare walls.

Max Ross pulled his BMW into the lot and parked next to me. His brother Ford was in the passenger seat.

"Hey, Kincaid," Max said as he and his brother climbed out. He spotted my phone in my hand. "Still working?"

I stashed it in my pocket as we all started heading for the entrance. "I'm putting together a quote for a big place here in Sewickley. One of those mansions. Just making a few notes. How about you? Did you get your permit problems cleared up so you can film on Mount Washington?"

Ford grinned like he'd just won the lottery and clapped his brother on the back. "Max worked his magic and got everyone to play nice."

"All in a day's work," Max said with a shrug.

"Don't undersell yourself," Ford said. "You pulled off a damned miracle."

Last year, when Ford had sealed the deal to have his family produce his movie, I'd wondered how the brothers would handle working together. The potential for chaos had been palpable, but they'd exceeded everyone's expectations, even when they'd had to tackle a recent tragedy.

With Ford as the director and Max managing the marketing and promotion, they were an unstoppable team. When unexpected problems arose, they proved to be masters of quick thinking and resourcefulness, with emergency string-pulling coming naturally to Max. Even the stunts were in good hands with their youngest brother, Sean. And of course, their father's involvement as the head of Ross Film Productions only added to the impressive collaboration.

Ford ran a hand through his brown hair. "I love seeing Pittsburgh from up there. In my opinion, this city has one of the best vistas in the world. From the top of Mount Washington, you have a perfect bird's-eye view of the spot where all three rivers converge. It's gorgeous. I've been dying to incorporate that shot into *Ghost*." Ford pulled open the heavy oak door and ushered Max and me inside.

I stopped. "Wait. Where's Emma tonight?" I asked Max. His niece wasn't with him. "I thought you were going to bring her along. I haven't seen the squirt in a couple of months."

"She and Sonya got last-minute tickets to the ballet." Max shrugged. "They're looking forward to a night out together."

I headed toward the back of the restaurant with Ford and Max on my heels, and pushed through the swinging door into Dante's territory—his gleaming kitchen. He was the chef as well as my brother's business partner.

Dante placed some cartons of eggs on the counter and then waved us over. "Good to see you. Glad you all could make it tonight."

"Wouldn't miss it," I said. "This is usually my favorite meal of the week. What are we making?"

"Cheese soufflé. I have baguettes and a salad to go with it."

I rubbed at my beard. "A soufflé sounds intimidating."

"Aren't they supposed to be tricky?" Ford asked.

"Nah." Dante smirked. "Maybe fifty years ago when you had to whisk the eggs by hand, but with a decent mixer, they're easy. The secret is to buy quality—"

"Ingredients," Conner—my brother—interrupted as he came in from the cold room at the back of the kitchen. "You say that every week." He lifted his chin in greeting.

"Next week I'll have you make a Bittersweet Chocolate Soufflé," Dante said.

Someone pushed open the door leading in from the bar. It was Reed, the bartender—but his brother wasn't with him.

"Alone tonight?" Dante asked.

"My brother prefers to sleep." Reed sounded irritated. He flopped onto a tall stool and perched there like an angry crow.

"Sorry to hear it," Dante said. "I guess that means you get me as your cooking partner tonight."

Reed shrugged. "Works for me."

Dante watched Reed for another moment, then said, "Now that we're all here, we can get started."

Dante discussed fresh ingredients, room-temperature eggs, and the delicate state of the soufflé as it came out of the oven, but

Conner was only half-listening as he typed into his phone. The guy was always working.

"No loud noises or hard knocks, or your gorgeous soufflé will get lopsided, or worse, deflate entirely. If that happens, it'll still taste fine. But presentation is everything in this meal. You don't want it to go flat. If you're careful, your soufflé will look impressive as hell."

As I read through the recipe card, the directions seemed fairly straightforward. We needed to combine cheese and other ingredients on the stove to make the base, then allow it to cool before mixing in whipped egg whites, bake it, and voila: a soufflé.

Bake it, and *voila*. A soufflé.

I joined my brother Conner at one of the cooking stations Dante had set up for us. "You ready for this?" I asked.

"Give me just a second," Conner said as he continued typing something on his phone.

"Work?" I asked.

"Yeah. Finishing up an email to a supplier." A moment later, he pressed 'send' and then put his phone away. "Sorry about that. He needed a reply. Let's get started."

We only ran into problems when Conner added the whipped egg whites to the cheesy mixture. Instead of folding them in, like Dante had told us to, Conner grabbed a metal spoon and started rapidly stirring the eggs and cheese together.

"Conner," I said, "you aren't supposed to—"

"Conner, stop!" Dante yelled as he rushed over to us.

Conner halted and frowned. "Am I doing something wrong?"

Dante took the bowl from him, his tone gentle but firm. "The key here is to handle the egg whites with care. Too much force and you'll destroy all the bubbles, leaving you with a flat soufflé. Let me show you." With that, he exchanged the metal spoon for a large rubber spatula and deftly demonstrated the proper folding technique. With a flick of his wrist, he lifted the heavier cheese mixture from the bottom of the bowl, gently laying it across the top of the egg whites.

He repeated the process two more times, and then pushed the bowl to Conner. "Here. Try it again. Fold it together until you don't see any white streaks."

Conner shrugged, then tried again.

"Better." Dante nodded approvingly. "Much better."

My phone chimed. Another message from John Murphy. I shot off a quick reply.

"Work?" Conner asked as Dante headed back to cook with Reed.

"Yeah. I'm trying to win a bid on John and Chrissy Murphy's renovation project."

Conner snorted. "You'll need all the luck you can get with Chrissy. She's notorious for flaking out. John, on the other hand, can be a real hard-ass, but he's putty in her hands. If you want to succeed, you'll have to make sure you stay on her good side."

That put me on alert. "What kind of 'flaking out' are we talking about here?"

"The woman's never made a decision she didn't want to change five minutes later. Plus, she's constantly giving me advice on how I should run my restaurant."

That could be a problem. If I won the contract, I'd have to be careful about documenting any changes she requested. "Thanks for the heads-up."

Conner poured the cheesy mixture into the special soufflé pan with tall, straight sides. The delicate blend was puffy and pale yellow, with a light and airy texture.

"I heard a rumor," Conner said, "that Heather moved in with a guy who runs a construction company. One of your competitors."

I shook my head, but I wasn't surprised. "Classic Heather move. She probably only started seeing him because she hoped it would irritate me."

"Does it?"

The look of doubt in his eyes had me scowling at him. "Hell, no. I'm not hung up on the woman. I'm glad to be rid of her."

He nodded, looking pleased. "I'm just relieved you came to

your senses and called off the wedding. That woman might even be more self-centered than Mom was."

I shifted uncomfortably. "It'd be a tossup." Heather had completely fooled me when we were together. Even now, I felt like a complete jagoff for believing her lies. I'd been willing to change everything about my life based on her deceit. The idea of it still made my stomach churn. Maybe I had been too eager to be in a stable, committed relationship, too desperate to ignore the warning signs. Heather had caused enough damage already, and I didn't want her lies to alter my outlook on life or change me as a person. But most of all, I didn't want to be hurt like that again.

At least Conner and I were on the same page about one thing for a change. We were both relieved Heather was out of my life.

We put our soufflé in the oven and then joined the others. For the next half hour, we hung out drinking wine, talking, and watching Dante work his magic on the perfect salad.

"Cut up the baguette, why don't you?" Dante said as he handed me a bread knife.

As I sliced, the click of a woman's high heels announced a new presence in the kitchen. I glanced up to see my sister, still wearing her business clothes. "Hey, Courtney. I didn't know you were dropping by tonight." I set down the knife so I could give her a hug.

"Conner invited me. He said you'd feed me. I'm starving."

"Did you come straight from work?"

She nodded. "We're having trouble getting approval for the next step of a drug protocol, and I had to talk to someone on the west coast. The three-hour time difference kept me there late." She lifted her nose and inhaled deeply. "Something smells scrumptious."

"The soufflé will be ready in about ten minutes," I said, handing her a slice of baguette. "In the meantime, you can snack on this."

Without hesitation, she tore off a chunk and took a bite. "Delicious," she said, savoring the flavor. But then she paused and changed the subject. "Hey, remember my friend Lianna? She's the one who got divorced last year. Her bonus finally came through, and now she's ready to build that addition to her house. Has she contacted you yet to schedule an appointment?"

I nodded. "I'm stopping by first thing tomorrow morning to meet with her and take measurements."

Courtney narrowed her eyes at me. "I expect you to treat her right. She's a friend."

I gave her one of those 'what the hell are you thinking' looks. "As if I'd treat anyone badly. You know me better than that."

"She's good people."

"I know; I remember her. She was a sophomore when I was a senior. She even went to the prom with a friend of mine…Steve." We'd all hung out together that night—me with my date, and Lianna with Steve. She hadn't said much all night. "She was kind of quiet back then." Not to mention cute. "What's she like now?"

Courtney paused and seemed to choose her words carefully. "Nice. Intelligent. Kind." She stared at me. "Like I said, treat her right. I like her."

It didn't slip past me that Courtney didn't mention that Lianna was beautiful, which she was.

That seemed…strange. Courtney had been urging me to get back in the dating game since barely a month after my breakup with Heather. Did talking about Lianna mean she considered her off-limits, being a mutual friend? Or was Courtney employing some kind of reverse psychology tactic on me?

I wondered.

"I'm nice, too," I reminded her, ratcheting up my charm to get a reaction out of her. "Everyone always says so—have you forgotten?"

She gave me the stink-eye. "There's nice, and there's nice. No flirting. You haven't been out with anyone since breaking up with your evil ex-girlfriend, and I don't want Lianna to be your rebound. Don't make me choose between you and her, because you won't like the choice I make."

"Ouch. Message received."

Be nice to Lianna, but not *too* nice.

2

REKINDLED FLAMES AND
REMODELED SPACES

As I bit into my bagel and settled down to check my email, the doorbell rang. I couldn't help but cast a longing look at my cup of steaming coffee before reluctantly making my way to the door.

I had a hunch it was Kincaid Gillette. Promptness was to be expected, but fifteen minutes early seemed excessive.

"You're early," I said as I pulled open my front door. I froze. This wasn't Kincaid. It was his older sister, Courtney. The tall redhead looked immaculate in a pale blue dress and suit jacket that brought out the green in her eyes.

Courtney held out a book. "No; I'm right on time. Remember? I said I'd drop by this morning and bring you my copy of our book club book."

I smacked myself in the forehead with my palm. As I glanced at the cover of *The Prime of Miss Jean Brodie*, I wondered how was I going to read the whole thing in time. "It's a movie, too, right?"

Courtney rolled her eyes. "Yes. But the book is substantially different, so you can't get away with watching the movie instead."

"Can't blame a girl for trying," I said with a grin. "Do you want to come in? Have a cup of coffee?"

Courtney glanced at her watch. "I don't want to be here when Kincaid arrives. He'll think I'm checking up on him."

I raised an eyebrow. "Are you?"

She avoided my gaze. "Of course not. I just need to get to work. I ran a sample overnight and I'm dying to check the results."

"Go." I shooed her away. "Cure cancer, or whatever it is you do there."

"Right on the first try." She waggled her fingers as she headed down my front steps. "Bye."

As I walked back to my kitchen, my cell phone rang. I glanced at it to see my mom's smiling face on the caller ID. I tapped the screen and accepted the call, proving that either I was a devoted daughter, or temporarily insane.

"Hi, Mom. This is an early call. Is everything okay? No one's hurt?" I slid back onto my stool and finally sipped my java.

Divine.

"Oh, my. We're fine. Did I scare you by calling before eight?"

"A little. Listen, I can't talk long—"

"I know you have to leave for work. That's why I'm calling now, to catch you before you walk out the door."

"Actually, I—"

"I wanted to make sure *you're* okay."

I stilled. This couldn't be good.

"Okay?" I noticed I had a hangnail. "Okay about what?" I opened a kitchen drawer and pulled out a manicure set.

"Didn't your brother call last night? He said he would. He's taking Felicity for another ultrasound today because she's decided she wants to know the gender after all. I just wanted to check in and make sure you're doing okay. I know this has been tough on you."

I tamped down my irritation. Mom was trying to manage me again. Treating me as though I couldn't handle any updates concerning Felicity's pregnancy. I began bouncing my leg in agitation. "Of course, I'm okay. Why wouldn't I be?" I squeezed the clippers and nipped off the offending hangnail.

"I thought you might feel jealous." Her words hung in the air.

I winced as I accidentally cut off too much cuticle, and a small bead of blood appeared on my finger. Mom had the amazing talent of being able to irritate me without even trying.

"Don't be silly," I replied, keeping my voice light. "I'm not jealous. Troy and his wife have every right to have kids, and I'm happy for them. It's no big deal, really." I shifted restlessly on the kitchen barstool, wishing Mom would drop the subject. "Besides," I added with a forced smile, "you know Troy will make a great dad."

"Of course, he will. He's always been such a good son." Mom's happiness seeped into my ear like honey. I only wished she'd stop obsessing about my infertility. It wasn't as if my ability to procreate defined me as a person.

I shoved down my irritation. Of course, I was happy for Troy. I loved my brother—although perhaps not his wife. Felicity could be insanely manipulative. I'd never understand what Troy saw in her.

"Listen, Mom. We need to wrap this up. Someone's coming over to work up a bid on that addition I'm building." I crossed my kitchen and rummaged through a cabinet for a box of bandages for my finger.

"That's great news. Which company?"

"Gillette Construction," I replied, ripping open the paper wrapper of the bandage. The scent of antiseptic brought back memories of childhood scrapes and Mom's cool, steady hand soothing away the pain.

"Good choice. That's Kincaid Gillette's company, right? He has an excellent reputation. Didn't you go on a date with him back in high school?"

"Not with him," I clarified, feeling a twinge of discomfort at the memory. "We double-dated for prom when I was a sophomore. I was his friend's date."

Mom's silence stretched between us. She had something more she planned to say in this call, I could feel it in my bones. Finally, Mom broke. "I think you should get a second opinion."

Ah-ha. Mom's real reason for calling. "Mom, it's been nearly three years without a pregnancy. Paul's swimmers were fine. It's me. And besides, I'm single now. I've come to terms with my infertility, and I'm content with the path my life is taking. I plan to become the best program manager my company has ever seen, and go back to school for my MBA. Pretty soon, I'll be running the place."

"But Dr. Walker never found a reason. I think you should have gone to see someone younger. Someone who keeps up with the newest research."

I wrapped the bandage around my fingertip. Did Mom really want to talk about this again? She was always second-guessing me, and it drove me nuts. "Mom, I like Dr. Walker. You like Dr. Walker. He's known me for my entire life. For Pete's sake, he delivered me when I was born. I know he's old-school, I've done my research and he's up-to-date on the latest treatments."

"I know, but—"

"No 'buts.' Dr. Walker was doing all the right tests. I took my temperature daily to track when I ovulate. I've become so attuned to my own cycle that I can almost feel my egg pop out of my ovary. I took drugs to boost my ovulation, even though that meant I might have twins or even triplets."

"And Paul—"

"—had his sperm checked. No issues. He wasn't the problem. I was. Dr. Walker ran tons of tests. What did he find? Nothing he could fix." Well, that wasn't quite true. He'd detected a minor issue with my viscosity—a word I now hated. I'd taken an antibiotic to address *that* particular concern, but in retrospect, I now wondered if my "viscosity" issue had come from some infection I'd picked up from my asshole cheating ex-husband. After all, that's what antibiotics addressed, right? Infections.

"Maybe if you saw a different doctor…"

My fingertip throbbed. "I've accepted it, Mom. I'm infertile. You need to accept it, too. Stop hoping I'll get pregnant. That ship has sailed."

"Am I being too pushy? I'm sorry. I didn't mean to upset you. I only want what's best for you."

I lifted my chin and squared my shoulders. "Then ask me how work is going. Ask me about the addition I'm building. Ask me about anything else. Just quit bringing up the whole baby thing."

I glared at the cardboard box sitting on the counter as if it was responsible for all my frustration. Maybe tackling it would help me vent some steam.

I grabbed a knife from the block and sliced through the tape with a quick flick.

Mom sighed on the other end of the phone. "Did I mention I found a new tiramisu recipe? It's delicious."

I almost whooped with joy at the change of subject. "I love tiramisu. Can you send me the recipe?" I turned on my speaker-phone and started pulling paper-wrapped bundles from the box. Bits of white Styrofoam from the box's interior sprinkled onto my countertop.

"What's all that rattling I hear?"

"Sorry about that. I'm opening a box labeled 'kitchen' I came across in the garage last night. I really hope some of my missing gadgets are in here."

I immediately spotted the silicone-coated whisk I'd been missing. Next came my cookie press. Then I unwrapped a coffee mug and inhaled sharply. "My Favorite Girl," was emblazoned on the side.

"Is something wrong? Did you hurt yourself?"

I huffed. "Just a bad memory."

"Paul?"

I let out a derisive snort. "Who else? I found a coffee cup he gave me." I scowled as I dropped the cup in the trash can with a loud thunk. I definitely wasn't Paul's favorite girl anymore, and the last thing I needed was a reminder of that fact. "I hate how stupid he made me feel."

"I know, Sweetie. The man's an ass. I never did like him. How about I come over and we can smash that cup together? Turn it into something cathartic?"

I couldn't help but chuckle at the idea. "I like the way you think, but I'll pass. Too bad you never told me how much you disliked him."

"I'll never keep my opinions to myself again," she teased.

I imagined a future where Mom verbally dissected every man I dated and groaned theatrically. "Not that. I learned my lesson. I'll be more careful from now on. I won't be taken in by a pack of sweet-sounding lies."

"I'm so sorry he wasn't the man you thought he was. Just know that you're not stupid. He was the one who messed up, not you."

"Thank you, Mom. That means a lot to me. But it's hard not to feel foolish for trusting him for so long. He had me convinced that we were building a life together, but it was all a façade. His lies changed the trajectory of my life by preventing me from making informed decisions, and it's difficult to come to terms with that. Nevertheless, I'm trying to keep moving forward, and your support means a lot to me. People let you down. You move on. Words to live by."

I stared at the box as though it was an unexploded bomb. Would it contain any more unwelcome reminders of my ex? Did I want to risk detonating another emotional incendiary device? On the other hand, I might recover some of my long-lost kitchen tools. One last attempt, then, to end the box excavation on a high note.

With a deep breath, I reached in and selected a random object. I closed my eyes and waited a beat before I peeked inside my hand.

A smile lit up my face. "Jackpot!"

Mom paused mid-sentence in her description of an estate sale she wanted me to attend with her. "What happened?"

"I found my missing garlic press. It's a small victory, but it feels like a big win this morning."

On that positive note, I turned my attention to my wall calendar, a task I had been dreading. I might as well tackle it now and get it over with.

I flipped the page, revealing the month of May, along with a new photo of Pittsburgh. This one was of a bright red trolley gliding up the steep side of a mountain. The Duquesne Incline. When my eye landed on May 1st, I let out a groan.

"Your garlic press? I thought you'd have been happy about that." Judging by the waver in her voice, Mom seemed to be clutching at this tidbit as though it was a life preserver and our conversation was about to go down for the third time.

"A small victory in my quest for a fully functional kitchen," I said, forcing a lighthearted tone. "Who knows? Maybe I'll even find my missing can opener next."

There was a reason I had been postponing this minor task. Today was May 1st. The plain white square on the calendar looked perfectly normal, but seeing it still made my stomach feel queasy. I'd never forget what had happened on this day.

I let out a sigh. I should tell Mom what was bothering me. "This is a tough day for me. It was exactly one year ago when I found Paul in bed with that woman." I dropped that little conversational bomb without considering the effect it might have on Mom.

Mom gasped, then recovered quickly. "Well, maybe you can search for something more uplifting in that box. Maybe a magic wand that can erase bad memories?" Her laugh sounded forced. "Or, even better, a recipe for a magical potion that will make your ex disappear."

My entire world had changed when I'd come home early to prepare an elaborate dinner to celebrate Paul's promotion. I wasn't sure who'd been more surprised. Me, to discover my husband had started celebrating without me. My husband, whom I'd caught with his cock buried inside another woman. Or Gloria, the aforementioned penis receptacle.

As I'd stood in my bedroom doorway in stunned silence, my mouth gaping in shock, Paul had squawked, "This isn't what it looks like." And Gloria had slapped him across the face yelling, "You said you were getting a divorce!"

"A divorce?" I'd parroted.

I'd seen the awful truth of it on his face.

Fury had filled me. "Good idea. Let's make it official." I'd left without saying another word.

Now, the doorbell rang, providing me with the chance to give this conversation the burial at sea it needed. "Sorry. I have to go. Kincaid is here."

I ended the call, then sighed, disappointed in myself for the way I'd handled everything. I'd have to visit her later and smooth things over.

I glanced down at my clothes and nervously brushed bits of Styrofoam off my slim-fitting, knee-length black skirt. It was silly to feel flustered about seeing Kincaid again.

I bet he barely remembered me. Sure, we'd double-dated at his senior prom, but other than that, we'd only ever had one class together in high school: gym my sophomore year. He'd been two years ahead of me and hadn't seemed to notice me except when we'd competed in a badminton match—which I'd won. That was it. The highlights of our social interactions.

It didn't matter if he remembered me or not, though. Today he was here to bid on my construction project, not to reconnect.

I hurried through my century-old house, the timbre of my heels changing from sharp to hollow as I stepped off the ceramic tile and onto the hardwood floor. I glanced around my living space. Everything was in order.

This time, I paused to look through the peephole rather than assuming I knew who was out there. Kincaid's face was turned away as he took in the expansive view of the town of Sewickley spread out below him.

Kincaid wore crisp khakis and a dark blue polo-style shirt that fit snugly around his muscular biceps, and he had a clipboard tucked under his arm.

I unlocked the door as he spun to face me. His green eyes flickered in—recognition? Appreciation?

His neatly trimmed beard looked good. The man was decidedly sexy. Over the years of living in the same town together, I'd noticed his beard appeared in the fall and disappeared again sometime in the spring. He'd probably be shaving it off again soon. It suited him, but so did his clean-shaven look. I had to admit, though, his rugged good looks and full lips seemed even more masculine with that beard. I wondered briefly if it would be soft if I kissed him. Not that I would, of course, but a woman wonders about things like that.

Kincaid appeared to freeze for a moment as he met my gaze. Then, he unleashed his killer smile—the one that always tugged at something deep inside me. When he turned it on me, the corners of his eyes crinkled, and I couldn't help but notice that his was a face that smiled often. Even his green eyes were in on it, seeming to light up with an inner warmth. Something inside me melted just a bit at being on the receiving end of that smile.

"Lianna. It's great to see you again." He paused as he seemed to take me in. "I don't think we've spoken since prom night. What was that? Ten years ago?"

I took a step back so he could come into my home. "More like eleven, but who's counting? Did you forget? We also had gym together that year."

"That's right. I remember now. How's Steve these days?"

"Steve Hanson?" I shook my head. "You'd know better than I would. I haven't spoken to him since he left for college. You two were pretty good friends as I recall."

Kincaid shrugged noncommittally. "Sure. Sewickley High is a

small school. You end up knowing just about everyone in your class. Besides, we were both on the football team."

I'd always loved attending the games and hanging out with my friends in the stands. "Whatever happened to him? His family moved away after he graduated. We lost touch."

"He went to Temple University," Kincaid said. "Lives in Brooklyn now. In the Williamsburg area. Married. Two kids. His wife's involved in the art scene there. They seem happy."

"Williamsburg," I repeated, having no trouble envisioning Steve as a hipster. "Nice. Good for him. It sounds like he has a wonderful life."

As Kincaid stepped into the foyer, his eyes darted around, taking in the surroundings. "You have a nice place. Have you lived here long?"

"Just a few months. I bought it last summer, and I'm still settling in. But I really love it here. I want to build an addition off the kitchen. Come on back. I'll show you what I had in mind."

I led him to the back of the house. He walked so silently that I had to glance back to make sure he was following me. I caught his gaze flick up to examine my crown molding with interest.

"Nice woodwork." Once we reached the kitchen, he took a moment to survey the space. "You want to add a first-floor powder room and laundry room. Do I have that right?"

I nodded. "That's the plan. I've been envisioning it ever since I bought the place. Having only the one bathroom upstairs is a problem when I have guests. Plus, moving the washer and dryer up from the basement will make my life a lot easier."

Kincaid looked around the kitchen, taking note of the various cooking implements and utensils. "I see you like to cook," he said with a hint of amusement in his voice.

"What gave me away?" I glanced at my clean countertops, but nothing was out of place. No crumbs on the table. No supplies sitting out. What clues had he seen?

"That bag of onions in the bowl. The stoneware garlic keeper. The J. A. Henckels knives in the block next to the stove." His mouth twitched and then he smiled. "I have a set just like them."

I raised my eyebrows in surprise. "You cook, too?"

Kincaid nodded, a wry smile playing at the corners of his mouth, and lifted one shoulder in a casual shrug. "I started taking Dante's cooking classes at Not a Yacht Club last summer, and I'm starting to get pretty good at it. I enjoy good food, so I decided to take Dante up on his challenge and learn to cook."

"Good decision." I admired a person who spotted an area where they could improve themselves and took action to address it.

He gestured toward my back door. "Is that where you want your addition?"

I nodded confidently but couldn't help feeling a twinge of nervousness as I handed him my rough sketch. I fumbled with the papers in my file folder, worried that my lack of drawing skills might have made it difficult to convey my vision. "I thought it might look something like this, but it's just a general idea. I'm no architect—not by a long shot—but I know what I want. There seems to be plenty of room back here, and it would work well with the flow of the house." As I spoke, I couldn't help but wonder how much this addition would cost, but I pushed the thought aside. I was determined to make my home exactly what I wanted it to be.

He examined the sketch for a moment. "Can I keep this?"

"Sure. I made that copy for you."

He lifted his papers on his clipboard and tucked my design beneath them. "Let me take some measurements outside. It'll take me ten minutes or so." He glanced down at my high heels. "You're welcome to join me—"

I chuckled. "I'm not dressed to traipse around the backyard with you. I'd end up ruining my heels."

"I'll come back in when I'm done and take some interior measurements. Will you want the exterior to match the current clapboard finish, or did you have something else in mind?"

"Clapboard. I want the addition to look seamless. As though it's always been here."

"Got it." Kincaid scribbled some notes on his clipboard before pulling out a sleek, high-tech device. "This is my electronic tape measure. It's one of my favorite tools when I'm putting together an estimate."

As he stepped outside, I finally took another sip of my coffee, only to find it cold and bitter. I dumped it out with a sigh and turned to the task of unloading the dishwasher, stealing glances out the window to keep track of Kincaid's progress.

I watched him move around the yard with a sense of anticipation, wondering what he was thinking as he examined the foundation of my home. His strong hands moved across the clipboard in long, confident strokes, and I found myself getting lost in the rhythm of his movements.

His hair was fairly short on the sides, but in the back, it tapered to a point just above the nape of his neck. I couldn't seem to look away. If I stroked it, how would it feel? Soft, like one of my sister's watercolor paintbrushes?

Stop it. I needed to get a grip on myself. I turned away from the window and finished unloading the dishwasher. Unfortunately, it didn't take long, so it didn't provide much of a distraction.

As I gave in and peeked outside again, Kincaid leaned over to pick up his clipboard, showing off the muscled curve of his backside. I imagined running my hands over it, pressing him against me.

Stop it, girl.

Not going there. He was Courtney's brother, and I didn't want to mess up our friendship.

As I typed furiously on my phone, trying to focus on work and *not* on ogling the gorgeous man, the back door suddenly swung open. I jumped, almost dropping my phone. Kincaid stepped inside, wiping his feet on the rug before pulling a pair of elastic booties from his pocket and sliding them over his shoes.

"Everything looks good out there," he said, his voice low and smooth. He scanned the room before his eyes settled on the ceiling. "What's above this room?"

My heart beat faster at his proximity. "The master bedroom," I managed to say, sounding breathless even to my own ears. "My window overlooks the backyard."

"Have you considered doing a two-story addition so you can have a walk-in closet off upstairs?" he asked, his gaze holding mine. "Most hundred-year-old houses don't have much storage space, and if it's something you're considering, this would be a perfect time to do it."

I gaped at him. The man was an absolute genius. Could I really have a decent-sized closet? "That's brilliant. Right now I'm using two armoires. A real closet would be paradise." I lifted my hand to my mouth, biting on the edge of my fingernail before scowling at my bandage. "Would it cost much?"

"I can run the estimate both ways and you can decide," he said, his eyes still fixed on mine. The tension between us was palpable, the air thick with something that felt like desire. Of course, the man had just uttered the words "walk-in closet." He's lucky I hadn't jumped him.

I was more jazzed about getting a walk-in closet than I'd been about ogling Kincaid's nicely formed backside. What did that say about me? "I'd love that. Thanks."

"Lead the way upstairs. I'll need to take a few measurements in your bedroom, and I'd like to look at your attic as well."

I stiffened. I hadn't planned to have him in my bedroom, so I hadn't bothered to make the bed. I glanced at him, but if he was aware of my consternation, he didn't show it.

"This way." I headed back toward the staircase at the front entrance. What would Kincaid say if he knew he'd be the very first man to ever step foot into my new bedroom?

3

CHECKING THINGS OUT

Kincaid

I followed a few paces behind Lianna as we climbed the staircase, unable to resist stealing glances at her backside. She wore a knee-length pencil skirt that was probably supposed to be businesslike, but the slit up the back gave me a tantalizing glimpse of her creamy inner thigh that was downright distracting.

The woman had always been stunning, with her natural grace and quick wit, but seeing her again after all these years, I was struck by how much she'd grown into herself. Her long hair was swept up in a messy bun, with a few wispy tendrils framing her face. I couldn't help but feel a little nervous around her.

When we reached the top of the stairs, I trained my gaze on the mahogany banister, hoping to avoid getting caught staring at her ass. The wood was solid under my grip, and it helped me think about something other than Lianna Alverson's inner thighs.

I glanced up and found her watching my hand on the banister. "Your house has beautiful woodwork," I said, trying to distract myself from my attraction to her. "Great architectural details."

"I love that about this house. The details, I mean." Her throat moved as she swallowed. Was she feeling the same tension that I was?

"The bedroom's this way."

I followed her down a short hallway, keeping my eyes focused on the walls and door frames instead of her curves. When we entered her bedroom, I couldn't help but take in the cozy atmosphere.

"Nice fireplace," I commented, my eyes lingering on the hearth. An image of Lianna lying in her bed, bathed in the warm glow of the fire, flashed through my mind. I swallowed and pushed down the dangerous thought. "Does it work?"

"Sure does," she said, a smile curving her lips. "It's cozy up here in the winter."

"This is a great room," I said, looking around. The lavender-blue walls matched the bedspread, and the soft lighting created a warm and inviting atmosphere. On the dresser, a bottle of Chanel Number 5 perfume sat next to a folded stack of laundry, while a slightly askew white silk flower arrangement added a touch of charm. The armoires she had mentioned were enormous, and although the room was not very spacious, she had managed to make it her own.

My gaze wandered over to the queen-size bed, and I couldn't help but notice that one side was neatly made while the other was rumpled. It was evident that this was the bed of a woman who slept alone. As I glanced at the white body pillow peeking out from under the sheets, a thought crossed my mind: did she snuggle with it at night? The idea was endearing, but it also made me wonder what it would be like to be the one she curled up against, her body pressed close to mine, our legs entwined.

I shook my head, trying to erase the thought. No, this was a bad idea. Mixing my personal life with my business was a recipe for disaster. Lianna was Courtney's friend as well as a potential client, and I needed to keep things professional. I turned to her with a smile.

I'd been burned twice, and didn't plan to go back for thirds. When I'd first started my business, I'd been dating a great woman who'd had asked me if I had any work for her younger brother, who was an "excellent house painter." I'd hired him without checking his references, and he'd turned out to have a terrible work ethic. I'd had to fire him, and my girlfriend had been furious with me. Ex-girlfriend.

Lianna bent over to pick up a pair of shoes from next to her bed, and I found myself admiring her curves.

Shit, don't go there.

The second time I'd mixed business with pleasure, the woman I'd been dating had asked me to "help" her with a bathroom remodeling project. It turned out that her idea of 'help' was for me to do all the work while she watched. Or went shopping. She even expected me to provide all the building supplies from the "extras" she assumed I had stockpiled in a warehouse somewhere. As if I had extra bathtubs just lying around. When I'd provided her with an estimate for all the materials she'd need to buy, she'd freaked out and dumped me.

Mixing work and pleasure wasn't worth the inevitable fallout.

I pushed the memories aside, focusing on Lianna's stunning figure. I wouldn't repeat past mistakes, no matter how much I was tempted.

I yanked my gaze away from her and focused on the window overlooking the backyard. I needed to do my job, not ogle a prospective client.

She turned to face me. "What do you think? Does it look like you could add a closet?"

I cleared my throat. "I think so, but I need to take a few measurements first."

Once I finished jotting down the interior dimensions, I lifted the window sash. There was no screen in place, so I ducked down and poked my head through it. I shifted my weight and peered up at the roof. The shingles looked relatively new, so I'd probably be able to match them with no trouble. Before I finalized things, I'd need to get up in the attic and look around, but from what I'd seen so far, the house had been well-built and well-maintained.

As I pulled my head back inside the room, Lianna suddenly

turned away from me. Her gaze was focused on a folded pile of laundry, her eyes widened, and she started cramming it into her dresser drawer. Were those leopard-print panties? That's not what I'd have expected her to be hiding under that professional-looking exterior.

She closed her dresser with a thump. The stack of laundry was gone—neatly stashed away. She leaned one hip against her dresser as she faced me. "How does the exterior look?"

"No surprises, which is good news. I'd like to go ahead and check out the attic."

"Sure." Lianna pushed away from the dresser and headed toward the bedroom door.

As we passed the second bedroom, I glanced inside. She had it set up as a guest room. It also lacked a closet, just like her room, but it had an armoire.

The hallway had two steps leading up to a closed door. She pulled it open and reached up to tug on a chain. A weak lightbulb winked on, and I followed her through the door and up another staircase.

At the top, I stepped into a semi-finished attic. All it held were a few neatly stacked red and green plastic bins and a bulky dark green Christmas tree storage bag. At the far end, a window with plain white sheers let in the morning light. Dust motes floated above the unfinished wood floor. The roof had strips of rolled insulation tacked in place between the rafters.

I examined the area where a new roof would join with the existing one. Fortunately, I found no surprises here, either.

I wrote down more measurements, snapped some photos, tucked my electronic tape measure back into my pocket, and then turned to face Lianna. "I think I have everything I need. I'll be able to have your estimate ready in a couple of days. Perhaps as early as tomorrow evening."

"That fast?"

"You're catching me at a good time. I usually have multiple projects going on at once, but right now I only have two. A new one is scheduled to begin Monday, but another is winding down in the next day or two, so it all evens out. Besides, since you're Courtney's friend, I'll make you a priority."

"If I decide to go forward, how soon can you start?"

"As soon as the building permit goes through."

"That's awesome."

I couldn't help but notice the way her eyes sparkled with enthusiasm. "I'll contact you when I have the estimate ready so we can review it together."

Lianna checked her watch. "Sounds good. Either call or text, and we'll set up a time."

She led the way back down the attic staircase. At the bottom, she paused to let me pass and then pulled the chain to turn off the light. When she closed the door and turned to move past me, her heel went sliding across the hardwood floor. She fell right into my arms.

"My heel—" She glanced up at me, and our eyes locked for a moment. She was close. I could smell her bodywash—something floral and elegant. Maybe it was that perfume from her dresser. Chanel Number 5. She also carried the scent of toothpaste and coffee on her breath. Scents I associated with a morning-after romp in bed. Something I hadn't experienced in a very long time.

Lianna flattened her hand against my chest, and the warmth of her palm shot straight into me like a lance. Her eyes darkened as her pupils dilated in the dim light of the hallway. Or was it due to something else—like being in my arms?

I was attracted to her, but I couldn't act on it. She was a prospective client, my sister's friend. That made this situation a tricky one.

I definitely couldn't dip my head down and taste her lips, no matter how much I wanted to. No matter what her eyes were telling me right now. No matter how soft she felt pressed against me.

I swallowed and shuffled away from her. "Are you okay?"

Her mouth tightened into a frown as she turned away from

me. "I'm fine. My heel slid on the hardwood floor." She held onto my forearm as she balanced on one foot and pulled off the offending shoe. She wobbled slightly, so I put my hand under her elbow to steady her.

Lianna flipped the shoe over and examined the sole. "A nail head wore through the heel. I'll have to drop them off at the shoe repair shop before I can wear them again." She kicked off the mate, scooped it up, and then padded down the hallway to her bedroom. "I need to grab a different pair."

She opened the double doors of her wardrobe and then bent over and began poking around, causing her backside to wiggle provocatively.

I closed my eyes before they popped out of my head. When I heard the doors to her wardrobe click shut, I opened them again only to discover she was wearing a pair of red spiked heels and was sliding a red bracelet onto her wrist.

Holy hell—that was one sexy look.

She checked her wristwatch. "I need to hurry if I'm going to make my meeting on time," she said. She moved toward the door and carefully edged past me, almost as though she didn't want to risk brushing against me again. Now that I was attuned to the scent of her perfume, it seemed to hit me even harder this time around. When she went down the staircase, I followed like a dog on a leash.

I hesitated, both wanting to kiss her goodbye and knowing what a horrible idea that would be. Instead, I turned on my heel. "I'll be in touch." I headed directly toward the front door and pulled it open.

She didn't meet my eyes. "Bye," was all she said.

She closed and locked the door.

I took a deep breath of the damp spring air, but it did nothing to clear Lianna Alverson from my system.

Damn. This could be a problem.

4

DO IT!

Lianna

Later that evening after work, I maneuvered my car into one of the few remaining spots in the Not a Yacht Club parking lot. What was going on here? Tuesday nights weren't usually this crowded.

As I stepped out of my ride, I heard music coming from the enormous garage door-sized windows facing the Ohio River. That explained the crowd. Allyson, a local musician, was performing tonight, and she always managed to fill the place whenever she had a gig. She was slim, pale, with white-blond hair, and happened to be one of the sweetest people you could ever come across. What really made her stand out was that she had a set of pipes that wouldn't quit.

I headed into the ground floor bar to meet Courtney rather than upstairs to the restaurant. I scanned the room and spotted her at a high-top table.

"Hey, girl." I hung my purse on the back of the tall chair. "I didn't realize Allyson was singing tonight. How did you manage to snag one of the best tables?"

"It was Conner's. I was sitting with him, but he had to leave. You don't get to sit and relax for long when you're the one in charge."

I moved over on the seat. "I'm surprised you found him out here at all. He rarely takes a break."

"She's one of his favorite performers. Did you know he gave Allyson her start? He's friends with her dad and says he first heard her sing as a kid. He took a chance on her after she graduated from high school last year. He says hiring her was one of the best decisions he's ever made. She always draws a crowd."

"So, Conner takes a brotherly interest in her?"

Courtney looked at me blankly for a moment and then burst out laughing. "You're wondering if Conner has a thing for Allyson? Not likely. He treats her like a sister... and I should know since I've been on the receiving end his brotherly attention for my entire life. Besides, he's been hung up on someone else for years now."

"Really? An old flame?"

Courtney frowned and glanced away. "I shouldn't have said anything. It's his business. He wouldn't want me talking about it."

Interesting. I wondered who it was, but I didn't press her.

When Allyson's song ended, a long round of applause greeted her. "Thank you, everyone. If you'll give me five, I need to take a short break." She set her guitar on a stand and stepped off the small stage.

The room started to buzz with conversation. I settled back in my chair. "What's going on with you? This morning you mentioned running a test. Was it a success?"

Her lips pressed tightly into a grimace. "Nope. I spent the day trying to figure out why. I'll run it again, in case there was an error, but I'm pretty disappointed. But overall, my life is about the same as always. Work. Family. Book club. Not much has changed."

"What about Richard?" I didn't really like the man, but he'd stuck with Courtney longer than most. Nearly three months now. Most men were intimidated by her.

The corners of Courtney's mouth turned down. "I'm not sure.

We had a date two nights ago. It was a business event, and when it was over, he dropped me off at home and didn't want to come in."

"Was he tired?"

"I guess." Courtney shrugged in a manner that suggested resignation.

A server stopped by to take our drink orders. "Want to try one of Reed's new concoctions?" the woman asked. "He's offering a spectacular coconut-infused mojito, if you're in the mood. We grow the mint in our garden."

"Sounds perfect." I always looked forward to trying one of Reed's new drinks. He was a creative bartender and had invented a banana old fashioned with walnut bitters last year that was out of this world.

"I'll take another glass of this Cabernet Sauvignon." Courtney's wine glass was nearly empty.

"Will do." Our server spun on her heel and hurried toward the bar.

"How about you?" Courtney directed her laser-focused gaze onto me. "Did Kincaid stop by this morning to take your measurements?"

Recalling Kincaid's hands around me, keeping me from falling, I felt myself flush. I shifted in my seat, cursing my pale skin. Hoping the dim lighting of the bar would hide my embarrassment from Courtney, I replied, "Yes, he did." I leaned back in my chair, toying with my red bracelet. Should I tell her what happened earlier? Probably not the best way to start discussing our appointment this morning. "I didn't expect him to remember me, considering we haven't spoken since high school. But he did."

Courtney gave me an odd look.

The drinks arrived, and the server said, "Conner says this round is on the house."

Courtney looked pleased. "He's a good brother. Tell him thanks."

"I'll pass it on." She lifted the drink tray up to her shoulder as she left.

I took a sip of my coconut mojito. "Wow. Amazing. Reed has outdone himself. This is excellent." I took another sip.

"So, what do you think of my baby brother?"

Something about the gleam in Courtney's eye made me wary. "He seems to know what he's doing."

"He's a quite a guy, don't you think?"

What the heck? Was Courtney talking up her brother?

I took another sip to buy myself some time. "He has some good ideas. He suggested I make it a two-story addition and include a walk-in closet for my bedroom. That would be fabulous if I can swing the added expense."

A slow smile spread across Courtney's face. "I knew it. You're into him. I can tell."

My jaw dropped open. Courtney couldn't possibly have figured that out based on what I'd just said.

Before I could deny it, she held up her hand to stop me. "I normally don't get involved in other people's business—"

I raised one eyebrow in disbelief. "Yes, you do. You always think you know best."

Courtney scowled at me. "I do know best. Remember that." She flipped her long, sleek red hair behind her shoulder. "I was afraid if I didn't speak up you might think you shouldn't see him simply because he's my brother. I want you to know I'm fine with the two of you going out. He's a great guy. I think you'd be good together."

I gave a cartoonish head shake that almost knocked me off my seat. "Wait a minute. Are you telling me you wanted me to hire him just so you could throw us together?"

Courtney looked at me as though she was trying to decide if one of the circuits in my brain had just shorted out. "Of course not. I recommended him because he's the best contractor in the area. Just ask around. Everyone loves his work."

"Then why are you talking about us being 'good together?' You aren't making sense."

She leaned back slightly and stared at me. "You're a project manager. You know as well as I do that timing is everything. In chemistry, things need to be done in the correct order, otherwise you'll ruin what you're creating, and you'll end up with crap. Or worse."

"Worse?"

"You know—like accidentally creating an explosion. Or poison gas—like when you mix ammonia and bleach. Any number of bad results. Take your pick. People and relationships are the same way. In my opinion—as an armchair psychologist—it's time for you to make a change in your life. You need get back out there again."

I scowled at her. "What do you think I've been doing these past two months? I've been on dating apps. I've even met three different guys in person." Three different disappointments.

"I think you've been playing it safe. You showed me your Match profile. Really, Lianna, you can present yourself in a better light."

My eyes narrowed. "I'm new to all this. I thought my profile was pretty good. I don't want guys contacting me just because they think I'm hot. I want them to be interested in who I am as a person. Besides, if you think I need to improve my profile, you could simply tell me rather than sniping at me."

Courtney leaned forward and covered my hand with her own. "I'm sorry. That came out wrong. You know me; I'm too blunt. What I'm trying to say is that I think you're being overly cautious. I can't blame you. You've been hurt. I think you've been trying to dip a toe into the dating world when what you really need to do is dive in."

I squeezed Courtney's hand and then pulled mine away. "You may be right. I'll look at my profile when I get home and work on it."

Courtney sat up straight and frowned at me. "What about Kincaid?"

I gave her a perplexed look. "What about Kincaid? Are you kidding me? Not only is he your sibling, but he and I could be entering into a business deal. The last thing I want to do is complicate matters by getting emotionally involved with him. What if things don't work out? I would be stuck seeing him work on my house every day. That would be uncomfortable. And what about our friendship? Have you thought about what it could do to that?"

Courtney stared at me. "You *do* realize that you won't be there while he's working, right? You'll be at your office. Also, he has workers who do the specialized jobs. A plumbing crew. An electrical crew. A drywall crew. Tile. Framing. He has individuals who do all that stuff. He oversees everything and is pretty hands-on, but he isn't there all the time. Furthermore, you'd have a signed contract that would establish clear lines of responsibility for your house."

True. A well-written contract could keep things professional. Since Kincaid came so highly recommended, I shouldn't have to worry about shoddy workmanship. But what if there were other problems I couldn't predict?

Courtney grinned. "And if it works out and you two really click, we'd get to hang out at family get-togethers. I'd love that." She broke off as she glanced behind me, and her face split into a broad smile. "Rose! How are you?"

I swiveled around to see Rose approaching us with a man by her side. She must have had time to go home and change after work, because she wasn't wearing one of her sensible librarian outfits. Instead, she wore a summery light blue floral print dress that made her sapphire-blue eyes seem more intense than usual. I didn't recognize the well-dressed man at her elbow. A date?

A spark of relief flashed in Rose's eyes at our warm greeting. "Hi. This is Gregory."

Rose hadn't mentioned the guy at our last book club meeting, so I was guessing he was new. She and I usually discussed our dating successes and failures. "Are you here to listen to Allyson?" I asked.

"We have a reservation in the dining room upstairs," Rose said, "but we're early and our table isn't ready yet. Since Allyson is singing, we thought we'd wait down here."

Gregory rested a proprietary hand on the small of Rose's back, which seemed presumptuous of him. As the librarian of the public library's teen section, Rose believed it was her responsibility to behave as a role model. She certainly wouldn't appreciate some guy getting handsy with her in public. As if on cue, she sidled away from Gregory's touch.

"First date?" Courtney asked.

Gregory dropped his hand to his side and gave us a bright white smile. "Second. Does it show?"

Courtney lifted her wineglass to her lips and took a sip. "A bit."

"Would you like to join us while you wait for your table?" I gestured to the single empty chair.

Gregory used the opportunity to put his hands on Rose again and guide her toward the seat.

"Thanks." Rose slid onto the stool. "I love listening to Allyson sing."

Gregory moved to hover close to her, so Courtney scooted her chair over to give them more room. "Conner loves having her perform here. She always fills the place."

Allyson stepped back up onto the stage to a smattering of applause.

Rose glanced at Gregory. "Courtney's brother is one of the owners."

"Really? He has a great location." Gregory reached into his pocket, pulled out a business card, and handed it to Courtney. "Let him know that if he's in the market for a financial planner, I'd love to meet with him." He paused to look at his watch. To me, it seemed like a calculated move to draw attention to his pricey timepiece. I recognized the Breitling logo on the watch face. My ex-husband had loved them and had dragged me into countless stores so he could check out the new styles the elite watchmaker produced each year.

Rose stiffened and shot Courtney an apologetic glance.

Courtney narrowed her eyes at Gregory. She obviously wasn't impressed with Mr. Pretentious's dating etiquette.

Based on Rose's increasing discomfort, I doubted she'd ever go out with the guy again.

Gregory abruptly pulled his phone from his pocket. He glanced at it and announced, "Looks like our table is ready." He stepped back so Rose could stand. "It was nice to meet you. I look forward to talking to your brother. I have some great ideas I think he'll be interested in hearing about."

"I'll be sure to pass that on." Courtney gave him a tight smile. "Bye-bye, now."

Gregory tried to slide his hand to the small of Rose's back again, but she hurried after the hostess.

Courtney grimaced. "I hate awkward dates like that. I bet he wasn't so handsy on their first date. It can be hard to find a good guy. The bad ones are so good at pretending."

I let out a snort. "I can attest to that. Paul had me fooled for three years."

"Paul was an ass." Courtney's tone was flat. "It isn't your fault he lied to you. It's his."

"It's my fault for believing him. For swallowing his lies about business trips and long hours."

"That's on him, not you. You're well rid of him." She sipped her wine. "There are good guys out there."

"If you say so."

Courtney met my gaze. "Kincaid is one. You should go out with him. He's great."

I stilled, recalling that moment when I'd tripped and found myself in his arms—and wanted him to kiss me. For an instant, I'd been certain he would. When he hadn't, I'd convinced myself

I'd been mistaken. I had to admit, though—I'd been disappointed when he hadn't.

I frowned. "Stop trying to pimp out your brother. It's weird. Besides, it isn't as if he asked me out."

Allyson strummed her guitar, back from her break and preparing to start her next set. The conversation in the room diminished.

Courtney glanced at the stage, her brows furrowing with concern, then rushed to say, "But if he did—what would you say?" She stared at me intently, apparently trying to read my thoughts—or use mind-control. "It's time for Kincaid to put himself out there again. I'd hate it if you shot him down."

I narrowed my eyes. "What do you mean, 'get back out there again?' Did something happen to him? A bad breakup?" The last thing I needed was to deal with someone else's baggage.

That thought suddenly struck me as...wrong. Did I actually expect to meet someone who was a blank slate? Who'd never been in a relationship? Would I even want someone like that? Someone who'd never learned how to live with another person? Someone who didn't know how to take part in those day-to-day negotiations and compromises that couples always faced? Someone used to having things his way?

"Don't worry. No skeletons." Courtney sat back and stroked the stem of her wineglass. "Just a woman who deceived him. Nothing you haven't had to deal with yourself."

I let out a laugh. "No deep dark secrets, then? Just trust issues?"

She sighed. "After what Paul did, I expect you're going to have trouble trusting anyone. How could you not, after the man who promised to love, honor, and cherish you decided to betray you? Just remember, you aren't the only person who's ever been hurt."

"I get it. Everyone had baggage." I met Courtney's gaze. "If he asks, I won't reject him on principle."

When she grinned in victory, I held up my hand. "Not so fast. I still reserve the right to reject him if there's no chemistry."

Allyson strummed her guitar, and the room grew quiet again.

Courtney's grin didn't fade. "Oh, *please*," she murmured. "No chemistry? I saw the way you blushed when I mentioned him earlier. There's *definitely* chemistry."

5

THE PUSH

Kincaid

As I drove home, I put together a simple plan for my evening. I'd make dinner and then prepare Lianna's estimate. Easy enough.

Lianna had been a pleasant surprise. That dark wavy hair up in a messy bun. That smile that made her brown eyes sparkle with good humor. They were interesting eyes. If I wasn't mistaken, they held all the colors of a nice piece of mahogany.

And damn. That slit in her skirt. That image had invaded my thoughts all day.

I scrubbed my hand down my face and smoothed my beard. Focus, Kincaid. Focus.

Lianna didn't live far from the family with the sunroom renovation. If I finished up her estimate tonight, I could drop it off tomorrow night after I met with them and picked up their final payment.

What would she look like when she opened her front door? Would she still be wearing her work clothes? That straight skirt with the slit up the back had been hella-sexy, but I'd love to see her in something casual. Jeans or a pair of form-fitting leggings would be nice. Very nice.

Maybe she'd trip and fall into my arms again. Having her

body—both soft and firm—pressed against mine had been an unexpected bonus. And she'd smelled fantastic, too, fresh from her morning shower and wearing that amazing perfume. An image of Lianna Alverson's body beaded with water flashed through my mind.

Not going there. She was a potential client.

But then again, it wasn't every day that a gorgeous, intelligent, single woman hired me to build an addition. Come to think of it, this might be a first.

I entered my house and put my keys on the hall table. A flash of gray and cream fur flew down the staircase and then sprang to the top of the newel post.

Meeoww! Mick let out a Siamese cat command as he balanced on the square-topped post and stared at my shoulder with grave intent. I set the clipboard with my notes and measurements next to my keys and then edged closer to my cat. Mick seized the opportunity and immediately launched himself through the air to execute a perfect landing on my shoulder.

No claws. All pad. Ten out of ten.

I dipped my head forward.

Mick was already purring as he padded his front feet along the back of my neck and then draped himself across my shoulders like a yoke.

A warm, furry, purring yoke.

"Miss me?" I rubbed the top of Mick's head as I headed toward the kitchen. Mick pressed his head hard against my hand and purred even louder.

I flipped on the faucet at the farmhouse sink, washed my hands, and then moved on to the important work of preparing dinner with a furry audience member on my shoulders. I pulled the chicken breast I'd been marinating from the refrigerator, grabbed an onion and some garlic cloves, and then selected a knife from the J. A. Heckles block. Mick contentedly supervised everything with an approving purr.

I stared down at the blade in my hand. Lianna liked to cook, too, which I found attractive. This might be the first time in history that a man had been turned on by a woman's choice of kitchen knives.

I heated some olive oil in a skillet and then made quick work of dicing the onion.

Mick didn't approve of the onion. As soon as the sharp fumes hit his nostrils, he jerked his head back and then dropped to the floor.

"Wimp."

Mick shot me an irritated glare and proceeded to lick his paws and clean his face.

Using the back of my knife, I scraped the onions off the cutting board and into the pan, then squeezed two garlic cloves in my garlic press and added them the pan.

I never could have pulled together a meal this easily just a year ago. Dante's cooking lessons had really paid off.

The kitchen was redolent with scents of garlic and onion. I put the marinated chicken breast into the skillet, browned it, added some broth from a carton, and then set the lid on it and left it to simmer.

While dinner finished cooking, I made a salad and cut off a slice of whole grain bread from the loaf I'd picked up yesterday.

Just over ten minutes later, I plated the food, added a splash of white wine to my pan, reduced the liquid, and then poured it over the chicken.

Perfect.

When I was done eating, I quickly loaded the dishwasher. The bottom rack was full, but the contents of the upper rack looked remarkably similar to Lianna's. One coffee cup. One water glass. The only difference was tonight's wine glass on the top shelf.

One.

I grabbed my notes from the hall table and then headed upstairs to my home office.

Mick trailed behind me.

This was our nightly routine.

I sat at my desk, reviewed my handwritten notes, pulled up a template on my laptop, and began working up an estimate. It wasn't long before Mick climbed under my elbows and slinked onto my lap.

At first, he purred and stared intently at my computer screen. Then, he edged closer to the keyboard.

"*Mick.*" My voice rose at the end in a warning tone. "Stop. I'm busy."

The cat eased back onto my lap. This wouldn't last long, but I was nearly done with my work.

I stared at the measurements I'd taken and realized there'd be plenty of room to add some first-floor storage along the wall of the addition. Every chef could use more cabinet space. It took a few more minutes, but I came up with a couple of alternatives for adding some kitchen storage, giving her a small butler's pantry.

I imagined Lianna's reaction when I showed her this design. She'd be thrilled, I was certain of it. That was one part of the job I always enjoyed—finding small ways to give the client even more than they'd expected from a project. There were always some relatively quick and easy solutions for including storage in these older homes. I'd have my architect prepare the final plans, but from experience, I knew my drawing was pretty accurate.

This time when Mick began to edge toward my laptop, I let him. The cat moved slowly, as though he thought stealth was the key to successfully interrupting my work.

I saved the estimate on my computer as Mick crept from my lap and onto my desk. A moment later, he draped himself across my forearms, purring lustily as he settled in place.

The cocky cat thought he'd pulled something over on me.

I copied my standard contract, customized it with Lianna's name and project details, and printed everything.

Finally, I picked him up. Mick's blue eyes became slits of pure bliss as I flipped him onto his back and cradled his limp, furry body in my arms. This was what the cat had been angling for with all those stealthy moves.

I scratched Mick's chin, head, and shoulders. It was cat bliss—until it wasn't. Mick could go from being contented to irritated in a flash, and woe be to me if I didn't pick up on the cues. I'd earned a few scratches before I'd learned to read his body language.

My cell phone rang. Good timing. I rolled Mick out of my arms and onto the floor.

I pulled the phone from my pocket and glanced at the screen before taking the call. "Hey, Courtney. How's it going?"

"Good. I had dinner with Lianna. She says you stopped by her place today."

"Are you checking up on me?"

"Why not? It's my job. I'm your big sister." Her tone sounded casual.

Too casual.

"Nope. Not buying it. You haven't asked me about a client in months, and now you've brought up Lianna twice in two days." I picked up the documents from the printer and tucked them into a new manila file folder. I grabbed a felt-tipped pen, wrote "Alverson, L" on the tab, and tucked it into my clipboard.

"Maybe that's because you've never done work for one of my friends before."

I paused. "Does that bother you?"

Courtney gave a throaty laugh. "Don't be silly. Of course not. If it had, I never would have suggested she contact you."

"Then why so much interest?" I clomped down the staircase and deposited the clipboard on the hall table next to my keys, then headed toward the kitchen.

"No real reason."

That had been evasive. "Courtney? What's going on?"

"Can you manage to not be so suspicious, just this once?" she asked with a hint of frustration in her voice.

"Kind of hard when you're being all secretive."

"Am not."

"Are too. You suck at it. You always have."

"You know, that's kind of mean." Courtney pretended to be annoyed with me, but she was really bad at it.

"I call 'em like I see 'em. Spill. Just be direct with me."

She huffed out a sigh. "Fine. I was calling because I wanted to find out if you like Lianna."

I stilled for a moment, then picked up the wine bottle and poured some into a fresh glass. Now I'd have two of them in the dishwasher.

"Kincaid? Are you still there?"

"I was just trying to decide if I had traveled back in time again and was back in middle school. Are you sure you don't want to pass me a note in class?"

She let out a frustrated sigh. "You're being evasive."

"You're one to talk."

"Would it be easier for you to give me an answer if I told you what she said about you?"

I was about to sip my wine, but I paused. "Maybe. Depends."

"I asked her if you'd asked her out, and she seemed flustered."

I rolled my eyes. "Of course, she seemed flustered. You have as much tact as a bulldozer." I took a large gulp of wine. Shame to treat good wine that way. It should be enjoyed, not gulped.

I took another gulp.

"That wasn't the problem. She said she couldn't date you because she'd be your client and things could get complicated."

I went still. That was an interesting excuse. "Really?"

"But I convinced her that you're the best builder in town and there won't be any problems. Besides, you'll have a signed contract that handles any issues, right? That seemed to calm her fears." Courtney paused, and then rushed to get out the rest of it. "I know I'm meddling again, but she said she'd go out with you if you asked."

"Say what?" A warmth spread through my chest that I couldn't blame on the wine.

"You can't tell her I told you."

"You don't want me to tell your friend that you revealed the details of a private conversation to me?" I asked, sarcastically. "I wonder why? Courtney, what's gotten into you?"

"What's gotten into me?" she snapped. "When was the last time you went on a date? You haven't gone out with anyone more than twice since you ended things with Heather last fall."

"Courtney!" I said sharply. "Who or when I date isn't any of your business."

"Isn't it? You're my brother. Of course, it's my business." She sighed heavily. "Listen. You're attracted to Lianna. She's attracted to you. If you ask her out, she'll say yes. So, do it. Ask her out. And if it doesn't work out, she's a class act. She won't go all Heather on you."

I let out a snort. "Go 'all Heather' on me? Is that what you call it?"

"It works."

I grunted.

"Listen 'Caid. You and Lianna are both good people. You're well-adjusted, levelheaded adults. You should be able to date each other. If you're really worried, then make sure you're both clear about your expectations up front. In fact, I think that would be a great idea. You have trust issues. She has trust issues. Get it all out in the open and you'll both rest easier."

I frowned. "What do you mean, she has trust issues?"

"No, no, no. I'm not going there. I've already revealed way too much. If you want to know more about Lianna, it's up to you to get to know her."

I finished off my wine and set the glass in the dishwasher next to the other one. "Fine. I'll bite. I'll ask her out after we get the project details nailed down. Although, if she decides not to hire me, that might be awkward."

Courtney let out a satisfied hum that sounded remarkably like Mick's purr. "Perfect."

6

CONTRACT

LIANNA

When I came home from work on Wednesday, I changed my clothes, put on my favorite fluffy pink slippers, and headed downstairs to the kitchen. With luck, I could get dinner started before Kincaid arrived.

I opened my refrigerator to grab the chicken I'd left defrosting all day, but it wasn't there. Apparently, in my rush to leave this morning, I'd forgotten to take it out of the freezer.

I sighed. That completely destroyed my timetable for tonight.

When I turned and noticed the two stamped envelopes poking out of the top of my purse, I let out another sigh. I'd forgotten to put them in my mailbox when I'd come home.

As I headed for the front door, I considered my dinner options. Defrost something in the microwave? Order pizza?

Pulling my cell phone from my pocket, I checked the time as I opened the door. I walked forward without looking and barreled directly into Kincaid's chest.

My letters fluttered to the ground and landed next to a file folder Kincaid dropped as well.

He grabbed my elbow to steady me. Damn, he felt solid and warm. "Are you okay?" He held onto me as I caught my balance.

"I'm fine. Sorry about that. Running into you is like running into a brick wall. That's twice in two days you've kept me from falling."

He bent and picked up my letters and the file. When he stood back up, his eyes were crinkled at the corners with his grin. "With that kind of track record, you might want to reconsider living in a house on top of a hill. Either move somewhere else, or put up a sturdier handrail."

"Funny, Kincaid." I held out my hand for my envelopes.

He started to hand them to me, then pulled them back. "Were you about to leave these in the mailbox?"

"That was the plan."

He turned away from me. "I got it. You don't want to get your slippers dirty."

I glanced down at my feet. I'd forgotten how absurd my slippers might look to someone else. They were puffy and fluffy and pink, and they cheered me up whenever I looked at them. Plus, they were amazingly comfortable.

Kincaid seemed to like them, though. He trotted down the steps—twelve of them—then put the envelopes in my mailbox and lifted the metal flag on the side.

"Thanks for accommodating my schedule," I said as he reached the top of the steps. "I just got home a few minutes ago."

"No problem." He followed me into the house and back to my kitchen. "Do you work late often?"

"Once or twice a week. Tomorrow should be an easy day, which is rare." Things were ramping down now that the new software release was out the door. My company had better pick up another project soon, though. Too many people were idle at the moment.

"Easy sounds nice."

"Easy-peasy," I quipped.

The corners of his mouth curled up. "Lemon-squeezy."

I grinned. "That's supposed to be my line."

We kept smiling at each other for a moment, and then Kincaid cleared his throat.

"I put this together last night. I added a couple of new design suggestions I think you'll like." He thrust the folder toward me. "Everything is itemized on the last page so you can make a decision based on your budget."

I waved him to a barstool at the counter and took the one next to him.

When I saw that his design added a butler's pantry, my jaw dropped. "You can give me more kitchen storage space?"

A muscle twitched in his forearm. "I thought you'd like that."

I flipped to the last page to look at his estimate. Now, that was surprising. "This isn't nearly as bad as I was afraid it would be. Adding all that closet space on the second floor only adds a little less than fifty percent to your overall estimate."

I grinned as I bounced my pink-slippered foot up and down on the chair rung. This was fabulous.

"I added two closets, including one for the second bedroom. Assuming no significant issues, we're good to go. Your new plumbing and electrical systems help a lot. While the house seems well-maintained, we won't know for sure until we start working. Major complications are unlikely, but I can't guarantee there won't be any."

I read the contract carefully. "Can I scale back if you find structural problems after I've given the go-ahead?"

"Probably. We have checkpoints to discuss any changes you want to make. I'll let you know the cost and you decide."

Excitement percolated inside me. This was actually going to happen. "I like that a lot." I shifted on the barstool, squirming a bit. "That's similar to the way I work as a program manager. Checking in and adjusting plans, I mean."

"Yeah? I always find that it's best to be clear about expectations up front. Then there are no misunderstandings."

"Precisely." I turned my attention to the signature page of the contract. I stared at it for a moment and then set it on the counter.

"You don't have to sign today if you aren't ready. You're welcome to think it over for a few days."

"No." I stood, grabbed a pen from the kitchen drawer, then turned to face him. "I'm certain I'm in good hands. You have excellent references. Plus, I've known you since high school, and you're Courtney's brother." I scrawled my signature on the contract in a large, looping hand.

Kincaid grinned as he held out his hand for me to shake. "You won't regret it."

"I'm expecting something pretty damned amazing, Kincaid," I told him, only half-teasing.

"And that's what you'll get. I'll start working on the building permits right away. With luck, we'll be able to break ground on the foundation in a little over a week. Two at the most."

"This is exciting."

"The exciting part comes when construction begins. The next couple of weeks consist of paperwork and patience."

I sat on the stool, bouncing one fluffy-slippered foot up and down. "It's exciting to me. I've been dreaming about this addition ever since I moved in." A grin spread across my face.

"In that case, we should celebrate. Let me take you to dinner."

7

DINNER, NOT A DATE

Kincaid

Lianna narrowed her eyes. "Do you normally take new clients out to dinner?"

She had me there. "Only the ones I've known since high school."

"And how many fall into that category?"

I pretended to count on my fingers, then met her gaze. "So far —one. If I include you."

The corners of her mouth tugged up. "Are you asking me on a date?"

Was that a glimmer of hopefulness I detected in her eyes?

I watched her. I didn't want to rush this, but I didn't want to leave her wondering, either. I hated knowing Courtney had extracted a promise from her to go out with me if I asked her. I didn't want her to feel obligated. "Let's call it dinner for right now. You can decide later if you'd like to recategorize it as a date."

She pursed her lips as she considered my offer. I really liked those lips.

"Maybe it can be a pre-date?" Her sexy lips slid into a grin. "Sort of like meeting a person from a dating app for coffee."

"Just like that. Except that we've known each other since high school. And you're friends with my sister."

"Exactly. So, it's almost identical." That pert smile of hers slayed me.

"Do you like Chinese food?"

"I do." She glanced down at her fluffy pink slippers. "I should probably put on some actual shoes."

"Don't do it on my account. Those are adorable, and they look comfortable as hell."

Her cheeks turned a bit rosier. "They are, but I might get some strange stares. I'll be right back."

We both stood at the same time and ended up brushing against one another. I caught another scent of that perfume.

She hurried upstairs. A minute later, I heard a thump from her bedroom above me.

My phone chimed.

Courtney: Have you seen Lianna yet?

Me: She just signed the contract. We're heading out to dinner.

Courtney: She said yes??? Let me know how the date goes. :-)

Me: Absolutely not. And it isn't a date. It's dinner.

Courtney: Spoilsport.

I silenced my phone so she couldn't keep bugging me, and then tucked it into my back pocket just as Lianna came back into the room.

"Feeling less comfortable now?" I asked.

She gave me a strange look. "Say what?"

"Weren't the slippers more comfortable than those shoes?"

"Actually, yes. They were." She chuckled. "But these ones

aren't bad either." She grabbed her purse and asked, "Who's driving, you or me?"

"Me. Dinner was my idea, after all."

"Good point. After you, good sir."

I smiled at her teasing tone. "A chivalrous gentleman should always let a lady go first," I replied with a wink.

"Well said." She gave me a saucy grin.

At my truck, I opened the passenger door for her. My Ford sat high off the ground, and she had to step onto the running board to climb inside, causing her jeans to tighten over her backside.

I went to the driver's side door as I pondered her perfectly rounded ass. "You mentioned you're a program manager," I said as I slid behind the wheel. "Tell me about your job."

She thought for a moment. "I work for a company that develops software solutions for other companies. My job is to coordinate all the work and liaise with the client. Mostly, I manage expectations and put out fires."

I let out a huff of laughter. "You just described *my* job. Except for the software part." I spotted two kids playing catch in front of a nearby house, and I eased my foot off the gas pedal as a precaution. When I reached the end of the street, I turned onto the main road and drove downhill toward the village.

"Actually, that's a great analogy. Your homeowners are like my clients, except I also have my own department head, the director of projects, and my company's CEO to please."

"Whereas I have to please the homeowners, building inspectors, contractors, and neighbors."

"Neighbors?"

"Noise complaints. Community rules. Historical society rules —which won't be an issue for you since you don't live in a historic district. It varies from job to job. Despite all the headaches, I really like running my own company."

I caught her staring at my forearms, so I tightened my grip on the steering wheel. She looked away and licked her lips. A faint flush of color warmed her cheeks.

If I wasn't mistaken, I'd just caught her thinking some decidedly naughty things about me. The thought drove me crazy.

"I like being in charge." I gave her a sidelong glance. What would she be like in bed? Would she let me take charge there, or would she challenge me for control? Either option sounded good —or both.

"Good to know. I like a man who knows what he wants."

Was she flirting with me? I shot her a grin. "Do you, now? I feel the same way; I happen to like a woman who knows what she wants."

She glanced at me, a faint smile playing on her lips. "I don't like conflict, so I try to find a solution that works for everyone. A win-win scenario. My goal is to find the option that makes everyone happy."

"Does that mean you're a control freak who hates to argue?"

Her grin was lightning fast. "That's an accurate description. What about you? Why do you like renovating houses?"

I considered the question as I drove through the main intersection in Sewickley and spotted an open parking spot near the restaurant.

"I like being in control too, but I always keep the other person's wants and needs at the forefront." I fixed my gaze on hers.

"So, as your client, my wants and needs will always come first with you?" A smile played on her lips. "That's good to know."

I parked the truck and turned to her, meeting her eyes. "And that's not just for my clients," I said. "I can promise you that if we decide to date, you'll always come first."

She shot me a playful smile, but then hid it behind a stern expression. "I'll come first?" She blushed again and this time the color went partway down her neck. This might be my new favorite activity. Flustering Lianna.

"Exactly."

She cleared her throat. "That's good to know." She seemed to be having trouble with her mouth. The way the corners were twitching made it look like she was trying hard not to smile. "That's probably why you have the reputation for being the best contractor around."

"Flattery will get you everywhere." I opened my door and climbed out.

"Truth isn't flattery," Lianna called out just before I shut my door.

As I walked to the front of my truck, she met me on the sidewalk.

When she slid her hand in mine, I looked down at her in surprise.

"I think we're a lot alike in when it comes to work," she said. "We both love what we do, and we give it our all."

I squeezed hers back. "I should warn you, I've been accused of working too hard."

Her eyes snapped to meet mine. "Me, too." We stared at one another for a long moment until the restaurant door swung open and a young family stepped outside. The mom clutched a takeout bag in one hand and had her other arm occupied with balancing a pink-beribboned toddler on her hip. The dad held the hand of a boy of about five.

"Can we go to the candy store now?" the boy asked.

The dad stopped dead in his tracks to stare down at his son. "You can't still be hungry."

"Yes, he can," the mom said. "That kid will eat us out of house and home."

"Candy!" the pink-beribboned toddler crowed. "Gummy worms! Red hots!"

The dad turned and headed in the direction of the candy store. "What's your favorite?"

"Chocolate."

The dad grinned broadly. "That's my boy. A chip off the old block."

The boy grabbed his dad's hand with both of his and swung from it. "A chocolate chip?"

"You can each have something small," the mom said breezily as they headed down the street.

Lianna watched them, her expression wistful.

I held open the door for her, but as we made our way to a booth, I couldn't help but notice her tense posture and subdued demeanor. Something had changed, but I wasn't sure what.

It didn't take long for us to settle in at our table and place our drink orders. Red wine for her, beer for me. We discussed what we wanted to eat, but nothing more. It was as though Lianna had mentally gone somewhere else.

When the drinks arrived, we ordered dinner, and she sipped her wine slowly. She regularly touched the stem of the glass and toyed with the base.

Our easy back-and-forth banter from a few minutes ago had vanished, and I wasn't sure how to get back to it.

"Tell me about your life," I said. "What've you been up to since prom?"

A whisper of a smile flickered across her face, but it didn't linger. "I graduated from Sewickley High."

"Congratulations," I teased.

The corners of her mouth twitched. "I graduated from Penn State with a bachelor's in information systems technology. But I found that I preferred program management once I started working. Over time, I've taken on more responsibility, and I recently earned my PMP certification after completing the training and testing."

"PMP? What's that?"

"Project Management Professional. It's sort of the gold standard in certifications when it comes to project management. In order to maintain it, I'll have to take continuing education classes. I'm Agile certified as well."

I waggled my eyebrows. "I don't know what that means either, but I like the idea of dating an agile woman. It conjures some interesting images."

She gave a mock scowl. "Get your mind out of the gutter,

Kincaid. Agile is a framework for project management. It focuses on communication, flexibility, and collaboration."

I narrowed my eyes. "That actually sounds intriguing. Why is it I've never heard of it before?"

"It's a term you'd probably only run across if you're involved in software development. Although, Agile is starting to make inroads in other fields."

"You'll have to tell me more about it—later. Right now, I'd like to know more about you."

Her grip on the stem of the wineglass tightened as she spoke. "I went through a divorce last year," she said, her eyes fixed on the glass as her thumb rubbed up and down its stem.

I placed my hand over hers, taking care not to spill her wine. "I didn't mean to make you uncomfortable."

"No, it's okay. It's probably best that you know." She let out a sigh. "A year ago, I came home early to make a surprise dinner to celebrate Paul's promotion and found him in our bed with another woman."

My body tensed at the thought. "He brought her to your house? To your bed? That's beyond the pale, even for cheating."

"Wasn't it, though?" she said with a pained laugh. "I left him, of course. He signed the papers without a fight. Ninety days later, everything was final. He bought out my share of our house. No great loss. I never wanted to set foot in that place again." She sipped her wine. "I used the money for a downpayment on my new place and moved in last fall."

"Have you dated anyone since then?" I didn't want to be her rebound.

She shrugged; her eyes fixed on my hand resting on hers. "I've been on a few dates since the divorce, but nothing's clicked. A couple of second dates, but no third ones."

That was promising.

"What about us? Do we click?"

She finally met my eyes. "Perhaps." The corner of her mouth

twitched, and then a smile broke through. "There's definitely a potential for clicking."

Our server appeared, balancing a tray above one shoulder. We let go of each other's hands as she set two platters on our table and removed the silver domes covering them. "Enjoy." She hurried away.

Lianna deftly opened a flat container and extracted a thin, pancake-like wrapper. She laid it out on her plate, added a spoonful of thick, dark-brown sauce down the center, and piled on a generous helping of the Mu-Shu chicken. With practiced ease, she rolled it into a burrito shape. When she caught me watching her intently, she paused. "Have you never tried Mu-Shu before?"

"Oh, I've had it. I was simply enjoying watching you. You have beautiful hands."

She stilled. "No one's ever complimented my hands before."

"That's hard to believe. They're very graceful."

She grinned devilishly and then affected a husky voice. "If I make another one for you, will you turn to putty?" Her voice was so rich and sensual it conjured images of an old video clip of Marilyn Monroe singing happy birthday to President Kennedy.

I stared at her for a moment with my mouth gaping and my tongue all but hanging out before I managed to corral my thoughts. "Jesus, Lianna. That voice. It should come with some sort of warning label for extreme sexiness." I shifted uncomfortably in my seat.

Her saucy grin turned up a notch. "Sorry. Too much?"

"Never. That was exactly the right amount." I shook my head in bemusement. "And I'd love it if you'd make me one of those Mu-Shu things."

"Take this one." She slid it onto my plate and then set about making another. She kept glancing up at me, and I couldn't tear my eyes away. What was wrong with me? It wasn't as if she was doing a striptease.

"My friends and I used to do Marilyn Monroe impressions."

Lianna rolled the second pancake into a burrito shape and then licked a bit of brown sauce off the end of her finger. When I swallowed reflexively, she made a devilish grin. "I love that recording of her singing to President Kennedy."

"You were pitch perfect."

"Thanks." She bit into her Mu-Shu chicken, so I followed suit.

"This is delicious," I mumbled.

"I'm glad you like it, not that I can take much credit. All I did was assemble it. The hoisin sauce is what gives it all the flavor."

"That's the brown stuff, right? I like it. I've never tried cooking Chinese food at home."

"It's actually pretty easy. You should try it sometime."

Now that whatever had been troubling her had dissipated, talking with Lianna proved to be effortless. Natural.

Everything about this woman captivated me. Her laugh. The graceful way she tilted her head as she listened to me. Her insightful comments. Her wit. It was all perfect. She'd been like this on prom night too, not that her date had noticed. Mine had though, and that had been a problem.

"What about you, Kincaid? You haven't told me anything about yourself tonight."

"You're friends with my sister. What has she said about me?"

"Not much, oddly enough."

I moved my empty plate to one side and rested my elbows on the table. "I went to college to study engineering, but hated it. I ended up taking a lot of business and architecture classes and earned a business degree. Now I put it to use running Gillette Construction."

"Ever married?"

The server appeared at that moment and dropped off the bill.

"Almost," I said as I picked up the check. "I got engaged last year, but it fell apart."

"Oh, no. I'm sorry to hear that. I hope the breakup wasn't too traumatic."

Frowning, I glanced at the bill and slid some twenties into the folder, buying myself some time. Lianna had been honest with me, and I owed her the same. "We got engaged when she told me she was pregnant," I said, grimacing. "But a couple of months later, I found out it was all a lie. She'd faked the whole thing."

"What?" Lianna went still.

"One of my friends spotted her out drinking with her girlfriends and overheard her tell them she wasn't really pregnant. When I confronted her about it, she admitted everything."

Lianna looked furious. "That's despicable."

I fixed my gaze on her. "I should warn you; I have some trust issues. That's why I'm being upfront with you."

She frowned as she nodded. "I appreciate that." She began twirling her empty wine glass by the stem. "Were you disappointed she wasn't pregnant?"

"At first, I was simply angry that she'd lied to me. Tricked me. We broke up, and I went to a weird place in my head. It was like I'd lost both her and the baby all at once, and I missed the baby even more than I missed her, but that's stupid, because the baby never even existed."

"No. It isn't weird at all. Losing the dream of a baby can be heartbreaking." The flash of pain that swept across her face clutched at my heart.

Had she lost a baby?

An instant later, her face turned to stone, as though she'd slipped on a mask.

"Ready to go?" She didn't wait for my answer, but immediately stood. She shuffled from foot to foot and glanced toward the front door.

"Sure."

As we passed through the restaurant doors, I took her hand in mine. I was relieved when she didn't pull away.

The family we'd seen earlier was parked next to my truck. The mom was buckling the daughter into her car seat as the dad stuffed a big bag from the toy store down the block into the rear of their SUV.

My shoulder brushed against Lianna's as we walked down the sidewalk. For a moment she began to relax and seemed to enjoy being close to me, but then something changed, and she straightened her spine and edged away.

This time when I opened the passenger door, she scurried inside and yanked it shut.

We drove the short distance back to her house in silence. As soon as I parked, she scooted out faster than my cat could dart through an open front door. I froze in the midst of turning off my engine to stare at her in surprise.

"Thanks for dinner," she said, her gaze fixed on my hand resting on the key, rather than meeting my eyes through the open passenger door.

I turned off the engine. "I'll walk you to the door."

"You don't need to. I won't be kissing you goodnight. I'm having second thoughts about this whole dating thing." She shut the passenger door with a decisive clunk.

Stepping out of the truck, I didn't know what had caused her to freeze me out, but I refused to let things end on such a sour note after such a promising start.

"I'll walk you to the door," I repeated.

She circled my truck, then approached me warily at the bottom of the steps.

I longed to recapture the moments of flirtation we'd shared, but I couldn't think of a way to do it.

I flipped my keys around my index finger. "I don't expect a kiss, but I always walk a woman to her door." When she still looked doubtful, I added, "No kissing. I promise."

She relented, but she didn't take my hand as we walked up the steps together.

As she attempted to slide her key into the lock, the entire bunch slipped from her hand and clattered to the ground. We both leaned down to retrieve them, and our heads collided with a solid thud.

"Ow." She rubbed her head as she wobbled.

I grabbed her elbow so she wouldn't tumble down the steps. "Are you okay?"

"You must think I'm a complete klutz."

I handed over her keys. "Nah. Don't forget, I've played badminton against you. You're no klutz."

"You remember that?" She seemed to relax a fraction.

"How could I forget? You stole the game from me."

"I won fair and square! I even made it to the semifinals."

"No. You absolutely did not win 'fair and square.' You had me so distracted with those shorts you wore that day that I could hardly focus on the birdie."

She arched an eyebrow. "You've got to be kidding. Whose fault is that? Don't go trying to blame me for your teenage lack of self-control."

"You have to admit, you were being just a bit underhanded."

"You're just trying to make excuses. Clutching at straws. Rewriting history. I always followed the school dress code. It's not my fault adolescent-you couldn't stay focused. There was nothing inappropriate about my shorts. They were perfectly fine."

"Perfectly fine. Definitely." I waggled my eyebrows.

"Stop it." She jabbed me with her elbow, but not hard. The tension between us was gone once again.

This was how I liked her. Relaxed and sassy. "How about a rematch?"

"Do you have a badminton set?"

"Hmm. No. But there's always the paddle court. Tell me you play. All the women in Sewickley seem to play paddle."

"As a matter of fact, yes. I'm in the league up at the YMCA. You play, too?"

"I used to play tennis."

She eyed me doubtfully. "When's the last time you were on a court?"

"It's been a few months." More like a few years.

"You do realize paddle and tennis are very different, right? Being good at one doesn't mean you'll be good at the other."

"Yeah, yeah. I know. It's a mashup of tennis, squash, and racquetball." Mom had always tried to get me out on the court with her, but I'd rarely given in. The game wasn't for me.

"It's a really lively game. I doubt you'll be fast enough if you don't play regularly. It'd hardly be a fair contest."

"I've played paddle. It would be hard not to, growing up in Sewickley. Everyone here is obsessed with it."

"When did you play?"

"With my mom."

"When?"

"It's been a while." At least ten years—which was when Mom had left. "Play me. That way we can put this pesky rivalry behind us." I offered up my most endearing smile. "You know you'll have fun."

She let out a long-suffering sigh. "Fine. If you insist, we can play. Just don't expect me to go easy on you."

"Great. Let's meet after work tomorrow. Can you be there by seven?"

"Um... sure." She narrowed her eyes at me. "Is this another date?"

"I don't know. Is it?"

"I don't know." She glanced at her front door, and I suspected she was considering bolting.

"Then, for now, let's just call it a paddle match. Nothing more."

"A paddle match." She still sounded a bit doubtful.

"It's a date. A not-date," I amended. "I'll reserve a court."

That coaxed a smile from her. "A not-date. That sounds good." The flirtatious woman I'd sparred with on the way to dinner was back again. The one who kept disappearing on me.

Her honey-flecked mahogany brown eyes seemed less guarded as she locked gazes with me. She must have liked what she saw, because she rocked toward me slightly, her lips parting.

She wanted to kiss me just as much as I wanted to kiss her.

Time to remind her I'd already promised not to. At her request.

I leaned so close that our lips almost brushed, but then changed course and took the key from her hand. I backed away, slid it into the lock, and opened her door for her. "See you tomorrow." I handed the keyring back to her.

She took them, looking stunned and more than a little disappointed. "Good night?"

My mouth twitched in a suppressed smile. "Like I promised. No kissing. Or did you forget?"

Her eyes widened in realization. "Good night," she said softly.

"Good night." I turned away to conceal my smile and then trotted down her front steps.

Maybe it was for the best that we hadn't kissed yet. After all, the best things were worth waiting for.

8

PADDLE

LIANNA

The next day, as the sun dipped lower in the sky, I arrived at the paddle court parking lot behind the YMCA. Pulling in beside Kincaid's truck, I grabbed my backpack and paddleball paddle before making my way up the hill toward the court. That's when I spotted Kincaid chatting with Elyse Larkin.

Under normal circumstances, I adored Elyse. Loved her, even. Who wouldn't? She was dynamic and intelligent and amazing. But seeing her with Kincaid sent a sudden stab of red-hot jealousy right into the pit of my stomach.

My reaction left me reeling. Gut-level jealousy was a relatively new emotion for me. Other than the day I'd found Paul in bed with another woman, I'd never been the type to react that way. Sure, it was a normal response when catching your husband cheating, but it was a bit over the top to react this way when seeing a guy you liked talking to another woman.

I needed to get a grip. After all, Kincaid wasn't the one who'd cheated on me, so I shouldn't treat him as if he had.

Shaking my head, I tried to rid myself of the crazy, possessive thoughts. After all, Kincaid and I weren't even dating. With my backpack now slung over my shoulder, I continued toward the courts, keeping my gaze fixed on them as I trotted up the stairs.

As I approached, I couldn't help but admire how well Kincaid and Elyse complemented each other. Her pale blond hair contrasted beautifully with his dark complexion, making them an attractive pair. Elyse's dynamic personality was a bundle of energy and contradictions: a martial arts studio owner with a pilot's license. Any man would be lucky to catch her attention—if he could convince her to slow down long enough to notice him.

Although she looked stunning in her snug-fitting black top and azure blue leggings, I didn't think she was right for Kincaid. The man needed someone more down-to-earth. Elyse was a fireball, and she'd probably burn through Kincaid without even realizing it.

As Elyse approached me, she exuded mischief. "Kincaid tells me you're about to stage a rematch that's been brewing since high school. You'd better kick his ass, girl. I expect nothing less." As she drew closer, she lowered her voice so only I could hear. "It's such a nice ass, too. Try not to bruise it too badly."

I flashed a grin. "You look so sweet, but that mouth! Why aren't you blushing?"

"Talent, practice, and hard work." She grinned wickedly as she waved at Kincaid over her shoulder. "Good luck," she called out to him. "You'll need it." With a wicked smirk, she snapped a quick photo of us before jogging for the stairs. "That's to remember you by, just in case you destroy him and he goes into hiding from the shame."

"Your lack of confidence wounds me," Kincaid called after her.

"You'd better pray that's the only wound you have after Lianna's done with you," Elyse teased. "I hope you wore a cup." At Kincaid's mock-horrified expression, she let out a laugh and jogged down the steps to the parking lot.

"She's just trying to rattle you." I patted his forearm. "I'd never try to unman you intentionally."

He raised an eyebrow at my words. "Please don't," he said, mock-serious. "Let's not even discuss that possibility."

"Mum's the word."

Kincaid placed his warm hand at the small of my back and led me toward one of the gates that opened to the court. Despite my best efforts, his touch left me flustered. It had been so long since anyone had touched me like that. I tried to keep my composure, but Kincaid was a tactile person, and it wasn't easy to ignore the heat emanating from his hand.

"We have the back court for the next hour," Kincaid said, interrupting my thoughts.

I edged away from him as we passed through the gate. "That gives me plenty of time to kick your butt."

"I need to lodge a complaint. You have me at a disadvantage again, just like in high school. I'm calling a foul."

"What are you talking about?"

"Look at what you're wearing. You're killing me, here."

As I set down my backpack, I glanced down at my clothes and then scowled at him. "I'm wearing black leggings, a sports bra, and a t-shirt. Nothing special. Elyse's outfit was much more provocative."

"Was it? I didn't notice. Why do you look so distracting?"

"Only you can answer that one, Kincaid. I'm not responsible for your libido." I was struggling to manage my own, especially when he looked at me that way—like he was a mouse, and I was a morsel of cheese.

With his paddle, he dribbled the ball off the heated floor of the court like a basketball player. That was one of the unique aspects of paddle. You could play it outdoors on the specially heated court during the winter. The entire fenced court was slightly elevated to make room for the heating system. At least I wasn't cold anymore.

"Your serve, Kincaid."

He fumbled the serve, allowing me to take the point.

After scoring the fourth consecutive point, I paused. "This is pitiful, Gillette," I yelled across the court to him. "The score is forty-love. You'll never win if you stay all the way at the back of the court. This isn't tennis. Paddle is all about net play."

"You're killing me, Alverson!" Kincaid stripped off his light-weight jacket. He wore a snug-fitting gray t-shirt, and it was no surprise that it highlighted his athletic build.

Of course, it did.

He ran his hand through his hair. The man looked ridiculously pleased with himself, despite the fact that he'd just lost.

"That's the plan," I said. "Ready to throw in the towel?"

"Never."

For the next game, he followed my advice and moved closer to the net. He was able to keep the ball in play longer, but even so, I kept scoring.

"Game." I grinned broadly as I swiped my hand across my damp forehead.

"Best two out of three sets."

"Let's make it three out of five," I suggested, not wanting our time together to end too quickly.

"You're on."

After forty minutes of intense gameplay, our match came to an end.

"I won three out of four sets, Gillette. Looks like I'm the champ." He'd managed to squeak out a win in the third round.

Wiping the sweat off his face with the towel around his neck, Kincaid looked exhausted.

I retrieved two bottles of water from my bag and tossed him one.

He snagged it in the air, twisted off the lid, and raised it to his lips. His neck was arched as he gulped the water, and his Adam's apple bobbed as he downed it.

That was one sexy man.

He paused and poured some water into his palm before running it through his hair and down the back of his neck.

"Thanks," he said, grinning at me. "Love."

My heart fluttered at the endearment. "Love?"

He grinned. "Seemed appropriate. You kept calling out 'love' during the game."

I laughed, enjoying his teasing. "I was calling out the score."

"Whatever you say, love." He pulled me in closer with his arm around my waist and leaned in as if to kiss me. "May I?"

I stared at him, confused. "What?"

"I promised you I wouldn't kiss you."

"I—" I'd forgotten. In fact, I couldn't even remember why I'd thought kissing him would be a bad idea. Without thinking, I pressed my lips to his, feeling the saltiness of his skin and the warmth of his mouth against mine.

A bolt of desire shot through me. I could barely restrain myself from deepening the kiss. After that brief taste, all I wanted was to go back for more.

One kiss from Kincaid Gillette was definitely not enough.

If only we weren't standing in the middle of the paddle court.

I turned away, but I didn't miss Kincaid's broad grin. I licked my lips, savoring the salty taste he'd left behind.

Suddenly, I noticed Bev and Pam waiting for us, and I froze. The last thing I needed was for them to witness our little moment and spread it around the paddle circuit, but this kiss was prime gossip material.

I could feel my cheeks turning pink and avoided meeting their gazes while passing them. "Sorry to keep you waiting."

"No trouble." Bev barely concealed her satisfied smirk. "It looked like you two were having a blast out there."

"It's a perfect evening for paddle." My throat felt tight.

Pam chucked. "It's a perfect evening for many things." The woman had a devilish twinkle in her eye.

I wanted to disappear. Instead, I rushed for the stairs.

Kincaid grinned as he caught up with me. "Busted."

I glanced back at them and found them still watching us as they laughed and chatted. "This is bad. By tomorrow morning, those two will have spread the news of our kiss all over town." I started down the steps with Kincaid next to me. "You should tell your sister about us before she hears it from someone else." I paused. "Or should I?"

"She already knows."

That made me stop short. "Knows what?"

"That we had dinner last night. She's very happy about it. A little nosy, too. I told her to mind her own business."

I let out a snort of laughter. "I bet that went over well. You might want to alert her to the rumor mill, though, just in case she gets the wrong impression."

We headed toward our cars. "Wrong impression?" Kincaid asked.

"Well, it's not as if we're dating."

"Perhaps we should be."

I shook my head from side to side. "What if things don't work out? That could lead to problems, especially since you're renovating my house."

We paused by my car and faced each other.

"What if they *do* work out?" he challenged.

My stomach tightened as I recalled my reaction to seeing him talking with Elyse earlier. The surge of jealousy had unnerved me and highlighted some unresolved issues. "I'm not sure I'm ready to talk about it yet," I said, looking down at my feet.

"What's holding you back?"

Me? My baggage?

I licked my lips. "What we have between us," I gestured to him and then back to myself, "has the potential to turn into something substantial. I'm finding that kind of intimidating. It's not exactly part of my plan right now."

He stepped closer, his breath warm on my cheek. "Do you really need to plan romance? I thought it just happened." He tilted his head and looked down at me. "My advice? Let go and be in the moment."

I swayed toward him, tempted by his words.

But it wasn't my nature to be impulsive. Planning was

ingrained in me, and that included my approach to Kincaid. As much as I wanted to give in to the moment, I couldn't shake my need for order and control.

I escaped by opening my car door and climbing inside. "Maybe," I said through the open door, "but I'm a planner. Give me time to think this through." Then, I closed the door and drove away.

9

DRINKS WITH COURTNEY

Lianna

Late Saturday afternoon I found myself staring dumbstruck at my coffee date, Jared, hardly believing the words coming out of his mouth.

"I'm telling you, he choked. It was pathetic. He just froze on the rock wall like a dead fly hanging in a web. The kid refused to move."

A coffee grinder whirred as the barista prepared someone's drink, interrupting our conversation, for which I was grateful. I didn't know how to react to this guy. While I waited for inspiration, I sipped my chai.

The grinding stopped, and I still had nothing.

I wiped my mouth with a napkin. "Has your son ever climbed a rock wall before?"

A man bumped into our table, jostling us as he moved through the busy café . "Sorry," he said, looking down at us.

I nodded and accepted his apology, but my coffee date scowled at him before turning back to me.

"Of course," Jared said. "I've taken him loads of times. Whenever we used to go to the mall, he'd beg me to let him climb the rock wall. He loved it. Then I took him to the rec center last week, and he just froze, right in front of everybody. It was embarrassing. He says he never wants to go rock climbing again, but I told him he had to. If you fall off a horse, you get right back on. Freezing when you're just five feet off the ground is pathetic."

I winced at his harsh language. "Poor kid. It sounds like he had an anxiety attack. How old is he?"

"Eight. But he's been rock climbing since he was two. He always loved it. I used to take him every weekend."

My heart went out to the boy. "And he just froze all of a sudden, out of the blue?"

"Well, this was our first time since the divorce," he said, frustrated. "He's refusing to go to the rec center with me tomorrow because he's convinced I'll make him climb again."

"Will you?"

"Damned straight, I will. The only way to conquer fear is to face it head-on."

I tightened my grip on my nearly empty paper cup. "Something else might be wrong. How is he coping with the divorce?" I recalled how my own sudden fear of heights had surfaced after discovering Paul in bed with another woman and how my world had fallen apart. Thank goodness it had lasted only a few months. "Could his anxiety be a symptom of his stress? Have you considered taking him to see a therapist?"

"A therapist?" Jared looked at me like I'd just suggested he try ritual sacrifice. "You think he needs to see a shrink simply because he lost his nerve climbing a wall?"

I kept my expression neutral. "It might be more than that. Didn't you say that was the first time you'd taken him rock climbing since the divorce? That could be what's causing his anxiety."

"The divorce?" Jared's lips curled as though he'd just smelled something rotten. "It's not that," he snapped. "The kid lost his nerve, plain and simple. He'll be fine tomorrow. He just has to get over it."

I pressed my lips together. How did you even talk to someone like this? It was clear that he didn't want to hear any opinion other than his own. "I'm sure you know what's best." I drained my cup of chai down to the last cardamom-flavored drop. I was done with this conversation. I stood. "Thanks for meeting me."

"The coffee at this place is great, even if it's crowded." Jared stood up as well. "How about having dinner sometime?"

"Thanks, but no." I took a step toward the door and another couple swooped in to claim our vacated table.

He frowned. "Is it because I have a son?"

It's because you're a bad father. "It's not that. I don't think we connected. I didn't feel any chemistry."

"Hmph."

"I hope everything goes well with your son. Try to be patient with him."

We left the café and turned in opposite directions.

I didn't look back.

Meeting Jared for coffee had been a big mistake. Normally, when I first matched with someone on a dating app, we'd text and then talk on the phone to get to know each other so I could weed out the ones that weren't any good. Jared had been in a hurry to meet in person, so I'd agreed to have coffee with him.

What a disappointment. I'd nearly cancelled on Jared after that kiss with Kincaid. Now I wish I had. I'd only followed through with it because I'd scheduled it before Kincaid and I had met.

I glanced at my watch, realizing it was still early on a Saturday. With no plans for the rest of the evening, I felt a tinge of disappointment. I had kept my schedule clear in case things went well with bad dad, but now I had empty hours ahead of me.

Perhaps I'd stop by the Not a Yacht Club and grab a bite to eat.

Ten minutes later, I entered the NAYC bar and saw Courtney chatting with Reed, the bartender, at the counter.

"Hey!" I said, claiming the stool next to her. "Fancy meeting you here."

"Lianna! It's great to see you," Courtney said.

"Can I get you something?" Reed asked.

"A glass of Pinot Grigio, please," I said.

Courtney tilted her head. "Do you have plans for the evening?"

"Nope. I'm a free spirit."

"Let's have dinner together," she suggested.

"Sounds perfect."

Reed handed us two menus. "Do you want to eat at the bar? Or would you prefer a table?"

"Eavesdropping?" I teased.

Reed grinned. "I'm just trying to anticipate your needs before you can even articulate them." He winked.

"We'll stay here," Courtney said.

I glanced at the menu. "I'll have the Quinoa Salad with Feta and Asparagus."

"And I'll take the salmon," Courtney added.

As Reed left to turn in our orders, she turned to me. "Have you made much progress on *The Prime of Miss Jean Brodie* yet?"

Does two chapters count as a lot of progress? "Give me a minute while I wash up," I said as I stood. Maybe she'd forget about the book while I was gone.

As I walked down the dimly lit hallway toward the restroom, a man stepped out of the men's room. My heart skipped a beat when I realized it was Kincaid Gillette—but beardless. Something in my chest swelled with tenderness at the sight of him.

Clean-shaven Kincaid was just as sexy and bearded Kincaid.

"Well, hello, stranger. You look familiar, but I can't quite place you." My heart thumped in my chest. Had fate brought me here to see him?

He stroked his hand across his smooth cheek. "Do you like it?"

I couldn't help but admire how delicious he looked. "I do. But I like the beard too."

"Just checking. I aim to please."

"You do it quite admirably." The scent of his cologne wafted toward me, woods and spice, and I felt a rush of desire.

Suddenly, I was very happy I'd decided to come to the Not a Yacht Club tonight. That bad date was turning into a good night.

Kincaid's appreciative gaze swept over me. "So, tell me. Did the rumor mill grind us up or ignore us?"

I rolled my eyes. "It's tearing us to bits. Pam and Bev spread the news all over town that we're an item. It's my own fault. I'm the one who kissed you."

"The question is, did you enjoy it?"

I felt my cheeks flush. "Of course, I did." I glanced at his mouth, at the lips that curled into a smile.

"So did I."

Before I knew it, Kincaid had looped one arm around my waist and pulled me against him. Without another word, he kissed me.

Softly.

Gently.

Lips touching lips.

Caressing.

Tasting.

I sighed and melted into him. Chasing his tongue with my own.

I took a shuddering breath, wanting more of him. More of this kiss. More of this moment.

When a floorboard squeaked in the hallway, I jumped back from Kincaid. My heart raced as he looked at me with a slow smile.

"If Bev and Pam could see us now..." he murmured.

I felt a blush spread across my cheeks. "This is a bad idea," I said, pushing past him and running into the women's room.

By the time I came back out, Kincaid was gone. I tried to tell myself I was relieved—but that was a big, fat lie.

I heaved a sigh and headed back to Courtney.

"Was there a line?" Courtney asked when I sat down next to her at the bar.

"Yep," I lied.

"Did you finish *The Prime of Miss Jean Brodie* yet?"

"Nope."

She sighed. "You only have a few days. You need to hurry."

"Definitely. I'll read when I get home tonight." Maybe. "How's work been going?"

Courtney grimaced. "Terrible. We had a data breach. Someone hacked our server, and I'm worried my research could have been compromised."

"Do you think it was corporate espionage?" I asked.

"It's possible. I don't know. It's just scary to think that someone could steal all of our hard work."

I shot her a worried frown. "That's bad. That can destroy a company. My brother told me about a video game company that was hacked. A brand-new game they hadn't released was stolen and the thieves put it up on the internet for free. It ruined the company and it folded. All those people were out of work."

Reed delivered our food, and we continued talking as we ate.

"That's scary," Courtney said. "Maybe I should boost the security on my personal laptop, too. Just to be safe."

I nodded approvingly. "Troy can give you some advice."

"Your brother? I haven't talked to him since high school."

"He does computer security now. He knows more about it than anyone I've ever met."

Then a thought crept in—should I mention Felicity's pregnancy? It was a big part of their lives right now, but I couldn't shake the feeling of unease. Talking about my sister-in-law's pregnancy was a painful reminder of my own difficulties. Then again, not mentioning it might come across as odd. "His wife is expecting their first baby soon," I finally blurted out, my words catching in my throat.

"Really? Good for them." She didn't appear to pick up on my tension.

I took a bite of my salad as I tried to push back the mix of emotions that threatened to overwhelm me.

"Let me give you his number," I said, regaining control of myself. "He can tell you what to do to protect yourself." I took out one of my business cards from my purse and wrote Troy's contact information on the back of it.

"I wouldn't want to bother him."

"I'll say what he'd say: It's no bother. It's something he's happy to do for friends. He'd rather help you before there's a data breach than after," I reassured her.

I handed Courtney the card. "Call him as soon as possible. It's always better to lock the barn door before the horse escapes, but he can also help you if someone's already breached your security."

She tucked the card into her wallet. "I'll email him when I get home. Thanks." When she looked up, her worried face brightened with a welcoming smile. "Kincaid. I didn't know you'd be here tonight."

I whirled around to face him and shot him a scowl.

He grinned at me and then turned to Courtney. "Hey, sis."

She eyed us both. "Want to join us?" She raised one eyebrow as though daring him.

I wanted to kick her, but I decided that would only encourage her.

"Thanks, but one of my clients is having a housewarming party, and I'm heading over there now." He turned his attention to me. "Good news. Your building permit was approved. I'll stop by during the day Monday with my excavation crew, and they'll start digging your foundation on Tuesday."

I blinked. "That's fast."

"We were lucky. The timing worked out." He said goodbye and headed for the door.

I watched him leave.

"I heard you and Kincaid were seen together the other night." Courtney's voice had a singsong lilt to it.

"Were we?" I asked, feigning innocence.

"On the paddle court..." she said, clearly hoping I'd fill in the rest.

"I challenged him to a match." I reached for my wine glass. "And I kicked his ass," I said, shooting her a cocky grin.

She narrowed her eyes. "The more important question is, did you agree to go on a date with him?"

I glanced away. "Things are sort of complicated."

"But the two of you kissed on the paddle court?"

I froze with my wine glass halfway to my mouth and widened my eyes in mock-horror. "Did we? That's crazy."

Courtney smirked. "You like him. I can tell. And he likes you, too. Why are you fighting it? Go on a date. See where things lead."

"How's your salmon?" I asked, pointedly ignoring her suggestion. "This quinoa salad is perfection."

She arched an eyebrow. "Fine. I'll let it go. For now."

I munched on a bite of quinoa and feta. Maybe Courtney was right. Maybe I should give some serious thought to dating Kincaid. After all, all signs were indicating, 'yes.'

10

BUTTONING UP

Lianna

I'm the kind of person who likes to take their time and think things through. I'm not really into snap decisions—I prefer to analyze situations, come up with a plan, and strategize. You could say I'm a bit of a slow mover.

Kincaid, though—well, Kincaid moved fast. Even the addition was happening quicker than I'd expected. I had only signed the contract a week ago.

The man had an effect on me. He made me feel impetuous, and that scared me. What was this spontaneous kissing thing we had going on between us? First at the paddle court behind the Y, and then at the restaurant the other night? It was kind of nuts. Fun, sure, but completely out of character for me.

I wasn't some hormonal, oversexed teenager who couldn't stop thinking about a cute boy. I was an adult, with adult responsibilities and an adult job and an adult house. It was time I started acting more like one.

So, maybe Kincaid and I should give the whole relationship thing a try after all. Maybe if I scratched that itch, it wouldn't keep bothering me.

As I left work on Tuesday, a gust of wind sent my hair whipping into my face. A storm was coming. I checked my watch. My last meeting of the day had run late, but I still had plenty of time to make it to book club tonight.

I'd been restless all day today. I'd finished reading *The Prime of Miss Jeane Brodie* last night, and it had left me feeling emotionally off-kilter.

Well, to say that I "finished" the book would be an exaggeration. I only made it halfway through before admitting to myself that I couldn't complete it in time. Instead, I resorted to streaming the movie adaptation online. The protagonist, Miss Jean Brodie, was a cunning character who handpicked a group of girls to be her "special students." On the surface, it seemed like a kind gesture, but in reality, she manipulated them to fulfill her own agenda. This reminded me of how easily Paul had fooled me, which was a tough pill to swallow. I couldn't ignore how naïve and gullible I had been to fall for his lies.

When I arrived at my house twenty minutes later, I noticed two trucks parked in my driveway. One of them had a big backhoe on its back. The men who were excavating for the addition must still be here.

I parked on the street and climbed the steps to my front door before heading directly to the kitchen. Through the window above the sink, I saw two men unfolding a large blue tarp on my lawn, which snapped in the wind as it struggled to take flight.

As I opened the back door, a board nailed across the opening prevented me from moving further. Apparently, it was there to keep me from breaking my neck by falling into the hole fifteen feet below.

Peering into the gaping square that would be the basement of my new addition, I shouted, "Hi!" to the two men who were wrestling with the tarp.

They both stopped to look at me and I caught a glimpse of their worn work boots and sweat-streaked faces. "Hey, Ms. Alverson," one of them said, glancing at his watch. "Sorry we're still workin' n'at. Wool be ahta yer hair rul soon. I'll knock on yer front dwur once we git dis all buttoned up and give yinz an update. Gimme five minutes."

"No problem." I had some time to spare.

I'd been living in the Pittsburgh area all my life and could sling the Pittsburgh accent around moderately well, but this guy was an expert. When I slipped into using it, I tended to rely on some of the unique words we Pittsburgers used, like yinz for y'all, or gumbands for rubber bands, or buggies for grocery carts, but this guy went all in, like that guy on YouTube, the Pittsburgh Dad. There was no way I'd ever be able to replicate it at his skill level, so I didn't even try.

After closing the door, I watched as they dragged the tarp down a dirt slope into the basement of my new addition. I briefly wondered why the slope was there until it dawned on me that it must be the only way to haul the backhoe out of the hole once it had been dug.

When my doorbell rang a couple of minutes later I hurried to answer it.

"Hey again, Ms. Alverson. I'm Mac Tenner," he said in his thick Pittsburghese accent, reaching out his hand for me to shake. "I'm thuh lead for thuh excavation part a' yer projec'."

As I stepped outside to talk with him, I noticed the wind had picked up. "How's everything going?"

"Rhul good. We gawt thuh basemen' dug and thuh durway caht so yinz can git inta yer new cellar. We'll be pourin' thuh fuhters as soon as we git a dry day."

I blinked as I took a moment to translate that. He was saying they'd dug the basement and cut a doorway so I could get into my new cellar, and they'd be pouring the footers when once the weather was better.

He looked up at the darkening sky. "It's gittin' real dohrk 'aht 'er. Der's a big stuhrm cahmin. We put dahn tarps tuh make shure watter don't git inta yer cellar through 'at hole we caht. Thuh tarp should keep da skirls aht, but ya' never know. Jus' watch 'aht fur any furry trespassers." He barked out a laugh. "But not thuh ones dat come dahntahn every spring."

I was confused. He'd said something about the tarp keeping the squirrels out, which made sense. But that other part. Was he also making a joke about furry trespassers from the Pittsburgh Anthrocon convention? The one where people dressed up as furry cartoonish animals? "Are you talking about the furries from the Anthrocon?"

"Yeh. Dey're a hoot." Mac chuckled. "Yinz're in a rhul safe neighborhoot, but yinz gahta be careful, n'at. If yin'z down't gahta lock on yer cellar duwr, yin'z can wedge a chair n'at."

I'm pretty sure he was suggesting I wedge a chair under the knob of the basement door. "No worries. The door has a lock."

"At'll work. I tied dahn dems tarps myself, so they awtah hold, but dems spots where thuh fuhters are gonna tie inta thuh existin' structure gahta stay cry, too."

"Got it." I glanced at the ominous sky. "It looks like you finished up just in time."

Mac nodded. "G'night, ma'am. Don't get too soggy 'aht d'air.'"

"Goodnight." As Mac turned and hurried down the steps, large raindrops started falling.

I dashed upstairs to change out of my work clothes. As rain streamed down my bedroom window, I quickly donned a blue and white spaghetti strap dress and grabbed a lightweight white wrap from my wardrobe cabinet. Slipping into white kitten-heeled pumps, I grabbed Courtney's copy of *The Prime of Miss Jean Brodie* from my nightstand and headed downstairs.

Lightning brightened the sky as I hit the bottom step, followed by a loud crack of thunder. This was turning into a nasty storm.

I shoved my wrap into my huge purse. Perhaps I should call Courtney, my ride for tonight, and suggest she wait to pick me up so she could avoid the worst of the storm. We could be a bit late, and I hated thinking of her driving in this rain. Besides, it would probably let up soon.

My heels clicked on the floor as I entered my kitchen in search of my phone. As I glanced around for it, a flash of bright blue movement outside the window caught my eye. One of the tarps from my basement was attempting to escape across my backyard.

"Damn!"

I darted toward the back door, but then checked myself. That first step would be a doozy, what with that fifteen-foot drop.

Instead, I ran down my basement steps and then through the door leading outside.

I dashed across my backyard toward the flapping tarp, quickly becoming drenched. The tarp was fighting valiantly against the embrace of a pair of scrubby bushes at the edge of my property, so I grabbed it and tried to wrestle it into submission.

The stubborn thing flapped in the wind like a living creature. I wrapped my arms around it and pressed it to my chest, wondering how on earth I was going to manage to reattach it in this wind.

As I dragged it over to the enormous hole and peered down, I saw a green tarp down there too. One side seemed to be nailed securely, but the side along the dirt edge had been attached using a stake. As the wind gusted, the stake moved back and forth, steadily working loose.

I inched closer to the stake, clutching the blue tarp to my chest as I braced my other hand on the house and extended one mud-caked foot toward the loose stake. I gave it a hard shove and managed to push it deeper into the soil.

The green tarp immediately eased its violent flapping, but I wasn't sure the stake would hold in this downpour.

As I took a step away from the precipice, the heel of my ruined white pump plunged deeper into the soft soil. I wobbled and threw out my hands to catch myself, causing the blue tarp to flap free as I grabbed hold of the corner of the house with both hands.

I overcorrected and found myself teetering on the edge of my fifteen-foot hole.

11

RAIN STORM

KINCAID

I pulled into Lianna's driveway, grabbed some extra-long stakes and a mallet from the passenger seat, and headed out into the storm. Rain battered me as I rounded the corner of the house into her back yard.

I was alarmed to find Lianna precariously close to that newly dug basement. Her white dress was plastered to her body. She was gripping the side of the house and using her foot to shove a stake into the mud.

I rushed forward to lend a hand, but she lost her balance and teetered toward the hole. Dropping the stakes, I darted forward and grabbed her wrist, pulling her to safety.

Lianna let out a gasp of surprise that was barely audible over the sound of the hammering rain. "Kincaid!" Her fingers closed around my biceps, gripping them to keep from falling.

Adrenaline surged through me as my heart thumped in my chest. "What are you doing out here? You could have broken your neck!"

She leaned closer. I wrapped my arms around her and pulled her close, and the warmth of her body seeped into me.

I could hardly believe she wasn't hurt. "Are you okay? You didn't twist your ankle, did you?"

"I'm fine. If you hadn't shown up when you did, I'd be sprawled on my backside in that mud pit." She took a shaky breath and gazed up at me. Rain ran down her face like tears. "You're kind of like a superhero, showing up in the nick of time." The corner of her mouth crooked up in an attempt at a smile, and I found myself staring at her lips.

"Happy to help." My voice wavered as I spoke. My hand rested on her back. Everything about this moment felt like it was meant to be, as though the fates had brought me here.

"You always seem to be nearby when my shoes turn on me." The flirty look she gave me made my heart give a hard thump.

"Falling into a pit would have been a terrible way to abuse such an excellent backside." My hand glided down her wet dress and cupped her bottom, pressing her against me.

She laughed and wiggled a little, driving me crazy. I held her closer to make her stop.

"Don't tell me you showed up just so you could grope me, Batman."

"Batman?"

"He's the first superhero I thought of." Her forehead furrowed in confusion. "Wait. What are you even doing here?"

The scent that was uniquely Lianna battled with the scents of rain and ozone and mud, but her essence invaded my senses and drew me in. "I'm here because of the storm. It's a bad one. We were supposed to get showers, not this. I was worried Mac and his crew might have trouble buttoning things up."

She took me by surprise when she draped her arms around my neck and peered up at me. "I think I really like having you rescue me." Her eyes softened as she leaned closer to me.

A moment later she was kissing me. Not like that gentle, questing kiss we'd shared on Saturday at the Not a Yacht Club, but something deep. Ravenous. All I knew was that it made me want more.

She pulled away from our kiss, tilting her head back and grinning up at me. "I think you just won the girl, Batman."

As I stared into her beautiful brown eyes, the sound of the flapping tarp grew louder. I glanced down just as a stake worked its way loose and the edge of a green tarp broke free. It jerked like an enormous bird trying to take flight.

I released Lianna's hands from my neck, pressed them together in front of me, and kissed them. "Hold that thought. Why don't you go inside while I deal with this?"

"I'm already soaked. It isn't as if I can get any wetter." Then she gave me a sidelong glance.

Was that a double entendre? God, I hoped so. "I won't comment."

She chuckled as she kicked off a pair of white shoes caked with mud. "I haven't been outside in a rainstorm since I was a kid." She darted off toward a balled-up blue tarp bouncing across the lawn like a demented tumbleweed.

For a moment, all I could do was stare at Lianna, running through the downpour like a ten-year-old. When she reached the tarp, she didn't immediately pick it up, but instead stomped one foot down on it and then stood on top of the thing to hold it in place. Then she tilted her face up to the sky, arching her back as she opened her mouth to taste the rain.

My body flashed hot with a bone-deep craving that swept through me.

I wanted to pull this woman into my arms and make love to her right here in the rain. Instead, I grabbed the mallet and one of the extra-long stakes I'd brought with me, and hammered it through the metal ring of the green tarp.

I turned to find Lianna standing behind me, the blue tarp clutched to her chest. Rivulets of water streamed down her cheeks and her hair hung in thick, wet strands.

"Hand me that," I said. "I'll reattach it." I took the blue tarp, noticing again the way her dress clung to her. I drank her in, wanting to memorize this moment. My gorgeous little selkie, risen fresh from the sea, a temptation no man could resist.

I would have reached out to pull her back into my arms, but she preempted me by grabbing one end of the tarp I held and beginning to untangle it. "I think this one was covering that footer on the far end."

I managed to stop staring at her and turned to peer down into the pit to the spot where she was pointing.

"I'll reattach it." I walked around to the ramp the backhoe operator had made and trudged down it. It was slippery going and getting worse by the minute. My work boots would be caked with mud by the time I was done.

It took me a couple of minutes to get the tarp secured. Once I had the site covered up to my satisfaction, I slogged back up the ramp. Lianna watched me from above, her forehead pinched with worry.

I'd been right. Climbing out of the hole was even more challenging than getting in. The mud made the climb treacherous, and my foot slipped just as I reached the top of the ramp, causing me to drop down to one knee. It was clear that I wouldn't make it out of this pit clean.

I dug one hand into the mud to brace myself and rose to my feet. I still had another foot to traverse before I'd make it out of the pit.

Lianna extended a hand toward me. "Grab hold. I'll pull you out."

I hesitated, then took hold of it with my clean hand. Immediately, one of my feet began to slide back down the muddy ramp.

She grabbed my wrist with her other hand and leaned back, using all her weight to haul me the rest of the way up the slope.

I came stumbling out of the hole and slammed into her. She teetered at the impact, and I wrapped my arms around her to keep from knocking her over.

She started laughing. "Really, Kincaid. We need to stop doing this."

I couldn't resist her. I lowered my head and pressed my mouth against hers, burying my clean hand in her hair at the back of her neck and cupping her head. Her lips were cool and wet from the rain. I trailed kisses down the side of her throat, warming her skin with my mouth, and savoring the tantalizing slickness of her body.

When she let out a soft moan, I slid my other hand over her breast and cupped it, kneading it gently. Her nipple was already hard and erect beneath the clingy fabric.

She gasped at my touch and wrapped her cold hand around the nape of my neck, pulling me into her. She drove me wild with wanting.

"You feel so good, baby," I breathed. "Taste so good."

She took a deep breath and let it out in a shuddering groan. "Don't stop."

"That's the last thing I want to do."

A sharp tapping sound came. Tap-tap-tap. Then again. Tap-tap-tap.

"What's that noise?" Lianna mumbled.

I lifted my head from her breast and kissed her again. I didn't care what it was. Didn't care if the tarp ripped loose from the stakes. Didn't care if the house ripped free of the earth a-la-Wizard of Oz. Didn't care about anything except kissing Lianna. Tasting Lianna. Savoring the honey-sweet flavor of Lianna.

"Kincaid? That better be you out there kissing Lianna!" A woman's voice pierced the storm.

Courtney.

"The two of you need to knock it off right now. If you don't let go of each other, we'll never make it to book club on time."

12

LOVE IN THE TIME OF BOOK CLUB

LIANNA

One moment my arms were wrapped around Kincaid, and the next he was backing away.

I felt as though someone had just dumped a bucket of cold water over my head, which was almost funny since we were both soaked to the skin.

I whirled and glared up at Courtney from her perch at the open kitchen door. The woman wore an entirely too pleased smile.

"What are you doing in my kitchen?" My tone dripped with a sugary sweet inflection that didn't mask my irritation.

Courtney's eyes sparkled with delight. "Your car was outside, so I knew you were home. When you didn't answer the door, I worried that you'd fallen down the stairs and were lying unconscious on the floor. Imagine my surprise when I found you in the arms of a mud-spattered man." She raked me with her gaze. "I see he was getting a bit handsy with you, too."

I glanced down at the front of my dress and saw the splotch of mud in the unmistakable shape of a hand. It was directly over my breast. Talk about getting caught red-handed. I shook my head as I returned Courtney's grin. "I could never resist a man with tools." Then, I lifted up on my tiptoes and kissed Kincaid.

"Knock it off! That's my baby brother." Courtney slapped her hand over her eyes. "No more kissy-kissy, missy. I can't unsee that." She groped her way backward, feeling along the door with her free hand until she was able to slam it shut.

"If I'd known that was the secret to making Courtney disappear, I would have tried it years ago." Kincaid took me by the hand and led me around the house to the driveway.

The rain had eased to a slow, steady drizzle. This was actually rather pleasant—if you were already drenched.

"Did we really freak her out?" I entwined my fingers with Kincaid's. His hand was warm in mine.

"Nah. She's just having fun by pretending to be a prude. She prefers to hide her wild side, but it's there."

I cocked an eyebrow and gave him a crooked smile. "Do all the Gillettes have a passionate streak they keep under wraps?"

We stopped next to his truck, and he wrapped his arms around my waist, pulling me close. "I don't know about all the Gillettes, but this one certainly does have a passionate streak. I don't think I keep it hidden, though," he said.

He lowered his head, and his kiss sent a jolt of heat straight to my core. I found myself clutching at his shirt as my knees went weak. As I moaned, he let out a deep groan of frustration and pulled away from me. He steadied me by the elbows until I opened my eyes to stare up at him.

"I'm taking you on a date this Friday," he murmured in my ear. "A real one. Good food. Fancy tablecloths. The whole thing."

I bit at my lower lip nervously. This was really happening. "That sounded more like an order than an invitation."

"I was afraid if I gave you a choice, Courtney might never forgive you if you said no."

I couldn't help but laugh. He was probably right. "Well, we wouldn't want that, would we?"

"Definitely not," he agreed with a grin. "So, do I have a date?"

I leaned in closer and whispered, "I made a promise to Court-ney, and I never break my promises."

He grinned. "I'll pick you up at seven, love."

There went that little thrill again. It took a moment before I could think clearly. "Sounds good, but I should meet you. I'll be coming straight from work. I have a late meeting on Friday. I'm not sure how long it will last."

He nodded. "No problem. I'll make reservations and send you the details. Text me when you're on your way."

"Sure thing."

He glanced up at the front door. "You'd better get inside. Courtney will be opening the door and shouting for you any second now. It's one of her big sister tricks."

A moment later, the porch light started turning on and off.

I burst out laughing. "She must have been a pain in the neck when you were kids."

"You have no idea."

I took a quick look at Kincaid's sodden clothes. "Want to come in and get cleaned up?"

"If you were alone, I'd say yes, but with Courtney acting as a chaperone, I think I might as well head home. Besides, I don't have anything clean to change into." He leaned down and gave me a quick, chaste kiss on my cheek. "Have fun with your book group tonight. See you Friday."

Suddenly, the next three days seemed to stretch into an eter-nity. "If I can wait that long," I muttered.

He laughed. "Patience is good for the soul."

"Hey, I thought that was laughter. You know; 'Laughter is good for the soul?'"

"I just know it isn't temptation. That's the road to ruin."

I grinned. "My mom always said, 'When temptation knocks, imagination usually answers.'"

"You certainly provide plenty of fodder for my imagination," he said.

The front door opened. "Do I have to separate the two of

you?" Courtney called out. "Need I remind you we're already late for book club?"

Kincaid waved. "Sorry, Court. I'm leaving." He rounded his truck and opened the driver's side door. "See you Friday, little Miss Temptation."

"I can hardly wait." I smiled to myself as I turned and trotted up my front steps, pausing outside long enough to wipe my muddy bare feet on the sisal mat and drop off my ruined shoes. Even Courtney's scowl couldn't erase the smile from my face.

"What on earth were you doing out there, young lady?" Courtney placed her hands on her hips, fully embodying the role of an irritated mom. But her grin gave her away. She was clearly pleased to see that Kincaid and I were getting along so well.

"Just playing."

"You march right upstairs and get cleaned up. We're already running late."

"Ma'am, yes ma'am." I saluted sarcastically and headed up to my bathroom, immediately stripping out of my filthy dress. I filled the sink with water and a bit of detergent to let it soak before jumping into the shower.

I didn't bother to dry my hair because I didn't want to delay us any longer, and put it up in a sleek chignon. Taking inspiration from Audrey Hepburn from Breakfast at Tiffany's, I put on a fifties-style boat-collared dress that suited my hairstyle.

Ten minutes later, I breezed into my living room. "Aren't you ready to go yet?" I chided Courtney as I grabbed an umbrella from the closet and tucked it into my enormous purse. "You'll make us late!"

"Very funny." Courtney came out of the kitchen and stopped in her tracks when she saw me. "How do you manage to look so put together when you were covered in mud not ten minutes ago?"

"It's a talent developed over years of good, clean living." I ushered Courtney out the door and locked it behind us.

"Yeah. Right. I saw you out there with my brother. Nothing you were doing could be described as clean."

I ignored her comment as I settled into her BMW coupe and turned on the seat warmer. Despite the hot shower, I still wasn't completely warm.

The sky looked as if it were considering unloading on us again. When Courtney pulled up in front of Rose Oliver's apartment, she grabbed her umbrella as she climbed out of the car.

"Apparently, you and Kincaid can't keep your hands off each other. Does that mean you're finally going to date him?"

I scowled at her. "I'm not certain you deserve an answer to that question. You've been awfully pushy."

Courtney gave a frustrated groan. "Come on. Give. You're killing me."

"Fine," I said, using my best belligerent teenager voice. "I agreed to go on a date this Friday night."

"Yes!" Courtney gave a little jump of happiness as we headed for the door.

"You're losing all credibility with me as a cool and collected cancer researcher. You know that, right?"

"Totally worth it to get the two of you together," Courtney replied.

"Let's just keep everything about me and Kincaid between the two of us tonight. I don't know where this thing is going yet, and I'd rather keep it to myself for now."

"No problem."

As we approached the door, we didn't bother to knock. The sound of laughter from the adjoining room welcomed us. Rose, our book group leader, was in the midst of telling a story. Our book group had been meeting for over a year now, and I couldn't imagine life without this incredible group of friends.

Mara, whose hair was tipped with blue, co-owned a video game company and the local comic book shop. Sonya, our newest member, was a fifth-grade teacher. Both had recently become engaged to the Ross brothers and were now busy planning a double wedding in Turks and Caicos. I couldn't wait for the trip, as the brothers had arranged to charter a plane to take the entire wedding party there.

"You're here." Rose crossed the room with her arms extended for hugs. "I was worried you weren't coming. Welcome to *mi casa*."

"Thanks," I said, hugging her. "I love what you've done with your apartment. You've done a ton of work in the short time you've been here."

Rose beamed with pride, her cheeks turning slightly pink. "Oh, thank you so much! It's been a lot of hard work, but I'm really happy with how it turned out. I'm glad you like it too."

"I'm sorry we're late," I said. "It's entirely my fault. First, I had a problem at work that kept me late, and then I got caught outside in the rain dealing with a construction site emergency and got soaked. I had to take a shower and wash off all the mud."

"You should have seen her when I arrived to pick her up." Courtney's eyes lit up. "I've never seen her looking so dirty. She had mud in some pretty unusual places."

My cheeks warmed. Me and my big mouth.

Rose raised her eyebrows. "Sounds like a good story. Tell me more."

"I want all the details," Gertrude added from her chair. She looked like the queen of the group that she was, and we always made sure she had the best seat in the house since she was the oldest of us—by about forty years.

"Please, no," I said, putting on a mock-stern expression. "Courtney's been teasing me about it for the past half hour. I don't think I can take any more."

Rose pouted her disappointment. "You're no fun."

"Don't worry about being late." Mara patted my arm. "You know us. We'll always love catching up with each other before we start talking books. Why don't you pour yourselves some wine?"

I poured a drink, served myself some brie and crackers,

added a dollop of delicious-looking artichoke dip, and then claimed the seat in the middle of the sofa between Courtney and Rose.

"Speaking of our habit of chatting," Scarlet said, "I think it would be a good idea to add a bit more structure to our meetings. We've already spent fifteen minutes catching up with each other, so now I'd like to call our meeting to order. Later, when we sit down to enjoy Rose's perfectly prepared Scotch pies, we can discuss how they fit with the setting of *The Prime of Miss Jean Brodie* and chat more."

"So formal, Madam Mayor." Mara rolled her eyes. "This isn't a town council meeting."

Scarlet didn't seem bothered by the comment. "Let's try it this way tonight and see if we like it. I'm hoping it will keep us all a bit more focused. We always chat for at least an hour before we finally get down to business, and then we have to rush through the discussion in order to get to the meal."

"Sounds like a good plan," Rose said. "Let's do it."

Scarlet looked at the agenda she'd prepared. "First, is there anyone who didn't finish the book?"

Everyone turned to stare at me.

"Really? You all just assume I didn't read it?" I shook my head and then grinned. "I have to admit, I struggled with this one. It wasn't just because of work this time. It had more to do with the book itself."

"But it was so good." Sonya, the schoolteacher, raised her eyebrows in surprise. "I loved it."

I glanced away. "I really didn't like the character of Miss Brodie. As the story progressed, she became more and more manipulative, and the whole thing made me uncomfortable."

"That's exactly how you were supposed to feel," Sonya protested. "She was a horrible person."

Courtney gave a thoughtful nod. "I think it's because you don't have a manipulative bone in your body. You're completely straightforward and genuine."

"I don't know about that," I demurred. "I can manage to get my way when I want to."

Courtney just rolled her eyes. "Please."

Mara cleared her throat. "I have to admit, I hated the way Sandy betrayed Miss Brodie in the end. But really, someone had to put the woman in check. I suppose it was the imbalance of power between the girls and Miss Brodie that got to me the most. A teacher is supposed to be a mentor, not some sort of Svengali or Puppet Master." Mara shuddered. "That comic book series is popular, but it gives me the willies. The idea of having someone else manipulate your life—" she shook her head "—it's my worst nightmare."

Scarlet furrowed her brow. "What comic book series? I don't follow."

Mara shook her head in dismay. "You really need to read more graphic novels, Madam Mayor. The Puppet Master is a Marvel Comics supervillain."

"Is he?" Scarlet cocked an eyebrow. "How enlightening."

Mara smirked. "Don't forget, I'll be choosing our next book soon. I plan to have everyone read *Maus*."

"That's a great one." Rose bounced up and down slightly in her seat. "It's about a Jewish father's experiences as a Holocaust survivor during World War II. We have multiple copies at the library. They use it at the middle school in the advanced English class." She opened a leatherbound folder and pulled out a few sheets of paper. "I brought a list of discussion questions for *The Prime of Miss Jean Brodie*."

Over the next hour, we discussed the book, and my unease began to fade. Everyone seemed to universally dislike Miss Brodie and admire Sandy for taking a stand against her.

"That was my last discussion question," Rose declared.

"That's a relief, because I'm starving," Sonya said. "Whatever you made for dinner, it smells delicious."

"It isn't haggis, right?" Mara said, her tone a bit dubious. "You promised it wouldn't be haggis."

"Do you have any idea how hard it was to come up with a menu based on Scottish food?" Rose asked. "I think I pulled it off, though. I made little individual Scotch pies."

"Mmm. Does each one come with a shot of scotch?" I asked.

Rose chuckled as she pulled a baking sheet of little round pies from the oven. The aroma of savory spices wafted through the kitchen, mingling with the warm, earthy scent of baked mutton. "Nope. They're mutton. I've never cooked mutton before." She arranged the golden-brown Scotch pies on a tray next to two covered bowls.

"I also have neeps and tatties," she said, gesturing toward a pair of bowls. "They're more commonly known as mashed rutabagas and mashed potatoes. I've never cooked rutabagas before, either."

"As long as you skipped the haggis and black pudding, I'm a happy camper," Scarlet said.

"What's black pudding?" Sonya asked.

"Ugh." Rose's mouth curled in disgust. "It's a sort of sausage made with pigs' blood."

"Pigs' blood?" I asked. "That sounds as bad as haggis."

"No one can accuse the Scots of not using every bit of an animal they butcher," Mara commented.

We each took a plate from the stack on the counter and served ourselves before taking our seats in the dining room.

Scarlet raised her glass in a toast. "Here's to the three most important things in life: good friends, good food, and good books."

13

FIRE PIT

KINCAID

After washing away the mud, but not the memory of holding Lianna in my arms, I headed to Ford Ross's place for drinks. I knew anything that happened on one of my job sites was my responsibility, and I couldn't help but feel relieved my favorite client was safe.

When Ford opened the door, his dog Zephyr was right beside him. "Hey, man. Come on in. Grab a beer. Are you up for sitting outside by the fire pit?"

"I don't see why not," I replied as we headed to the back of the house, Zephyr trailing us. "That rainstorm passed. It's pretty nice outside."

"Mara thought I was nuts when I mentioned sitting by the fire pit to her. It was pouring when she left," Ford chuckled.

"Is she at book club?" That's where Lianna and Courtney had been going.

"Yep. Every month. Like clockwork. She always rushes to finish the book in time, but she seems to enjoy it."

"Just like the way we enjoy Dante's cooking class." I grabbed a beer from the fridge. "Gives us a place to hang out and actually

97

do something instead of just sitting around drinking or watching TV."

Zephyr's enormous ears went on alert, and he darted for the front door. Moments later, Dante walked in with the dog by his side. "Wait," I said, surprised to see him. "What are you doing here? I thought you had a kitchen to run."

Dante raised his middle finger toward me, but then I noticed the thick layer of white gauze wrapped around it. "Cut yourself?"

"Kitchen accident. The knife didn't like my technique. I decided to let my sous chef take over for the night. The guy's thrilled to be in charge."

"You're the boss. You might as well enjoy the perks," I said, chuckling. "I hope the cut isn't a bad one."

He shrugged. "I've had worse."

Ford slid open the back door, allowing the scent of damp grass and mud to waft into the house. Dante peered up at the dark sky. "You sure it won't rain anymore?"

"I checked the weather radar," Ford said as we walked outside. "There isn't a single cloud headed our way."

Zephyr trotted outside and sniffed the night air before heading toward a tree at the rear of the property. "I spotted you with Lianna the other night," Dante commented as we followed Ford.

"At the Chinese restaurant?" I hadn't seen him there. I shot him a puzzled look. "Where?"

"Near the restrooms at Not a Yacht Club."

I just stared at him, knowing exactly what Dante had to be referring to—the kiss Lianna and I had shared. "We have a date this Friday," I finally admitted.

Dante smirked. "You owe me!" he yelled across the backyard to Ford.

Ford was crouched next to the cold fire pit and whirled to face us. "You were right?"

Something was going on. I looked from Dante's grinning face back to Ford's pleased one. "What the hell are you two talking about?"

"I told Ford you and Lianna would be on a date within the week," Dante said. "He didn't believe me. We made a bet."

"You guys are assholes," I said.

Ford nodded. "We know. It's our thing."

"Wait. I'm not an asshole," Dante protested. "That was you."

"That's both of you," I clarified.

"I'm just glad you asked her out," Dante told me. "It's about damned time you dated a decent woman."

They made it sound like a scene out of an old western where the cowboy falls for the farmer's daughter—a woman of character.

My hands began to sweat. I couldn't understand why I was so nervous about pursuing Lianna. It had been much easier to hook up with Heather last year. But with Lianna, everything felt different. This decision seemed like it had higher stakes.

"When I went out with Heather last year that first time, there wasn't much at risk," I told them. "I didn't have anything on the line with her. But, with Lianna, I feel like I'm risking it all. Like I'm betting everything on one roll of the dice."

Ford twisted a knob on a tank of propane and then pressed the button next to the fire pit. With a whoosh, a bright ball of fire leaped into existence.

"Is it possible that you feel this way because you already know she's something special?" Ford asked.

My stomach tightened. "Maybe. I don't know." He could be right. After all, Lianna wasn't a stranger. I'd known her since I was seventeen, and I'd always been attracted to her.

Ford adjusted the flame and sat down on the stone bench. The light from the fire flickered over his features, giving him an other-worldly glow.

"Time will tell," he said. "But Lianna is a good person. She's one of Mara's closest friends."

His words were supportive, a pleasant change from last year when none of my friends had liked Heather much. It should have been a sign that Heather was not the right person for me. It was reassuring to know that my friends already approved of Lianna.

"I've only gone out with a handful of women since Heather and I broke up," I said, poking at the fire pit with a wet stick. It sizzled and popped. "Only a couple of second dates. No third ones. I'm having trouble trusting anyone."

Dante sat down on the bench next to Ford. "You don't need to assume all women lie."

"It's not that simple," I said, prodding a stone in the pit. "Heather really did a number on me with that fake pregnancy. I'm finding it hard to believe anything a woman says to me anymore."

Dante frowned. "Don't assume a relationship with Lianna will go south. She's a better human being—all around—than Heather could ever hope to be. So are you, for that matter. The two of you just might be perfect for each other."

Zephyr sat down next to my feet and leaned against my legs. Reflexively, I scratched Zephyr's ear as I considered Dante's words. "Yeah," I finally admitted. "Could be."

"Tell you what," Dante said. "Bring her to my restaurant Friday. I'll give you the best table. The one with that stupendous view of the Ohio River."

I lifted my eyebrows skeptically. "Isn't assigning tables Conner's domain?"

Dante chuckled. "Don't tell me you're afraid of your own brother."

"I'm not afraid," I said. "Just don't go blaming me if he gets pissed at you for it."

"Stop worrying, kid. Conner and I are like this." He raised his crossed fingers on his unbandaged hand. "Bring her. I'll make reservations for you at seven."

14

2ND FAVORITE

Lianna

When I arrived at the Not a Yacht Club on Friday night, I was full of nervous energy. I planned to tell Kincaid about my infertility tonight, and it had me on edge. I'd had to stay late at work and had come straight here, but I ended up arriving fifteen minutes early because the traffic on the bridge crossing the Ohio River was lighter than usual.

The downstairs was packed, but I was lucky enough to find a single seat at the bar where I could wait for Kincaid to arrive.

I'd hoped to be able to go home first, since Kincaid said the framing should be done today. I'd wanted to see it, but that would have made me late.

I scanned the room but didn't spot anyone I recognized. I pulled out my phone and sent Kincaid a quick text.

> Me: Already here. The place is crowded.

> Kincaid: I'm on my way. Be there in ten minutes.
> We have a reservation for 7.

Reed set a square napkin on the bar. "What will it be? I just invented a new martini, if you'd like to try it. It has fresh basil."

I raised my eyebrows. "Sounds unusual, but intriguing."

"If you don't like it, let me know and I'll give you something else."

"It's a deal."

Just as I finished speaking with Reed, I felt someone approach me from behind. An instant later, a heavy male hand clapped me on the back, causing me to jump in surprise.

"How's my second-favorite girl?" my ex-husband asked.

I cringed at the words and had to curb my impulse to elbow Paul in the stomach.

This is what I got for arriving early. I should have waited in my car.

Reed's head snapped toward the sound of Paul's inept greeting, and his grip on the martini glass faltered, sending it tumbling to the floor with a tinkling crash. Reed danced back from the shards, his eyes widening in surprise and irritation as he shot Paul a glare.

Paul didn't even notice.

"How's my least favorite ex-husband?" I gave him the stink-eye and shrugged off his hand.

He had the nerve to look hurt, the ass. I ignored him. Paul wasn't permitted to look hurt. Not after what he'd done. So why did I feel like I'd just kicked a dog? Years of caring about him, I guess. Old habits and all that.

Just then, my phone buzzed. I snatched it up like a lifeline, glancing at the screen. It was my brother Troy.

I opened the message and came face-to-face with a grainy black-and-white sonogram image.

Troy: Felicity changed her mind and decided she doesn't want to wait any longer to find out the baby's gender, so now we're letting everyone else know too. We're having a girl!

My stomach stopped its gymnastics. A girl? That was fabulous news. Not that a boy wouldn't have been fabulous news, either. It was simply exciting to know their baby would be here soon.

Me: Yay! I'm having a niece! Tell Felicity she'd better prepare for that baby to get spoiled!

Paul looked over my shoulder at the image on my phone. "Is that from Troy?"

"Yep." I held up the phone so he could see the image more clearly.

"A baby girl." Paul tugged at his ear. "Does that bother you?"

I scowled at him. "Do you really think I'm so petty that I'd begrudge them a baby simply because I can't have one?" I should have waited in my car. Stupid. What a seriously bad decision.

The couple next to me stood and headed to the hostess station, so Paul claimed the seat next to mine. "Of course, I don't. Sorry. Tell Troy and Felicity I said congratulations."

Yeah. When pigs fly.

Paul cleared his throat. "Meeting someone?"

"I have a date, but I'm early. He should be here soon."

Paul glanced down the nearby corridor. "Gloria's in the ladies' room."

My stomach began to churn again at the mention of Paul's new "favorite girl." It was galling to know the woman was still in his life, but really, which would be worse? Having my marriage destroyed because of a one-night stand, or having my husband stay with the other woman? Each scenario would have had its own special kind of pain.

After finding them together in our bed, I'd learned they'd been seeing each other for a while. I felt like a complete fool for not noticing anything suspicious before. I had never thought I would be so gullible.

I pulled a face and glanced toward the restrooms to see if I could spot Gloria.

"She's not that bad," Paul said, reading my expression. "I bet you'd like her if you got to know her."

I snorted. Actually snorted. I couldn't help myself. Paul seriously had a screw loose if he believed I'd ever like Gloria. The woman was a cheater, just like him.

A sudden thought turned my stomach sour. "Are you having dinner here?"

"That's the plan. You?"

No, no, no! The idea of having Paul and Gloria as onlookers during my date almost sent me running, but instead, I pulled up my big girl panties and pasted my smile in place. "The reservation is at seven."

Paul shook his head and grinned. "Sounds par for the course for you. You always plan ahead and show up early." He suddenly went still. His face flushed as he looked away.

Great. Now he'd made me remember the last time I'd arrived early to meet him—and found him in bed with that woman.

I bit my tongue. Literally. Total tongue biting going on here. It took tremendous willpower, but I managed not to utter a single word, despite wanting to lash out at him.

My plans for tonight were beginning to take on a surreal quality. Having a romantic dinner with Kincaid while Paul and Gloria sat across the room would be bad enough, even on a good night, but knowing my ex would have front-row seats while I told Kincaid about my infertility—that was too much to bear.

Maybe I should reconsider the baring-my-soul part of the plan.

Reed delicately set my brimming basil martini in the center of a white cocktail napkin. He tapped the counter next to the drink with a forefinger. "Tell me what you think of it. It isn't bitter, is it?"

I lifted the glass with care, admiring the paper-thin slice of lime and the floating basil leaf. How did he manage not to spill a drop? I could barely get it to my lips without making a mess.

A burst of fresh, sweet, tart flavor flooded my senses. I raised my eyebrows in appreciation. It tasted like springtime. I took another sip. "Perfect. Not bitter in the least. You've outdone your-self, Reed."

He grinned and gave me a subtle thumbs-up before turning to assist another customer.

Just then, Gloria sauntered over to us, wearing a pair of pink stiletto heels that matched her skin-tight dress. Despite my dislike for her, I had to admit that she looked adorable, the paragon of petite femininity.

I despised her. Pure and simple.

And Paul was a louse, any way you cut it.

To hide my grimace, I took another gulp of my martini.

"Did I give you two enough time to catch up?" Gloria claimed the barstool on the other side of Paul.

"Nearly. Lianna just got some big news. Her brother is having a baby girl."

Gloria wrinkled her nose. "That's great."

My breathing stuttered. "You don't want kids of your own?"

"I'm not mother material. I already know that about myself." As I absorbed that bit of information, Gloria glanced at Paul. "Did you tell her my news?"

I took in the telling sheen of nervous perspiration on Paul's upper lip and immediately knew I wasn't going to like this. "Nope. He didn't say a word."

"That text sidetracked us." Paul gave me one of those lopsided apologetic grins that used to work so well on me.

Not anymore.

Gloria smiled brightly. "I moved. Here. To Sewickley." She raised her hands in a ta-da gesture. "I found a place in town. The commute to my yoga studio will be a lot easier this way."

I closed my eyes to let the news sink in before snapping them open again. "Good for you," I lied. "Did you get tired of commuting from downtown Pittsburgh?"

"That, and I realized I needed to keep a closer eye on Paul. He doesn't do well when he gets lonely."

I arched one eyebrow. That had been his excuse for having an affair. He'd been lonely. "You can say that again." I could feel Gloria's eyes on me and worried she might have picked up on more than I meant to reveal.

Paul avoided my gaze as he set his drink on the bar. "We thought you should know."

Gloria turned that same considering gaze on Paul. "I'm famished. How long will we have to wait for a table?"

"You were right. I should have made a reservation. They're busy. They won't have a table available for at least another hour."

The knot of tension in my belly unraveled. They wouldn't be watching me on my date after all. I'd never have believed I'd ever think this, but thank the stars for Paul's procrastination. The habit had always annoyed me, but tonight it had been a godsend.

Gloria's bottom lip protruded slightly at the news. She fixed her gaze on Paul and then slowly dragged her finger down his upper arm.

It twitched.

"You know," Gloria drawled, "I've been dying to try the new sushi restaurant that just opened down the street. Since we have a long wait here, we might as well see if we can get in there sooner." She glanced at me and winked in a decidedly co-conspiratorial sort of way.

I tensed. Was Gloria trying to do something kind by taking Paul somewhere else?

"Might as well." Paul moved to stand. "Have fun on your date."

I shot Gloria a curious look. The woman had handled Paul to perfection.

Gloria gave me a tentative smile, along with a nod of acknowledgment.

So, maybe Gloria wasn't completely evil.

Just immoral.

And unethical.

After all, what kind of woman slept with another woman's husband? Maybe she and Paul were perfect for each other.

15

MEETING UP

KINCAID

As I approached the front entrance of Not a Yacht Club, the door swung open, and a man came out with a woman clinging to his arm. I almost did a doubletake. Wasn't that Lianna's ex-husband Paul? The woman with him appeared to be a fitness buff, wearing a tight pink dress that hugged her curves like a lover. Everything about her suggested high maintenance.

On the surface, Lianna and this woman had only one thing in common—they both oozed self-confidence. I swept past them and into the downstairs bar where I spotted Lianna chatting with Reed, one of the guys from my cooking class as well as the bartender here.

She looked stunning tonight. Her dark hair tumbled down her back in heavy waves, and she wore a summery top with slim-fitting pants. Perfect.

"Hi, love." I slid onto the stool next to her.

She tensed. "Hi, yourself." She shot me a tight smile that didn't reach her eyes. "Want to try my basil martini? It's Reed's latest invention, and it's delicious."

I raised an eyebrow as I glanced at the slice of lime and the basil leaf floating in her glass. Reed must be getting creative again. If he was trying it out on a customer, it had to be good.

"Sure," I said. "I'll live dangerously." I took a sip and raised my eyebrows approvingly. "This is great." I looked over at Reed. "Can you make me one, too?"

"You got it." Reed paused. "Conner says your drinks are on him tonight." Reed pulled out a martini shaker and added some ice.

I jerked my head back in surprise. "What's gotten into him?" I asked. "I don't think he's ever given me free drinks before."

"He doesn't tell me those sorts of things. He just says 'jump,' and I say, 'how high?'"

Lianna grinned. "Does that mean you didn't know that Courtney gets free drinks here all the time?"

"Figures. She was always his favorite."

The hostess approached us. "If you're ready, I can seat you now."

"Go ahead." Reed gestured toward the staircase to the restaurant upstairs. "I'll have your drink delivered to your table."

"Thanks, Reed." I rose to my feet.

"At least tonight won't be a complete bust," Lianna said as she stood. "Free drinks always make everything better." Her eyes went wide. "Oh, no. I can't believe I just said that. I was trying to make a joke. I'm sure tonight will be nice—gah! I mean fun." She shook her head. "Maybe I should stop talking now."

I grazed my hand across her back, noting her tense muscles. "You're nervous. Don't be. I saw your ex leaving, so I assume that's what put you on edge. I think Conner is offering to pay for our drinks as a way of saying he likes us together."

Had Lianna just stopped breathing?

I wanted to kick myself. "Sorry. I probably shouldn't have told you that."

"No. It's sweet." She wouldn't meet my eyes. Something was off with her tonight. She was tense as hell. Had seeing her ex messed her up this much? That was a bad sign. I didn't want to be her rebound guy. I had my eye on the boyfriend role.

I shifted to one side and slid my hand across her back as she moved past me to follow the hostess. Honestly, I'd take any chance to touch her. Her now-familiar scent of Chanel Number 5 wafted behind her as I trailed her up the staircase to the restaurant.

Watching that delicious apple-shaped backside sway as she climbed the stairs was becoming one of my new favorite pastimes.

After our muddy encounter at her house the other night, I hadn't been able to sleep. Even after I'd drifted off, she'd invaded my dreams. Incredible dreams, thanks to her.

I repeated to myself that I needed to take things slow even if that wasn't my typical approach to life. I really liked Lianna. A lot, actually. Enough to learn from my past mistakes with Heather—rushing into a relationship was a bad idea. Moving slowly was the smart, cautious thing, even if every particle of my being wanted to rush toward Lianna at lightspeed, consequences be damned.

16

A DATE WITH BUTTERFLIES

LIANNA

I followed the server to our table, which was located near a large window that provided a stunning view of the Ohio River. I started to take a seat on the left side, but Kincaid beat me to it and pulled out the chair. Who did that these days?

As our eyes met, a playful twinkle appeared in Kincaid's eyes. "Thanks," I said.

He sat down across from me, and our gazes locked for a moment. "You look amazing, as usual," he said, shooting me a charming grin that made my stomach flutter. Some of my tension eased. Did he have any idea what his smile did to me?

"You clean up pretty nice yourself." And he did. His dark hair and expressive green eyes made him look absolutely stunning. He was wearing a button-front shirt tonight that hugged his toned body perfectly.

The tension between us intensified. I was drawn to him as if we were connected by a magnetic force. I wanted him on all levels, not just physically, but emotionally. He made me feel special and comfortable. I already cared about him much more than was prudent.

But I needed to remain levelheaded for this. I couldn't let my emotions get the best of me or I might lose my nerve about telling him the truth. I needed to be strong.

I tore my gaze away and picked up my napkin, laying it across my lap. Looking into Kincaid's eyes had been a mistake. I couldn't look at him now.

Gradually, I started to notice my surroundings again. A bright flash of blue on the riverbank caught my eye. Was it a swimsuit? A plastic buoy? I leaned forward to get a better look. "Is that a kayak?"

Kincaid leaned forward as well. "Conner finally opened the kayak and canoe rental he's been talking about for the past two years. This definitely isn't a yacht club."

"I love kayaking." I sat back in my chair and savored the fresh green flavors of my basil martini. "My dad has a kayak. We used to go out on the river all the time, but lately it's usually just me and Zoey."

"Zoey's your sister, right? Does she live nearby?"

"She's a student at Pitt. She has an apartment near the main campus." A couple in their mid-forties, wearing life vests, stepped out onto the dock below.

"You and I should take a kayak out sometime."

My stomach did one of those somersaults. I wanted that. So much. But would he still be interested in seeing me after I told him about my infertility? I lifted the menu up to hide my face. God, I needed to get this over with. "That sounds like fun."

"How about Sunday?"

I slowly lowered my menu. I should tell him now. What if I agreed to go kayaking with him and then he was too nice to cancel even though he didn't want to see me again? I could just imagine the awkward silence that would drown us as we sat in that little boat in the middle of that enormous river. Misery.

"Kincaid—" I started.

Our waitress appeared and set Kincaid's basil martini in front of him.

"Hi, Becky," Kincaid said. "It's good to see you."

Becky smiled. "You too, Kincaid. Your brother mentioned you'd be here tonight. Can I tell you about Dante's specials?"

"Sure thing, thanks," he said, and Becky proceeded to recite the specials. She left us to decide on our orders.

Glancing at the river, I said, "The water view has put me in the mood for seafood. The ahi tuna sounds tempting."

"I want the snapper," Kincaid said as he set down his menu. Becky stopped by our table to take our orders and then hurried away.

My mouth felt dry. Was it just nerves? I took another quick sip of my martini. "There's something I need to tell you. I have to admit I'm nervous about it."

Kincaid went still. "Okay. I'm all ears."

"This is kind of hard for me, so just bear with me for a minute."

Kincaid nodded and sipped his water. As he leaned back in his chair, he brushed his thumb across his lower lip. He seemed so perfectly at ease, but it only made me more nervous. I needed to stop dragging this out and get it over with.

I couldn't meet his eyes. Instead, I stared at the basil leaf floating in my martini. "I really like you, but before we go any further, there's something important you need to know about me. It might matter to you." I swallowed, took a deep breath, and let it out. "I'm infertile. I can't get pregnant. I've been tested, but since my doctor couldn't find a cause, he couldn't do anything to help. I had planned to have more testing done, but then my marriage fell apart, and that derailed everything in the baby department. I just thought you should know, in case it's a deal breaker for you."

I finally looked at him, but he was staring out the window at the river. I couldn't read his expression.

When his eyes met mine, they tangled us up together, and I couldn't look away.

"I can tell this is difficult for you," he said, opening his mouth and then closing it again. He shook his head. "I'm trying to choose my words carefully."

I began to fill the awkward silence with anything that came to mind, trying to avoid the crushing weight of it. "My ex-husband, Paul, was tested too, and he passed with flying colors. Whatever the problem is, it lies with me." Kincaid's thumb slid back and forth along the rim of his glass, but then he stopped and looked up at me. I couldn't read his expression. Was that disappointment, disillusionment, or pain?

My stomach twisted into new somersaults, and I felt myself crumbling under his gaze. I was about to cry.

Kincaid suddenly pushed his martini glass aside, almost spilling it, and leaned closer. He extended his hand, palm up, toward me. I stared at it, avoiding eye contact, but I didn't move. I couldn't. I was frozen.

"I understand that you want children, and I'm sorry that you can't. That must have been a blow. Thank you for sharing that with me," he said.

I pressed my lips together, unable to trust my voice not to waver. Talking about this left me feeling too vulnerable, exposed, and defenseless. I simply shrugged.

His hand remained there, palm open, waiting for me to place mine in it. Should I take a chance?

I slowly uncurled my sweaty palms from beneath the table and lifted one hand. Tentatively, I reached out to touch him. Fingertips touching fingertips, then hand grasping hand.

"The fact that you were so upfront with me took me by surprise. Now I understand why my story about losing a baby who had never existed affected you so deeply."

Tears welled in my eyes, but I blinked them away and met his gaze. "It's hard to lose a dream."

"But that's all it ever was for me. A dream. When Heather and I got engaged, we hadn't been together long. Only a couple of months." Kincaid was the one to look away this time, and I sensed his discomfort.

He stared down at our linked hands before gliding his thumb across my knuckles. "It was too early in our relationship to decide to get married. We didn't know each other well enough. Honestly, things weren't even that serious between us. After we got engaged, though, everything changed. She wasn't who I thought she was. I realized we had different values and goals. I had been impressed by her drive and ambition, but I came to understand that impressing others was the primary goal of her life, to have the right clothes, the right house, the right fiancé." The corner of his mouth twitched. "It seems that I was close to what she wanted, but I wasn't ideal. She kept trying to improve me." His green eyes met mine. "When I told you about her that first night, you might have thought that her lie drove us apart. It wasn't just that. We were a bad match."

"I'm sorry. It must have been difficult to come to that realization." I knew the pain of being with the wrong person, with someone who wasn't who they seemed to be.

"I always assumed I'd have kids, but it isn't a make-or-break thing for me. After everything I went through with Heather, I've come to realize that sharing my life with the right person is what's really important." He rubbed his thumb across the back of my knuckles. "I know it's early in our relationship, but I want you to know that I could see myself being very happy with you. With us. Just you and me."

My fingers twitched involuntarily in his grasp. I wanted to snatch my hand away. How could he know that? "You can make such an important decision on the spot?"

He glanced down at our hands. "It's strange to be talking about this so soon with you, but when I think about you and what we might become, I only imagine the two of us." He glanced out at the river, and his eyes tracked the couple in the kayak. "That might simply be due to a lack of imagination on my part. I'm good at visualizing what a house will look like after I renovate it, and I know how I want my business to grow, but I'm not so good at imagining what my future will hold on a more personal level. I guess I don't spend all that much time thinking about stuff like that."

Hope fluttered in my chest, and my words came tumbling out. "Do you want to keep seeing me?"

He tightened his grip on my hand. "Definitely, love."

I stared at him in stunned silence, my mind racing to process the unexpected turn of events. I had braced myself for his rejection, not his acceptance. His next words took me completely off guard.

"Listen," he began, pausing for a moment to carefully choose his words, "if this ends up going somewhere—if we end up together—would you ever consider adoption? Is that even an option for you?"

Relief flooded me. My face broke into a wide grin. "Definitely. Paul was against all of it. Adoption, in vitro, surrogacy—he wouldn't discuss any of it."

"That was pretty selfish of him," Kincaid remarked, shaking his head. "It doesn't sound as though your happiness was all that important to him. It's hard to be with someone who refuses to talk about things."

My breath caught in my throat. "I suppose that's true."

"I want to say something important, and I want you to remember it. Whether we end up together or not, I want to make sure you don't ever settle for less than you deserve. Don't accept a man who doesn't put your happiness first. You should be with someone who makes you his priority. Can you remember that?"

I shook my head in bemusement, moved by his sincerity. "I have to admit, Kincaid, you're an amazing man."

"Promise me," he insisted.

My heart gave a thump. "I promise."

"Good." He nodded, looking satisfied. "I'm glad we got that out of the way. Now, I need an answer to that all-important question you neatly dodged earlier."

I stared at him, momentarily confused. "What question?"

"Do you want to go kayaking with me this weekend?"

17

WALKING ON STARDUST

Kincaid

As we lingered over dinner, the sun sank slowly behind the cliffs overlooking the Ohio River. Lights winked on to illuminate the graceful lines of the enormous steel bridge, and beneath it a barge crept downriver, its massive size making it appear to inch forward.

I admired the stunning woman across from me. Being with Lianna put me completely at ease. She looked lovely tonight. Her inner radiance lit her up, making her incandescent.

As I glanced out the window, the trail lights illuminating the path along the river flickered to life. Conner had installed the walkway last summer and embedded it with glowing chips, making it a popular spot for evening strolls.

"Would you like to take a walk along the river?" I asked.

She leaned her elbows on the table, her long, dark-brown hair falling forward to frame her face. "I'd love to. And thank you for dinner. It was so delicious, but I think I ate too much."

"I'll let Dante know you enjoyed his cooking," Conner said, appearing next to our table.

"Please do," Lianna said, looking up at him. "Everything was perfect."

"Thanks for the drinks," I added.

Conner shrugged as he tried to hide a smirk and failed. "I have to admit, our big sister suggested I comp them. I think she's already shipping the two of you. Sometimes it's easier just to go along with her."

I glanced at Lianna, and we both shrugged. "Not much we can do about her. She seems invested."

"Courtney is a force of nature," Lianna said.

Conner chuckled. "You could try to get her to back off, but she can be tenacious when she thinks she knows best."

"When we were growing up," I said, "I think she knew everything we were planning to do before we even did it."

Lianna's eyes danced with amusement. "She did mention that her little brothers kept her on her toes. She says you two were troublemakers as kids."

I shook my head in mock despair. "That woman never forgets anything. I bet she's still pissed that we turned her dolls into zombies."

Lianna stared at me a moment. "Zombies? Um, no. She never mentioned that particular transgression. I bet she was furious."

Conner shot me a mock frown. "Way to go 'Caid. Now she knows we were into zombies before they became cool again."

I feigned confusion. "Wait. Are you trying to tell me there was a time when they weren't cool? That can't be right. This is Pittsburgh, after all. Home of the very first zombie flick. *Night of the Living Dead*. They might have gone out of style in other parts of the country, but they've always been cool in the Burgh."

"Can't argue with you there." Conner rubbed the back of his neck.

I stood. "We were just about to take a walk along the river."

"It's a perfect night for it." Conner took a step back and ushered us toward the door.

The sun had set by the time we began strolling down the asphalt walkway. The little glow-in-the-dark flecks embedded in the pathway shone—some fainter and some brighter—giving it the appearance of the Milky Way. Dante and Conner had added the stones last year, and they had become a popular attraction around town. Not a Yacht Club had even hosted a spooky Halloween event with a haunted forest, which had attracted a lot of locals.

The warmth from the sun had dissipated rapidly after it dipped below the cliffs, although the asphalt still radiated some heat.

Lianna halted and rummaged through her large purse. A moment later, she pulled out a bright floral wrap. She quickly wrapped it around her shoulders and knotted the ends to hold it in place.

What else did she keep in that purse? I raised my eyebrows, impressed. "You came prepared."

She shrugged. "I hate being cold. I usually carry a pashmina with me wherever I go."

I draped my arm across her shoulders. "Body heat is more fun."

"Mmm. It is." She hugged my waist, and the knot kept her scarf from falling. "Maybe I should put you in my purse instead of the pashmina."

I relished the way she fit snugly under my arm, especially with the alluring scent of Chanel Number 5 that made me want to nuzzle her hair.

As we stepped under the trees, I asked, "Have you been down this path before?"

"Huh," she said, "it sounds like you're speaking in metaphor." I could hear the smile in her voice. "I'll answer both literally and metaphorically. Yes, I've walked along this path a few times. Your brother was brilliant to pave this section and add lighting. It's so beautiful and peaceful. I love it." She glanced at me and smiled tentatively. "And metaphorically, I'll assume you're asking if I've dated since the divorce, and that's a yes, too. I've met some guys, had a few dates, a couple of second dates. Nothing that stuck, though."

I nodded, surprised to get so much information from my casual question, but I appreciated it. I liked that she didn't shy away from difficult topics and was honest and forthright. "So, if things progress between us, am I risking being your rebound guy?"

She thought for a moment before shaking her head. "Nah, I think I'm past that stage. Although, I might have some residual trust issues."

"That makes sense. It can be tough to trust again after you've been betrayed."

"You've been there, too." She tightened her arm around my waist, and the pressure was reassuring. "Not the same kind of betrayal, but a pretty painful one."

"We have that in common," I replied.

The dense foliage muffled most of the sounds from the nearby highway. The glow stones along the path faintly illuminated the way, but they were dim. They ended just ahead, and the path continued deeper into the trees.

"We have better things in common, too," she said, turning her head to face me.

"Good point," I said, stopping on the path. "Let's focus on those." I tipped my head down and briefly brushed my lips against hers. Not a real kiss. Just a quick grazing of the lips.

The rhythmic lap of the water against the shore made me feel as though we'd entered a place separate from the rest of the world. I had the sense that if we kept going, we'd step into another universe altogether.

Lianna turned and pulled me along toward the end of the paved path. We stepped off the blacktop and onto the damp earth.

"It's peaceful here," Lianna said, gazing out at the water.

I kicked a small rock down the path. It hit a rough spot, changed trajectory, and went rattling off into the trees.

"A couple of weeks ago, I met a guy out here playing with his Labrador Retriever," Lianna said. "He was throwing a ball into the river so she could dive in after it. He said it was her favorite thing to do in the whole world. I believe him. I don't think I've ever seen a happier dog."

We reached a part of the path where the water had spilled over the bank and left behind a large mud puddle. The path turned away from the river here and moved deeper into the wooded area. A wooden pallet had been dragged over it, serving as a makeshift bridge. I eyed it with skepticism. "Do you want to keep going, or turn back?"

"More metaphors?" she teased. "Keep going, of course."

Clever woman.

Lianna tugged on my hand. "Don't tell me you're afraid of slipping and getting your shoes dirty." She stepped away and glanced down at my leather shoes. "Oh. Maybe you are. Those look too nice. I wouldn't want to ruin them." She shot me a mischievous look. "Tell me, Kincaid, are you as clumsy as I seem to be?"

I arched my eyebrows. "That sounded like a dare."

"Did it?" She darted across the pallet to the other side.

An instant later, I was standing next to her, wrapping her in my arms. Here along this darker part of the path, it was harder to see her face.

"So, you can't resist a dare," she teased. "That's extremely interesting. I should warn you: I'll use that against you. You'll be putty in my hands."

"It's you I can't resist. Not the dare. I don't think I mind the idea of being putty in your hands, as long as that means your hands will be on me." I pulled her closer.

I bent my head, just a little, and paused so our breaths inter-mingled. I waited for her to make the next move. She closed the distance, pressing her lips against mine. The hot jolt of passion that surged through me made my body tingle with awareness.

Lianna's lips were soft. Warm.

I tilted my head to one side and let out a sigh that whispered over her lips.

"If that's the reward I get for accepting a dare," I murmured "you need to do it on a daily basis."

She clung to me. "If that's the response I get for daring you, you can count on it."

I stepped back and tucked a strand of her hair behind her ear. "Do you want to keep going?" I peered down the path. It was hard to see very far since the woods were so dense, but I'm pretty sure we were facing more puddles of thick mud.

"It doesn't look like we'll be able to go much farther without getting muddy," she said. "The river's been running high this spring. This section of the path is a mess."

"Not going to dare me this time?" I teased her.

"How about I dare you to turn back with me? Will that give me the same response as last time?"

"You can count on it." I squeezed her hand and then let her go. "Lead the way."

She hesitated at the edge of the pallet. It was darker now, and this spot was in deep shadows.

"Having trouble?" I asked.

"I can't see anything, so I can't decide where to step," Lianna replied.

Without hesitation, I lifted her into my arms, navigating the wooden slats with ease, and placed her safely on the other side. We continued down the path until we reached a small clearing where I gently set her back on her feet. Lianna gasped in surprise before grinning up at me. She had enjoyed being carried; I could tell.

"You're very resourceful," she said, flattening her palms against my chest. "Quite the problem solver."

"What can I say? I saw a lady in distress and took action," I replied with a smile.

As we stood in the clearing, I couldn't help but notice the barge slowly disappearing from sight, concealed by the tall stand of pale flowers. It was a reminder that the real world was waiting for us beyond our romantic bubble, and a pang of remorse washed over me at the thought of our moment out of time coming to an end.

Lianna broke my thoughts, "Do you know that song '*Moon River?*'" she asked, staring out at the river.

"The one from *Breakfast at Tiffany's?*" I replied, grateful for the distraction.

"That's it. The composer, Henry Mancini, grew up just a few miles from here in Aliquippa. I've always imagined he was writing about this stretch of the Ohio River. It's beautiful."

I looked at her, seeing her face glow in the soft moonlight. I wanted to remember this moment forever, to imprint every feature of her just as she looked right now. "Not as beautiful as you," I said, "The way the light reflects off the water and shimmers across your hair and skin is mesmerizing. You look like you're sparkling."

She stepped closer and leaned in so her lips were inches from mine.

My heart thumped harder. We were nose-to-nose when an ear-blistering blast of a barge horn ripped through the silence.

Bla-a-at!

The sound hit us like a warning bell and she rocketed away from me.

"What was that?" She pressed her hand over her heart. "A barge horn?"

Out on the river, a smaller boat let out a short toot, as if in reply.

Lianna gave a whole-body shake. "I guess I scare easily."

Our eyes met. I pulled her into my arms, dipped my head, and nipped at her lower lip, teasing it. Pulling it between my lips.

She let out a nervous sigh as she slid her hand around my neck, caressing my nape with her thumb and brushing it against the grain of my hair.

We deepened our kiss as I slid my hand down her side. When my thumb grazed a strip of bare flesh between her waistband and her top, she gave a startled jerk.

She put her hand over mine, stilling my movements. "You're… this is…" She stopped and licked her lips, but she wouldn't meet my eyes. "That barge horn really put me on edge. I'm sorry. It's just—I thought I was ready for this, but I haven't been with anyone in a long time." She let out a gust of air. "This is getting intense for me."

I drew my hand away. "I don't want you to do anything you're not ready for. We can take things at your pace."

"Thank you." She leaned in and kissed me softly. "I appreciate that. I think I'm ready to head back now. It's getting late."

"Lead the way."

She squeezed my hand. "I'd like to see you again."

"So would I. How about Thursday evening? A group of writers from Saturday Night Live are performing at the comedy club in downtown Pittsburgh. Want to go?"

"Sounds perfect."

She led us to her car and stopped to face me.

I leaned toward her, planning to kiss her senseless again, but at the last minute, I changed my mind. I altered my aim and placed a quick peck on her cheek.

Lianna's eyes crinkled around the corners as she gave a slow smile. "Goodnight, Kincaid." She climbed into her driver's seat.

That was anticlimactic.

I watched her push the button to start her car, hoping she would look at me.

Thankfully, she did.

I rested my arms on the roof of her car and leaned down so I could meet her eyes.

She frowned as she rolled down her window. "What?"

I gave her a slow smile. "I dare you to kiss me."

Her mouth twitched. "I'm not the one who'll do anything for a dare."

"Not 'anything for a dare,'" I corrected her, "anything for a kiss." I leaned forward, resting my forearms on her open window ledge and leaning in.

Her lips met mine and we were kissing again. Falling into each other—again.

Music burst into the parking lot as someone walked out of the restaurant and she immediately pulled away.

"You're such a tease," I said.

She gave an impish grin. "See you Thursday." She waved and drove away.

18

COMIC RELIEF, INTERRUPTED

Lianna

Last Friday's date had been perfect. Better than I'd dreamed it would be.

Sure, running into Paul and Gloria had thrown me off my stride. Even now, imagining them as onlookers while I had that conversation with Kincaid made my stomach flip.

But everything had worked out after all. Kincaid hadn't ditched me.

I still couldn't believe how well he took the news about me being infertile—something I had barely dared to hope for. I suppose a faint hope must have existed somewhere deep inside me; otherwise, I wouldn't have bared my soul. Instead, I would have distanced myself from him and figured out how to end things.

Kincaid's touch and his kisses had left me reeling. I'd felt so off-balance that I'd had to put on the brakes. Maybe that barge horn had been a sign for me to slow things down. I hadn't slept with anyone since my ex. I was a woman of strong appetites, so celibacy wasn't the issue. It was timing. I needed to clear my head before I let Kincaid into my life, and my bed.

I was excited about seeing him tonight. Nearly a week apart

was too long. Now that I knew we might have something real between us—something real that had the potential to grow and last—I wanted to get on with it, embrace our future—or at least explore the possibilities, because Kincaid was something special. I knew it deep in my heart.

As I was leaving work, a text came in.

Kincaid: My truck is making strange noises. Do you mind driving tonight? The comedy show is in Pittsburgh.

Me: No problem. I hope your truck is okay.

Kincaid: Me too. My mechanic can't get to it until Monday.

I went home and changed into something more comfortable for a date night—jeans and a cute red top. When I arrived at Kincaid's, he came outside before I could even turn off my engine. He looked scrumptious in his jeans and a Steelers t-shirt. I loved his toned, tanned, and muscular arms. Something about his forearms turned me on.

Man, I needed to sleep with this guy before I exploded. Hopefully, tonight would be the night. "I'm really excited about the comedy show. It sounds like it'll be a lot of fun."

"I'm glad you're excited. The shows I've seen at this venue have all been great, but there was one a few years ago at a different place that was terrible. There weren't many people there, and I almost walked out, but I felt sorry for the guy."

"That was kind of you. It must be difficult to perform on stage and face an audience that expects you to make them laugh. I don't think I could do it."

"My family isn't filled with class clowns. We're all on the serious side. Maybe it's because we mostly raised ourselves. Dad was never around, and Mom was what you might call a 'free spirit.' She let us run wild, so it was up to us to develop some self-discipline."

"You don't strike me as a free spirit kind of guy. You're focused and hardworking, like my dad. My mom wasn't a helicopter mom, but she always knew what I was up to."

"Are your parents still together?" he asked.

"Yeah. They live about ten minutes outside of Sewickley."

"Mine got divorced as soon as I graduated from high school, and my mom moved away. I think she was counting down the days until then. As the youngest, I always felt like an afterthought. All of my siblings have names that start with C. Christopher, Conner, and Courtney. My dad put his foot down and said he kept getting the names mixed up. No more C names. My mom got her revenge by naming me Kincaid. Dad always said it was just to spite him."

"She sounds like quite a character."

"I suppose so. All I know is that neither of them had much interest in being parents. Why they had four of us is beyond me. My oldest brother Christopher ran off to New York to avoid the responsibilities they always foisted off on him. After that, Courtney stepped in and handled it all pretty well. She likes being in charge."

"I've noticed."

"Maybe that's why Conner and I have a rocky relationship. He always resented having to watch me when we were little. Now that we're adults, he sometimes thinks he still gets to boss me around."

"Where are your parents now?"

"Dad moved to Florida, and Mom ran off to some island."

"An island? That sounds adventurous."

"That's probably what she thought too. All I know is that none of us ever see her anymore."

"My family life was completely different. My mom was there all the time. She drove us to ballet lessons and lacrosse practice. She was my sister's Girl Scout leader. You name it, she did it. She even volunteered to be the room mother every year when we were in elementary school."

"My parents never even went to parent-teacher conferences."

I grinned, shaking my head as I tried to imagine anyone stopping my mom from attending conference day. "Whereas my mom was on a first-name basis with all my teachers. She still exchanges Christmas cards with loads of them."

Kincaid laughed at that. "Our families are nothing alike. You have just one sister?"

"And a brother. Troy is married and lives outside of Washington D.C. Zoey is at the University of Pittsburgh studying art history. She hopes to open an art gallery someday." I scanned the road for a spot to park on the street, but didn't see one.

"Are you and Zoey close?"

I shrugged. "Not really. She's a few years younger than me, so we aren't as close as we might have been if we were closer in age. We tend to have an on-and-off relationship. I guess we're typical sisters. I'm probably closer to my brother, but I don't see him much these days."

I gave up on finding a parking spot on the street and pulled into a nearby parking garage.

"Thanks again for driving," Kincaid said. "It's always hard to find a place to park my truck in the city. It's so long that it doesn't fit into many spaces."

"I'm happy to do it." I took his hand as we headed toward the venue. "I checked out the progress on my house after work today. I love coming home every day and seeing something new."

"Additions are always exciting. We're right on schedule, too. The roofing crew was there today, and the plumber finished up a couple of things. My favorite electrician will be there tomorrow to start the wiring."

We stopped at the end of a short line of people waiting outside the comedy club to be let in. When the door opened, everyone moved inside.

The attendant scanned Kincaid's tickets on his phone, and we quickly settled into our prime seats in the second row of the small venue with only four rows facing the tiny stage. The room buzzed with excitement as the emcee took the stage, signaling the start of the show. Each comedian showcased their unique style, and the audience was thoroughly entertained.

By the end of the show, Kincaid and I were giggling like a pair of teenagers.

"Do you want to grab a drink?" he asked.

"Sure. There's a charming place down the street with a library-themed section. Their drinks are always perfect," I replied.

"Great drinks and great atmosphere," he said, squeezing my hand. "It sounds like you have your priorities straight."

"I always appreciate a creative bartender. This place never disappoints."

A short time later, I led us through the entrance of The Public Library.

"I know this spot," Kincaid said. "It's great."

As we made our way through the crowded main floor, I caught our reflection in the mirror behind the shelves of assorted spirits towering two stories above the bar. We climbed up past the second-floor dining area with its bookshelves, antler chandelier, and an enormous taxidermy bear, to the considerably quieter third floor. With our pick of seats, we settled at the bar.

The dark-haired bartender handed us a list of drink specials. I scanned it for something new and settled on a Cake Martini. Kincaid ordered Suntory Toki, a Japanese whiskey.

When my drink arrived, complete with rainbow sprinkles on the rim, I grinned with delight. It looked decadently delicious.

Kincaid looked at it dubiously. "Have you tried that one before?"

"Nope. I get a different drink every time I come here."

As Kincaid took his first sip of whiskey, his phone vibrated on the counter. Not with a text, but a call.

"Who's calling me so late?" He flipped it over, and I saw

Chrissy Murphy's name on the screen. He let out a frustrated sigh. "Sorry, I need to take this. It's a work call."

I nodded and he answered, "Hello?"

The bartender flipped on a blender, and Kincaid frowned. "Do you mind if I put it on speakerphone so I can hear better?" he asked.

"That's fine," I said.

"Can you repeat that?" He said to the person on the other line.

"I said, John just called from Japan and was raving about his bathroom there. He says it has heated mirrors that don't get foggy when the bathroom fills with steam, can you believe it?"

"I've heard of those," Kincaid told her. "If you want them, I'll need to get the electrician to come back to run the additional wiring before the building inspector comes on Monday. I don't know if he's available or not. If he isn't, you need to be aware that adding them could delay your entire project because we'd have to delay the inspection."

"I'll take that risk," Chrissy said. "This is a must-have. John loves them."

Kincaid nodded, lifted his phone, and pulled up his calendar.

"Let me call my crews and see what we can reschedule. I'll contact you tomorrow and inform you about the cost and timeline implications," Kincaid said.

"But the inspector isn't due until Monday," Chrissy noted. "You have all of tomorrow to add a few wires. That should be enough time."

Kincaid scowled at his phone. "I need to see if I can move people around to do this. My electrician is already scheduled to work on another job."

Chrissy sighed. "Can't you just have him do this first?" She sounded irritated. "It's quick and easy."

Kincaid's jaw tightened, and he massaged the bridge of his nose with his index finger and thumb. "Yes, it's quick, but if I move him to your job, I'll have to ask another client to postpone their work. These changes can have a ripple effect."

"Fine," Chrissy said, her pout evident over the speakerphone. "Just let me know what you can do. I'm counting on you."

The line went silent. I assumed she'd hung up.

Kincaid rubbed his hand over his face. "Adding the wiring should only take an hour or two," he mused, scrolling through his team's calendar. "If my electrician is willing to work overtime, he could do it. But I don't want to push another client's project back to accommodate Chrissy. Hopefully, it won't come to that."

"Is it the same electrician who's currently working on my house?" I asked.

"Yes, it is," Kincaid confirmed. "If I pull him off your job, it'll affect your timeline since you have a building inspection coming up. Let me figure this out for a minute."

After a few texts, Kincaid, gave a sigh of relief. "I was able to work it out."

"Does that happen often?"

He let out an irritated laugh. "Dealing with homeowner changes at ten at night? Fortunately, not often, but she's been more indecisive than most."

I sipped my Cake Martini, and Kincaid's gaze fell to my mouth, lingering there.

"Is this the same homeowner you mentioned before? The one who's pregnant and whose husband is always traveling?"

"Right on the first guess. I was working with her husband at first, but with him in China, she's my point of contact now. She calls at least a couple of times every day with a list of questions and concerns. She's kicked out my work crews twice now because she thought they were doing something the wrong way."

I raised my eyebrows. "Were they?"

"Nope. She doesn't know a lot about construction and gets spooked easily. It's frustrating because I was counting on this job to generate some buzz for me. Chrissy's working with a local interior designer, and her house is scheduled to be featured in the Pittsburgh Home Reno magazine this coming February. That is— if my crews don't refuse to work for her. No one likes being kicked off a job by the homeowner. If she does it again and they end up walking off the job, I'll be screwed. Word will get out that I missed deadlines and lost the Murphys their magazine feature. That could ruin my reputation."

I let out a sigh and shook my head. "You're really in a tough spot. Have you considered the possibility that her pregnancy might be making her anxiety worse? Hormonal changes can really make it a rollercoaster."

Kincaid shrugged. "Maybe. I need to set up a meeting with her to see if we can find a way to get her to stop panicking all the time. I don't want her to lose the magazine spread because she keeps changing her mind about things."

"Good idea. I bet you can reassure her that you know what you're doing. You have a great reputation. That must have played into their decision to hire you in the first place."

His gaze dropped to my mouth again, and I felt my heart skip a beat.

"I can't resist," he said as he leaned closer to me.

He lifted his hand and trailed a finger down the side of my face, sending shivers down my spine. I leaned in, and our lips met, the kiss deepening quickly.

The flavors of his Japanese whiskey and my cake-flavored vodka melded to perfectly complement the kiss, and a luscious heat spread through my body.

He cupped my face, and I felt myself falling into his gorgeous green eyes. "You make me happy, Lianna Alverson."

A smile sprang to my lips. "That was so sweet."

"You're sweet." He grinned, "Especially after drinking that Cake Martini."

When the bartender set our check in front of us, Kincaid glanced at his watch. "I didn't realize it was so late. We should head out so you can get to work tomorrow."

I pulled up in front of Kincaid's place a little while later and cut the car engine, my mind racing with thoughts of him.

I knew exactly how I wanted the night to end—or rather—

continue. I needed to get this man naked, finally, and the first step of my plan was to have him invite me inside.

It had been over a year since I'd had sex. I hadn't missed it much, truth be told. Out of sight, out of mind. At least, I hadn't missed it until Kincaid had walked into my life. Now? It was just about all I could think about.

Before I could reveal my nefarious and decidedly decadent plans for him, Kincaid leaned across the center console and kissed me. The sparks flew between us, igniting a fire that had been simmering all night.

My body turned liquid. He slid his hand along my side and pulled me even closer. His long, lingering kiss left me gasping for breath and desperate for more.

But before I could suggest we take things inside, headlights filled my rearview mirror, and I heard the crunch of gravel under tires as a car pulled up behind us.

Kincaid swore under his breath. "It's my brother. What's he doing here?"

I looked back. Sure enough, I recognized Conner in the driver's seat. My heart sank, and I slumped back in my seat, trying to hide my disappointment. "Does he stop by often?" I asked, trying to sound casual.

"Almost never," Kincaid replied, looking just as bewildered as I felt.

"I hope everything's okay," I said, trying to sound concerned.

Kincaid's hand brushed against mine, sending shivers down my spine. "I'm sorry," he said. "I'd planned to invite you in."

I couldn't resist leaning in for one more kiss, savoring the taste of his lips and the feel of his body against mine. But with Conner's headlights lighting up the car's interior, I knew it was time to go.

"I should probably be heading home now," I said, my voice barely above a whisper. "I have an early meeting."

"Can I see you this weekend? Take you out to dinner?"

I shook my head, disappointed. "I can't. I promised Mom we'd go antiquing in Lancaster, Pennsylvania this weekend. We leave tomorrow after work."

"Ah, that's too bad," he said.

"I know. I'd really like to see you, but we won't get back until Sunday evening."

He looked disappointed too. "I'll miss you. How about Monday? Could you pick me up from the Not a Yacht Club after my cooking class? My truck will be with the mechanic, and I'll need a ride home. What if you join me for dinner there? Dante says we'll be making a gourmet version of Mac and Cheese."

I flashed him a grin. "Sounds delicious. I love Mac and Cheese. How can I refuse? Text me Monday when you're ready for me to come by."

"Sure thing."

Kincaid climbed out of my car, and as I drove away, I stole a glance in the rearview mirror to see him watching me.

19

MAC AND CHEESE—DANTE'S STYLE

Kincaid

Lianna had been away all weekend, and I found myself missing her more than I had anticipated. I took advantage of the opportunity to tackle some yardwork and threw myself into mowing, mulching, and trimming until I was covered in sweat and grime, and my property looked amazing. When Lianna got back, I'd offer to help with hers too.

Mick lounged either in the sunroom or on the porch, watching me with sleepy cat eyes. Every time I took a break, he'd roll onto his back and stretch, as if mocking me and my foolish human endeavors.

Monday morning, I sent Lianna flowers to let her know how much I'd missed her. She called, probably to thank me, but we ended up playing phone tag.

Later that evening, as Conner and I worked on our recipe in Dante's cooking class, I kept glancing at my phone, hoping for a message from Lianna. Finally, fifteen minutes before dinner was ready, I sent her a text.

135

Me: The gourmet mac and cheese will be ready
soon. Can you still have dinner with me and give
me a ride home?

"This is so full of flavor and cheesy goodness, it's gonna be your favorite mac and cheese, ever," Dante said.

Lianna: Of course! I'd never let you down.
Besides, I'm starving! Be there in ten.

I grinned, feeling a sudden surge of adrenaline. Couldn't have timed it better.

I added a plate for her next to the two I'd already set out. When Conner returned from the bar, I noticed something off about him.

"Kennywood's open," I told him.

He glanced down at his pants, grimaced, and zipped his fly. "Thanks." He gestured toward the third plate on the counter and raised an eyebrow. "Are we expecting someone?"

"Lianna. She's giving me a ride home tonight. My truck's in for repairs."

He looked surprised. "Again?"

"What do you mean? It's new. This is the first time I've ever had to take it in."

"No," Conner said. "I meant Lianna. You're seeing a lot of her."

Not as much as I'd like. "I guess."

I tensed, waiting for him to start his usual sniping. But instead, he surprised me. "Sorry again about dropping by last Thursday. If you'd let me know you had a date, I never would have shown up like that."

His apology caught me off guard. I shrugged. "It's okay."

"What about work?" Conner continued. "Everything going okay? Is Chrissy causing problems?" His attempt to have a brotherly moment was a relief. Perhaps, we could avoid our usual arguments for once.

I let out a low laugh. "She's exactly as you predicted. The other two jobs are on schedule and running smoothly. Hers is giving me a headache, but I have a meeting with Chrissy to discuss the changes she's been making. Once we finalize things, I can create a new timeline."

Conner scratched the back of his neck with a frown. "Sounds like a lot of work. Don't let the Murphys take advantage of you."

My back tensed. Did he think I didn't know how to run my business? "That's why I had them sign a contract. Everything will work out in the end."

The kitchen door opened, and Lianna walked in, still wearing the gray pants, white shirt, and blazer she must have worn to work. "Hi, everyone."

The guys all greeted her, and Conner went to sit with Reed and Dante, giving me some alone time with her.

"What smells so delicious?" she asked as she came over to me. "I'm starving."

"Dante's Gourmet Mac and Cheese and Grits," I said, my lips meeting her cheek. "We're waiting for it to cool."

"Long name," she commented, glancing at me with a faint smile. "Maybe we could come up with a better one."

"True, but it describes it perfectly." I gestured toward the stool next to mine. "Come on, sit down and relax."

She looked exhausted, but I knew better than to mention it. "Did you come straight from work?"

"Yep." One side of her mouth lifted in a lopsided smile. "It's been a long, strange day. Things are hectic there with upper management meetings."

"Is something big going on?"

She shrugged. "'I'm not sure. There are too many secrets floating around, and I'm being kept out of the loop. I was supposed to have a meeting with the director of our division this afternoon, but he canceled at the last minute. I'm beginning to wonder if there's going to be some big shakeup in upper management."

"That sounds nerve-wracking." I rubbed the back of my neck. "Do you think it would affect you?"

"Probably not," she said with another shrug. "Not unless I mess up."

"Then you know what to do," I said, wanting to be supportive.

She raised an eyebrow in question.

"Don't mess up," I said firmly, trying to inject some confidence. "Ensure your work is flawless and go above and beyond with everything you're in charge of."

She nodded thoughtfully. "That's good advice. Complacency is a killer. The way my marriage fell apart was proof of that. I still regret not recognizing the warning signs."

I was a little surprised by the analogy. "Really? Like what?"

She shrugged. "I'm still not sure. Him growing distant, maybe. Like the way he'd go off and play golf with a buddy after not seeing me for a week. It was as if he was intentionally distancing himself from me, but when I commented on it, he made me believe I was being clingy and possessive."

"It's not all on you. Your ex could've spoken up instead of shutting you out. It's not your fault he didn't communicate."

She nodded, considering my words. "I try to tell myself that. But what if I'm missing something now? At work? What if the fact that I don't know what's going on behind the scenes means my job's at risk?

The weight of her worry was palpable. I rubbed her back and zeroed in on the knots I found there. "Hedge your bets? Update your resume? Start putting out feelers for a new job?"

She sighed and leaned into me, relaxing into my impromptu shoulder rub. "Yeah. That's good advice." But then she shook her head abruptly. "Enough of that. I'm here with you, and I'd rather not worry about work right now."

I dropped my hand. "I'm happy to change the subject. I got your text. I'm glad you like the flowers I sent you."

Her eyes softened, and that smile of hers seemed to brighten Dante's kitchen. "Thank you again. The pink roses and lilies are gorgeous. I brought them home from work with me. They're in my car right now, and I plan to put them in my bedroom so I can see them first thing in the morning and last thing at night."

I liked the intimacy of having my bouquet watching over her as she slept. "Your bedroom sounds like the perfect spot. On the mantel over the fireplace."

She blinked, and when she spoke, her tone became flirtatious. "Before the week gets away from us, I want to schedule a date with you. Can you come for dinner at my place this Friday? I'll cook."

My lips twitched as our eyes locked. "You couldn't keep me away. Maybe I can bring you more flowers for your bedroom."

Her sexy, endearing smile made my heart race a little faster.

Conner came over and served himself, and I noticed the others were eating now, too. The casserole must have cooled enough to eat, so I served Lianna some of Dante's Gourmet Mac and Cheese and Grits.

As I handed her the plate, she inhaled deeply. "This smells amazing." She finally took a bite, and then her face lit up with a smile that made me feel as though I'd just given her the moon. "This is delicious. So cheesy and full of flavor."

"I heard that," Dante called out, beaming. "I'm glad you like it. The grits are my secret ingredient. And the four kinds of cheese. And the garlic. Hell—I guess it's the whole combination." The big man brought over the large bowl of salad he'd prepared and served some to Lianna and me.

Reed came over with a glass of red wine and handed it to Lianna. "For you. One of your favorites. It's on the house."

"Thanks. You're all spoiling me. Tonight is an unexpected treat." Lianna's eyes glowed with contentment as her exhaustion faded away. "Do you guys always eat this well on Mondays?"

"Sure do," Ford said. "It's what keeps us coming back to Dante's classes."

Lianna took a sip of her wine and then turned to me and dipped her head in mock supplication. "This meal is a million times better than the frozen pizza I normally would have made after working late. A lot more fun, too. Thank you."

"It's the least I could do," I said. "After all, not only are you driving me home tonight, but you're also making me dinner on Friday."

She took another bite and let out a soft moan. "Mmm, I'm not sure I can impress you now. You've set the bar pretty high."

I leaned in closer, my eyes locked on hers. "Don't worry, Lianna. You've already made a huge impression on me."

Her lips curved into a playful smile. "Oh really? Do tell."

I chuckled. "Well, for starters, there's your smile. It could light up a room. And your laugh. It's like music to my ears."

Lianna's dimples deepened. "So, it comes down to looks?"

"And charm. And quick wit. Besides, I have to admire a woman who can wipe the floor with me on the paddle court." I gave her a wink.

"Those are much better reasons to be impressed with me," she said with a saucy grin.

When we were done with dinner, Conner and I divided up the leftovers between the three of us so Lianna could have some for lunch tomorrow. Then she and I said our goodbyes to everyone and headed out the door.

Once we were finally alone and standing next to her car, I couldn't resist pulling her into my arms. She felt so good there, and I could tell she was tired from her emotional day. I'd been taking things slowly with her, but the wait was wearing me thin. Still, I wouldn't push her tonight. I didn't want our first time together to happen when she was worn out and emotionally drained. It needed to be special. Memorable.

But that didn't mean I couldn't indulge in a little flirtation. I leaned in and our lips met, tongues tangling together. Her hands ran up my back, pulling me closer to her. I could feel her body pressing against mine as she leaned back against the side of her car.

Suddenly, the front door of the Not a Yacht Club opened and Reed walked out. We quickly broke apart, but the mischievous glint in Lianna's eye told me how much she'd enjoyed both the kiss—and getting caught.

As I opened the car door for her, our eyes met, and we exchanged grins like two teenagers caught in the act. "You're pretty smooth, Kincaid," she murmured with a chuckle as she climbed into the car.

We drove away, both lost in thought and comfortable silence, enjoying each other's company. Eventually, Lianna broke the silence. "I appreciate you letting me vent about work tonight. It's good to have someone to talk to. You give good advice."

I squeezed her hand where it rested on the center console between us. "Anytime."

She took my hand in hers, intertwining our fingers. I sensed there was something else on her mind, so I gave her space to talk. "Sorry I brought up that stuff about my ex," she said. "Something about what's going on at work is triggering my self-doubt."

Her apology took me by surprise. I neither expected nor needed one. "Don't worry about it. I'm not bothered in the least."

But as I took in her troubled expression, I knew I shouldn't simply dismiss her apology, so I elaborated. "We all have our baggage. None of us is a clean slate. You struggle with self-doubt and trust, and I have my own issues with depending on people and being lied to. I've been let down too many times, first by my flaky parents, and then by a fiancé who manipulated me by lying outright. It's made me cautious and guarded around people."

As we stopped at a light, she turned to face me. "But you haven't been like that with me."

I looked away, then back at her. "Maybe that's because you haven't triggered any of my deepest fears. You haven't broken a promise or lied to me."

"Of course not." She almost sounded offended. The light

turned green, and she drove on. "I take my commitments seriously, and I'm not manipulative. That's just not who I am."

I nodded slowly. "I know. And that's a big part of why I'm so attracted to you. You're genuine."

She glanced over at me and squeezed my hand. "So are you. I think we have something here."

"Here?" I teased. "Only in Pittsburgh? I hope that means you don't have plans to leave anytime soon."

She chuckled. "Not me. I have roots in this city. I love my job. I love my house. I love my life. I plan to live here for a very, very long time."

She pulled up in front of my house, but didn't turn off the engine like she had last time. "See you Friday for dinner?"

"You couldn't keep me away."

2 0

ARRIVING AT LIANNA'S PLACE

Kincaid

On Friday evening, I felt as eager as a teenager. I grabbed the bouquet of flowers from the passenger seat of my truck and tucked a bottle of wine in the crook of my arm, then I took the steps to Lianna's front door two at a time.

As I waited for her to answer the doorbell, I turned to take in the view from her porch. This was one of my favorite things about Lianna's house—this amazing vista of Sewickley and the Ohio River beyond it.

As I gazed down the hillside and over the tops of the hundred-year-old trees, I could see people bustling along the street below, their faces unidentifiable from this distance, granting them a sense of anonymity. The scene reminded me of the model train exhibit at Phipps Conservatory and Botanic Gardens, where a miniature train chugged through Pittsburgh's landmarks, such as the Duquesne Incline, the baseball stadium, and the skating rink in Market Square.

The doorknob clicked, and I turned to face Lianna. At the sight of her, I stilled, drinking her in. She smiled, looking adorable in a pink and white fifties-style apron, complete with little pink ruffles down the sides. She even had a streak of flour on her cheek.

"Hello there, June Cleaver," I teased, grinning from ear to ear. "Or are you Lucille Ball?"

Without thinking, I moved toward her, driven by a powerful impulse that I couldn't ignore. I wrapped my arms around her, holding her close, and nearly dropped the wine bottle in the process. She laughed, taking it from me to keep it safe.

She examined the label, nodding approvingly. "A French Cabernet Sauvignon? Dropping it would have been tragic."

"Good save." I bent my head to kiss her. The scent of the flower bouquet engulfed us, blending with her Chanel Number 5 perfume.

Lianna let out a hum that told me she liked my greeting. Her body melted against me in a way that made it impossible to release her. I kissed her softly at first, then I teased her lower lip with my tongue. When she opened her mouth to me, I nearly groaned in pleasure at the taste of her. God, she was sweet. I pulled her even closer as I thoroughly and happily made love to her mouth.

Her enthusiastic response thrilled me.

I'd been thinking about kissing her ever since she'd dropped me off after my cooking class on Monday. Hell, it was worse than that. I'd been thinking about kissing her since I'd come here to give her an estimate.

Lianna was fast becoming an obsession. Now that I had her in my arms again, the last thing I wanted to do was let her go. This moment was too perfect. Judging by her response, she seemed to want this kiss as much as I did.

Since we were still standing on her front porch in full view of the town, I reluctantly pulled away, my heart hammering in my chest as I released her. I took a small step back, just far enough so that our bodies were no longer pressed together, but close enough to touch.

That kiss was—unexpected.

"Lucy, I'm home," I quipped, tugging at the tiny pink bow at the neck of her fifties-style apron. Did women actually still wear these things?

Apparently so.

Damn, but it was sexy. What was the top part of it called? A pinafore? A bib? Something like that. My imagination ran wild as I imagined her naked under the apron. I had to close my eyes for a moment. Was it to savor the image or to banish it? If it was the latter, I was failing.

"Aw, Ricky," she teased back, her voice sounding husky and sensual from the kiss. I opened my eyes to see her gazing intensely at me, her cheeks flushed with color. "More flowers? They're gorgeous." She didn't even glance at them. Her eyes were too busy devouring me.

I'd be the Ricky Ricardo to her Lucille Ball any day. Especially if she used that sexy voice on me.

She seemed to realize she was staring and glanced down, suddenly remembering the bottle of wine she'd rescued. "Thanks for this."

"You said you were making something Italian. Does red wine sound good?"

"Perfect." She ushered me inside.

As soon as we closed the door behind us, shutting out the outside world, her expression tensed. Her hands fluttered nervously, smoothing out her apron. I caught her glance and wondered if she was nervous about tonight, about being alone with me in a private setting. I hoped she didn't feel any pressure from me.

"What's cooking? It smells amazing," I said, trying to lighten the moment.

As if my words grounded her and gave her something to latch onto, her tension evaporated. She beckoned me toward her kitchen in the back of the house and led the way.

"Lasagna. I just need to take the foil off the pan and put it back in the oven to brown."

"It smells amazing." My mouth watered.

"Take a seat," she said, gesturing toward the barstools at the L-shaped granite counter jutting into the room.

"I want to take a look at the drywall first." I handed her the flowers. "Do you mind?"

She exuberantly buried her nose in the bouquet of white daisies, lemony alstroemeria, and yellow roses. Her eyes sparkled with joy. "Do I mind if you check up on the work your crew did? Have at it. I'll put these in some water while you're gone."

I entered the laundry room first, making my way to the new powder room before returning to the kitchen. "The walls look perfect," I said.

Lianna was reaching for a vase from an upper cabinet, her entire body stretching as she did so.

God, she looked lovely. Beautiful beyond words.

I had to swallow before I could speak again. "I should inspect the drywall on the second floor too, but that can wait until after dinner."

"Good plan," she said, filling the crystal vase from the kitchen faucet. "Hungry? Have some snacks while we wait for the lasagna."

I grinned with satisfaction. It had been a while since a woman had taken care of me like this. Having Lianna pamper me was a welcome change.

I settled onto the barstool as Lianna slid a cutting board bearing a crusty loaf of bread she'd already sliced onto the counter between us.

She turned to a cabinet and deftly extracted a bottle of olive oil along with some dried herbs and sea salt, mixing them together in a small dipping bowl. "Try this," she said, setting the dipping oil next to the bread.

I tore off a piece and dipped it in the oil concoction, savoring the perfect combination of flavors. "Delicious." I took a second piece, enjoying the warm, homey atmosphere of Lianna's kitchen. A braided bundle of garlic hung from a hook near the window, a bright red tea kettle rested on the stove, and a row of red canisters sat tidily on the countertop.

"Do you have Monday off for Memorial Day?" Lianna asked.

"Absolutely. My crews deserve time off with their families."

Lianna opened a drawer, retrieved an old-fashioned corkscrew, and handed it to me. As she turned toward the oven, I cut through the foil on top of the wine bottle.

"Maybe we can do something together," she suggested.

Just as I began twisting in the corkscrew, she opened the oven door and leaned over.

Damn.

That was a spectacularly short skirt under that apron. And that bottom. Lord. It looked perfectly heart-shaped whenever she leaned over that way.

She straightened up and placed the lasagna pan on top of the oven. I swallowed hard, feeling the discomfort of my sudden erection. What was wrong with me? I was acting like a fifteen-year-old boy. How would I make it through dinner if I couldn't control myself?

I needed to think of something boring, something completely nonsexual, but nothing came to mind. All I could think about was Lianna naked under that apron, or naked without it, or naked and leaning over the kitchen countertop with that heart-shaped ass—

When she leaned over again and slid the pan back into the oven, I thought my head might explode.

She turned and glanced over her shoulder at me, "Did you hear what I—" She stopped abruptly.

Busted.

Her eyes widened when she caught sight of me staring at her with the undisguised lust that I knew had to have been written all over my face, but she didn't look annoyed. She looked—well, she looked pleased.

That was good. That was very good.

I uncorked the bottle, and the thick popping sound made me jump. Lianna straightened and smoothed the front of her skirt before removing two wine glasses from a nearby cabinet. She sauntered back toward me, placing them on the counter between us.

I poured a taste into her glass and then pushed it closer to her. "Tell me what you think of the wine, love. I want to hear your impressions."

Her mahogany eyes sparkled. "You mean, like in a wine tasting?"

I nodded, relieved to engage in a less toe-curling topic with her. "I want to know what kinds of wines you prefer."

She lifted the glass and held it up to the late spring sun shining in through the window. After taking a deep sniff, she gave me a playful smile. "Clear with no cloudiness and a gorgeous nose. Now for the important test." She took a sip and closed her eyes, her expression thoughtful. It was a delight to watch her, so serious yet so playful.

"What's the verdict?" I asked, unable to stop drinking in the rapt expression on her face.

"It's a delightful wine," she intoned with her eyes still shut, "rich and full of complex notes. I detect a hint of blackberry and— is that thyme?" She opened her pretty brown eyes, merry with humor.

"Do you approve?"

"Indubitably." She held out her glass, and I topped it off, then filled my own.

"This one is from a vineyard in Napa Valley."

She glanced at the label. "I don't recognize it, but then again, I'm notorious for never being able to choose wine at a restaurant. I usually just pick whatever Cabernet Sauvignon or Pinot Noir they recommend. If I stop at the Wine and Spirits store, I ask someone there to help me choose."

I took a sip. "Tell me about your week. Any news about the hush-hush goings-on at work?"

She gave an irritated sigh. "Nothing I've been able to glean.

Everyone's being so secretive. One of my team members is leaving for Colorado Springs. Her fiancé got stationed there."

"Interesting," I said, raising an eyebrow. "Did she tell you anything about her new job?"

"Just that she's excited to work with a defense contractor. It's the perfect opportunity for her."

"I'm trying to do the same with Gillette Construction—get it on the right path, I mean. With the magazine article that the Murphys lined up about their renovation, I expect more high-end contracts to come my way. I love working on custom projects like that."

"Fingers crossed it all works out for you. Did you have your meeting with Chrissy yet?"

I shook my head. "No, she had to reschedule for next Tuesday. But the good news is that she hasn't kicked one of my crews out in over a week."

"That's progress, I suppose."

21

DINNER

LIANNA

I took in this man. This surprising gift that the universe had dropped into my life.

I liked Kincaid. In fact, 'like' seemed too tepid a word to describe my emotions. Words like 'need,' 'want,' 'desire,' and 'obsess' were much more fitting.

And his kisses. They were simply divine. The man made me feel things I hadn't felt in ages. Paul had been a good enough lover, but our lovemaking had become routine during our three-year marriage. Mechanical. Kiss this spot here for this reaction, nibble that spot there for that response. Wait for this particular sound… there it was… and then the finale.

Paul had stopped trying, and because of that, our lovemaking had become stale. Boring. He'd taken me for granted.

Taken us for granted.

Our passion had vanished. And our lovemaking had become infrequent toward the end. Had he been cheating on me all along? Had he brought other women into our bed before Gloria?

Did it even matter anymore?

As soon as I'd caught them together, I'd made an appointment with my gynecologist to be tested for any sexually transmitted disease he might have passed on to me. It killed me to have to admit to people that I'd been so deeply betrayed. It made me feel like a fool.

I took another sip of Kincaid's delectable Cabernet Sauvignon, determined to keep all thoughts of Paul and Gloria out of my mind. This moment was mine, and I wasn't going to allow them to ruin it. I was well rid of the man, and I wouldn't let him intrude on my life any more than he already had.

I tore off a piece of bread and dipped it into the oil blend. "I hope you like garlic, otherwise, tonight might be a problem. I was a bit heavy-handed when I added it to the lasagna." I bit into the oil-drenched bread.

The corners of his lips lifted. "I love garlic."

"That's a relief." I licked a bit of olive oil off my thumb with the flick of my tongue. "Tell me more about the Murphy project."

He watched me intently, taking a moment before answering. "That one is a whole-house renovation."

"That one? Are you working on more houses than mine and theirs?"

"I almost always am. I have several others in the pipeline. I finished up a sunroom addition two weeks ago. My other active one is adding a new first-floor bathroom to a house in Sewickley. A lot of these older homes only have one bathroom."

"Just like mine."

"Exactly, but you're adding a bit more."

"So, you do all sorts of jobs?"

"All shapes and sizes. Some are major overhauls, some are additions, some are kitchen renovations, and some are simpler, like replacing drywall. We do it all."

The timer went off. I turned toward it and picked up my red silicon oven mitts. I opened the oven door and the delicious aroma of lasagna hit me full in the face as I leaned over to extract the pan.

I could feel Kincaid's gaze on me again as I straightened. I glanced back, and sure enough, he had his eyes pinned to my backside. The man certainly didn't hide his interest. He'd been watching me all night, and the way he was looking at me now made me flush from more than the heat of the oven.

For a moment, I tried to suppress the curling tendril of desire smoldering inside me. I'd gone without sex for over a year, and tamping down my sexuality had become more habit than anything else. A self-defense mechanism.

One—I suddenly realized—that was no longer necessary.

I immediately stopped resisting. Instead, I let that hot little ember take hold. I wanted this man. I wanted him more than I'd wanted any man in a very, very long time. Why suppress my desire? Why not enjoy it? Why not let the sexual tension between us build until neither of us could withstand it any longer?

Wouldn't that be delicious?

I set the oven timer once again and sauntered back over to my barstool. "Now it just needs to cool for a bit. About ten minutes should do it."

At my words, Kincaid grinned, his lips curling crookedly, a hint of cockiness in his raised eyebrow. "Ten more minutes? How ever will we fill up the time?"

A sudden barrage of images filled my mind. Illicit, carnal images that made my heart flutter and my knees go weak. Not to mention the effect those smoldering eyes were having on my lady bits. They were screaming for attention in a way they hadn't done in—forever.

Before I knew it, Kincaid stood and wrapped those muscular arms around me in a satisfyingly strong embrace.

I slid my hands up his delicious forearms and held on for dear life as he lowered his mouth to mine. As our lips met, desire jolted through me, and I clung to him as my knees threatened to give out, a deep, throaty sigh escaping my lips.

Heat rushed through me in intoxicating zips, setting my skin on fire.

Kincaid's hard, muscled body pressed against mine, and his hands slid down my sides, cupping my bottom and pressing me against him. He took a few steps backward, pulling me with him as he moved toward the back of the sofa in my adjoining living room.

He stopped there and lifted me slightly, setting my bottom on the edge of the sofa's back. My skirt crept up as I instinctively wrapped my legs around his waist, lost in a moment of passion.

He let out a deep moan, pressing even closer to me.

My fingers fumbled with the buttons running down the front of his shirt, but I only managed to undo a couple before he grabbed the shirt by the bottom and dragged both it and his undershirt over his head. I thought I heard a couple of buttons ping off the wooden floor, but the sight of his bare chest drove every other thought from my mind.

Lord, but this man was perfect, his skin tanned from hours spent on job sites working in the sun. As I stared, his pectoral muscle twitched, and I leaned closer, touching my tongue to the spot. He let out a low, growling moan as I kissed my way closer to his right nipple, swirling my tongue around it, then pulling it into my mouth.

Kincaid plunged his fingers into my hair, cupping my nape and pulling me against him. He pulled at the bow behind my neck, releasing the top of my pink apron. I tilted my head to one side, granting him better access to the bow. As it fell loose, he pulled my pink blouse free of my waistband, dragging it off over my head.

I'd worn a low-cut, lacy pink bra, and his gaze locked onto it. He pulled away, just a little, and cupped my breasts, rubbing his thumbs over the outline of my erect nipples that jutted against the satiny fabric.

I released a hiss of pleasure at his touch. He lowered his head as he teased one breast free and pulled it into his mouth, evoking a soft groan from me. He nipped and teased and suckled until I was nearly wild with wanting him, then he pulled the other side free and repeated the process.

He pulled his head away and gazed down at my breasts,

pressed up by the cups of my bra. I watched his thumbs move over my nipples, and was overwhelmed by the erotic sight of those massive, capable hands sliding over my soft skin.

He peered at my cleavage more closely and then smiled. With a flick of his fingers, he released the front clasp of my bra.

As he smoothed a hand over my newly liberated breasts, I shrugged out of the bra, letting it fall behind me onto the sofa. A moment later, Kincaid stepped back and yanked my skirt down my hips, leaving me dressed only in my panties and the pink apron still tied at my waist.

Kincaid's eyes devoured me, and he let out a low growl of appreciation. A shiver of pleasure ripped into me, striking at my core.

Then he did something that surprised me. He took the ties to the pinafore of my apron and lifted them up in place, tucking them behind my neck again and quickly tying them.

He ran kisses up my neck. "I've been imagining you this way all night," he murmured, his breath hot on my ear. "Naked under that apron. When you bent over the oven, I thought my head would explode. Will you do it again now? Bend over for me?"

Oh. My. God. Heat filled me. I wanted him. Wanted him now. I nodded.

"Tell me if this is too fast for you. If you want me to stop," he said softly.

"No," I whispered.

He froze.

"I mean, don't stop. Keep going."

With strong, firm hands, he grabbed me by the hips and turned me around, so I was facing the sofa. He tilted me forward, raising my bottom in the air and bending me over the back of the couch. I felt so exposed. So wanton. A wave of heat swept through me, and I trembled, desperate for him.

He pushed his knee between my legs, nudging my feet farther apart. His hands slid up the outside of my thighs and then cupped my bottom.

My breath came in gasps. I couldn't touch him with my back to him, but his hands were firm and strong on me. He ran his fingers under the thin elastic of my thong, then slid one finger down the string, down to my core. When the back of his hand brushed against my sex, I nearly jumped out of my skin.

He rested his other hand on the small of my back, and I trembled.

"You're perfect, Lianna." He ran his fingers through the wetness gathering between my legs, coating them with it. One fingertip circled that needy, greedy little bundle of nerves, coming close, closer, but not quite touching it—until he pressed there, making me let out a gasp of pleasure. I pressed my hips back, thrusting into his hand.

He went back to circling that pearl of sensation, teasing me until I was writhing and moaning in pleasure. He dipped a finger inside me, and my knees would have buckled if I hadn't been leaning over the couch. He moved inside me. Teasing. Swirling.

He added a second finger to the first, moving them in and out, driving me mad with desire. Pleasure pinged inside of me, making me wild with want. I needed to touch him too, to feel his hard muscles under my hands. I tried to push myself away from the sofa and face him, but he pressed me back down. "Stay like this." His voice sounded raw with passion. "Please. You don't know how much I've wanted to touch you this way."

The naked desire in his voice sent shivers of want coursing through me, so I complied.

His fingers entered me again, sliding in and out. I began moving against them, meeting each stroke with a thrust of my own.

Kincaid stopped for a moment, and I heard the zipper of his jeans and the rustle of fabric. Then I heard the sound of what had to be a foil packet ripping open. "Is that a condom?" I asked.

"Yes." Then he paused. "Is it okay? You don't want me to stop, do you?"

I tightened my grip on the back of the sofa. "If you stop, I just might have to kill you."

He let out a low chuckle. "In the interest of keeping you from becoming a murderer, I'll continue."

The kitchen timer started beeping.

I felt him hesitate. "Don't you dare stop, Kincaid."

"Not stopping."

The tip of his erection pressed at my entrance, and I suddenly realized I hadn't even seen his cock. He was about to put it inside me, and I didn't even know how big it was.

"Wait."

He froze. "What? I thought you said not to stop."

I twisted a bit to meet his gaze. "I just realized I don't know what I'm getting myself into."

"Say what?"

I could feel my cheeks turning a bright shade of pink. "I mean, I haven't seen, well, you know…" I trailed off, feeling like a total prude. "I have no idea what to expect." The word "package" felt too awkward, "dick" too crass, but "thingy" sounded way too ridiculous for the situation. What had I gotten myself into?

He grinned. "Oh, I can promise you, you'll be satisfied."

I froze. Did that mean he was big? "Maybe if you just let me see for myself." I started to turn, but he grabbed hold of my hips and held me firmly in place.

"Actually, how often in your life will you ever be in this situation? I think you should close your eyes and find out—in the best way possible."

I let out a groan and dropped my head onto the back of the sofa. "You didn't just say that."

He slid his fingers back inside me again, and my body, traitor that it was, thrust back against him. "Less talking, more doing."

He moved closer, sliding his length along my folds. His considerable length.

I gasped. "Oh, my."

He was well-endowed, that was for sure. He pressed against

my opening, and then, just that fast, he slid smoothly inside me. With each thrust, he pushed deeper and deeper into me. Filling me.

I lost myself at that moment, letting out gasps, moans, and mewls as pleasure took over. Faster than I expected, I found myself plunging into the abyss of an orgasm.

My response took me by surprise. Yes, I was having an orgasm—an amazing one at that—but I wanted more. Much more. All of him. I wanted this to go on and on. I pressed back against him to extend my exquisite ecstasy, and he filled me wholly and completely.

My orgasm continued as my interior walls thrilled and contracted, drawing him into me. He gripped my hips with both hands as he thrust deep inside me, and then the muscles of his legs that were pressed against my backside bunched and stiffened as he froze, finding his release.

I collapsed, folding over the back of the sofa, and Kincaid fell onto me, his body slick with perspiration.

His heart thudded against my back. As it began to slow, the beeping of the oven timer began to pierce my hazy brain.

"Is that the lasagna?" he murmured, planting kisses down the side of my neck and lifting away from me slightly so his weight was no longer pressing down on me.

"Mmm. I think we've let it cool long enough."

He laughed, his chest rumbling against my back. "Good thing you already took it out of the oven. It would have been a tragedy if something that smells so delicious had been ruined."

I sighed happily. "It would have been worth it."

I could feel his lips curl into a smile where they were pressed against my neck. "True, but I like to have my cake and eat it too. And you are a most delicious piece of cake."

The delicious scent of garlic and cheese drifted into the living room. Suddenly, I was famished. "I'm starving. Let's have dinner."

He stood and then pulled me to my feet. "And then, perhaps, a second helping of you?" He waggled his eyebrows at me, and I couldn't help but laugh.

I reached for my skirt, but he halted me with a firm grip on my hips, pulling me closer to him.

"Would you mind indulging my fantasy a little longer?" he asked, his lips grazing my neck. "I'm dying to sit across from you at your dining table with you wearing nothing but that apron and pink thong."

I arched my neck to meet his gaze, then glanced down to take in the broad expanse of muscled chest. "I can certainly see the appeal. I will if you will." At his raised eyebrows, I grinned. "Let me run upstairs to the bathroom first. Can you turn off the oven timer for me?"

"Got it."

"It's too bad I don't have a first-floor bathroom," I teased.

"I blame your boyfriend. He needs to work faster."

Grinning, I turned and hurried up the stairs, where I cleaned up and avoided looking in the mirror. I was afraid if I saw how wanton I looked, I'd lose my nerve.

As I descended to the dining room, I saw that Kincaid had set up plates and silverware on the table, thoughtfully covering each chair with a towel. "To keep our bare bottoms from getting cold?" I jested.

"Or leaving butt-prints. It seemed wise."

I took him by the hand and pushed him into his chair. "Why don't you get comfortable while I grab the salad?"

As I turned away from him, I gave my hips a bit of a wiggle. He let out a moan. "You're killing me here."

I pulled the salad from the fridge and then joined him. His eyes were pinned to the pinafore top of my apron. I glanced down and saw my nipples making two little tents in the fabric. "The refrigerator was cold."

"Right." He glanced down at his lap. "I don't think that's the only explanation."

"Naughty, naughty. Let's try to make it through dinner." I

pushed the salad bowl closer to him and then began serving the lasagna with a large spatula. I nudged a stringy length of cheese onto my plate and then licked the sauce from my finger.

Kincaid made a "tsk" noise. "If you want me to eat this dinner, you need to stop licking your fingers. It's unbearably erotic."

I made a show of picking up my napkin and wiping my hands on it. "Better?"

"Possibly." He paused, obviously thinking. "Actually, no. Not better at all. I like watching you lick them."

I let out a mock sigh of consternation. "Have some lasagna. That might distract you."

He looked doubtful, but he still pressed the edge of his fork into the lasagna and took a bite. He closed his eyes for a moment. "Perfect. Is that Italian sausage I taste?"

"Half Italian sausage, half ground beef. Do you like it?"

His mouth was still full, so he simply nodded.

"I made dessert, too. Tiramisu."

He furrowed his brow. "That's the coffee-flavored dessert, right?"

"It is. Do you like it?"

"Love it. It's one of my favorites."

My lips twitched. "That's a relief. Mine too."

We managed to finish eating, but I found it a challenge. I didn't know about Kincaid, but I could hardly wait until we could move on to the next part of the evening.

When we were done, he stood and picked up our plates. "You put the lasagna away and I'll rinse the dishes." He padded barefoot and bare-ass naked to the sink.

Oddly enough, my heart gave a flutter at that. He wasn't going to leave the mess in the kitchen for me to clean. He wanted to help. It was the sexiest non-sexy thing he could have done. How had I been lucky enough to find someone like him?

As he began to rinse, I found myself staring at him, transfixed. It was like watching a piece of art come to life. He was so beautiful, so perfect. Was there anything sexier than watching a gorgeous, naked, well-muscled man rinse the dishes? What had I done to deserve a moment as absolutely perfect as this one?

He turned to me, a dishtowel draped over one shoulder, and I had to catch my breath. The way his body moved was hypnotic. He shifted his weight, causing his glutes to ripple under his skin, and I had to force myself to look away.

I quickly finished putting away the leftovers and wiping down the counters all while admiring the view. I couldn't keep my eyes off him.

With an impatient sigh, I gave up on cleaning. We'd done enough for now, and I had other things on my mind.

"Should I start the dishwasher or wait until later?" he asked as he finished loading the last dish.

"Go ahead and start it," I said, my voice barely above a whisper.

He bent over to add detergent to the dishwasher and then straightened and turned it on. He turned and pinned me with a devouring gaze as he snatched the dishtowel from his shoulder and tossed it haphazardly onto the counter.

This was one smoldering hot man, and he had one smoldering hot look in his eyes. I watched his gaze drift over me. He licked his lips, and then a devilish smile spread over his handsome face.

I had the feeling that expression meant something scandalous was on its way.

"Kincaid? What has you grinning like that?" My entire body flushed with heat.

"It's time for dessert. Tiramisu, you said. Right?" An expectant gleam twinkled in his eye. "I can hardly wait."

22

AND DESSERT

I couldn't keep my eyes off her. "I love tiramisu. It's soft and sweet and delicious. Just like you."

Her gaze heated. "You want dessert? Now?" She seemed surprised. Given the ideas percolating in my brain, she'd be even more surprised once she heard them.

"Absolutely."

Lianna turned her nearly naked back to me and removed the tiramisu from the refrigerator. I'd been right. The sight of her in nothing but that apron and the pink thong was perfection. She moved with grace and ease, and I admired every curve and line of her body.

When she turned to face me, she held a large crystal bowl. Layers of oval ladyfinger cookies lined it, and a thick layer of cocoa powder dusted the top. She'd even placed what looked like a sprig of mint leaf in the center as a decoration. My mouth watered to see her holding it.

She looked like a pin-up in a 1950s centerfold. Lianna, wearing nothing but that apron, holding that decadent dessert—it was like something out of an erotic fantasy.

She carefully placed the bowl on the island and then removed two dessert plates from the cabinet next to her. The muscles of her legs tensed and flexed deliciously as she moved, and I caught my breath. This woman was pure perfection.

Through sheer force of will, I shifted my attention away from her body long enough to pull open the drawer closest to the dishwasher. Inside, I found the spoons I hoped would be there and grabbed two.

As I handed one to her, my eyes lingered on her face, drinking her in. *"Bon appétit."* I tore my gaze away and moved my spoon toward the bowl, eager to savor the delicious dessert, but she batted it to one side.

"Don't be so impatient." She mock-scowled at me, but her expression quickly softened and she grinned broadly. She served portions into two bowls. "I'm glad to know you can't resist my cooking," she teased, digging her spoon into the dessert.

To my surprise, she held her spoon out to me, offering me the first taste. I stared at it for a moment, then opened my mouth, eager for the treat. Unfortunately, her aim was slightly off, and the cold mascarpone cheese mixture landed on the corner of my mouth. I gave her a playful scowl. "You need to work on your aim."

She looked at the blob of dessert with a hint of irritation, then leaned closer to me. "Let me get that for you," she murmured, flicking her warm tongue over the corner of my mouth. A jolt of desire shot through me. Maybe she wouldn't be shocked by the ideas percolating in my brain, after all.

"It's good, isn't it?" I said. I scooped a spoonful and offered it to her. She hesitated for a moment, then opened her mouth. I slid the spoon inside, and she closed her eyes, letting out a sigh of enjoyment. "Yummy," she murmured.

I could hardly tear my eyes away from her for the fraction of a second it took to scoop another bite of tiramisu. This time, I dipped a finger into the spoon and slid it across her lips.

Her eyes widened in surprise, then she licked the sweet concoction away. "What was that for?"

"I want to taste it on you." I dipped my head to devour her soft, sweet mouth.

I pulled her closer, pressing my body to hers. She let out a low moan as she wrapped herself around me.

"Bed," I demanded. I wanted her sprawled out on it, open for me and begging me to take her.

"Upstairs." She grabbed my hand and dragged me toward the stairs.

As we passed our discarded clothing, I paused to grab my bowl and handed it to her so I could pick up my jeans. "Don't eat that. I have plans for it."

She held the bowl aloft and raised an eyebrow at the jeans dangling from my hand. "Planning on going somewhere?"

"I have another condom in my pocket."

The corners of her mouth curved up with delight. "I have a new box upstairs." She tugged my hand again, pulling me toward the stairs. As I followed her, I was treated to a view of the narrow band of her pink thong smack dab in front of me. The sight of it nearly drove me wild.

She pulled me into her snug, intimate bedroom. It was a sea of lavender blue and white, with a bouquet of lilies and pink roses placed prominently on the fireplace mantel.

Exactly where I'd imagined them.

They were the first thing she'd see in the morning and the last thing she'd see at night. Something to make her think about me. Had I inspired her dreams? Had she touched herself as she imagined me touching her? The thought increased my desire tenfold.

She pulled a package of condoms from her nightstand and handed one to me. Her eyes locked with mine as she slowly backed toward the bed, still holding the spoon aloft in one hand. Her other hand tugged at the bow holding her pinafore in place. When it fell, she glanced down at her bared breasts. "Oh, my," she said in that breathy Marilyn Monroe voice that did crazy things to my self-control. "Your favorite apron seems to be falling off me. How will I ever manage to entice you to kiss me now?"

She stared slyly at the spoon poking out of the bowl, and then met my eyes as she dabbed tiramisu across first one nipple, then the other, leaving behind a streak of the decadent dessert.

She set the spoon back in the bowl on the nightstand as I stalked closer, my gaze fixed on her perfect breasts.

I pressed her back against the edge of the bed, and she dropped down onto it. I lowered my body, bracing a hand on either side of her as I dipped down. Nibbling, licking, tasting. Coffee and sugar and complete and utter deliciousness.

She let out a soft moan. Once all the delectable tiramisu was gone from the first breast, I shifted my attention to the second one.

Lianna wrapped one leg around me and pulled on my arms, dragging me to her mouth. I kissed her willingly. Passionately. She opened to me as I teased her lips with my tongue and then caressed the interior of her mouth.

She pressed her entire body against mine and wrapped both legs around my waist, holding me fast—exactly where I wanted to be.

Heat filled me as she rocked her hips against mine. I was pressed against that juncture between her legs and felt as though I might explode from the intensity of my desire.

I reached one hand down, looping it under her leg and bypassing her thong so I could touch the slick moisture I knew I'd find there. I let out a moan as I touched heaven, and she bucked against me as I stroked her hard nub.

When I pulled away long enough to open the condom wrapper, she wriggled out of her thong. She was perfectly, beautifully, bare to me.

She sat up on the edge of the bed as I rolled on the condom and she slid her hand over it as well, drawing it to the base with me.

When she met my gaze, her eyes were dark pools of want and desire. "I need you inside me."

"As you wish." I nudged her legs apart with my knees and then reached down to part her folds, dipping my finger inside her.

I loved seeing her this way, sprawled half on, half off the bed, her legs wide for me. Her passionate response made this incredibly arousing. Knowing I could take this rational, composed woman to a point where she was moaning with pleasure and want made me feel both powerful and humble. I shifted forward and pressed my tip to her entrance.

She wrapped her legs around me, pulling me closer, and urging me to enter her. I could tell she wanted me to move faster, but I remained unhurried, drawing out the moment as I entered her slowly, inch by enveloping inch, prolonging the pleasure as she moaned for me to fill her.

"Please," she begged.

"You want more?" I teased her. "You want me all the way inside you?"

"Yes. Now."

I pressed slightly, but only gave her another inch or so. I wanted to draw this out. To prolong the moment for both of us. She tried to press into me with her hips, but I resisted.

"Please," she whimpered.

I pushed all the way into her with one deep thrust, giving us both what we desperately needed.

Lianna let out a deep moan of pleasure as she met me thrust for thrust. I reached between us and pressed my thumb against her clit.

She bucked in response. "Kincaid."

A moment later she arched her back and threw back her head. Her inner muscles started convulsing and pulsing around my length, pulling me over the edge as well.

My heart thundered, and I tightened my grip on her as I buried myself as deep as I could go. A throaty cry of release burst from me as I arched my back, the muscles down my spine tightening in triumph.

When I came back to myself, I looked down at her where she lay sprawled across her bed, her eyes closed, and her smile glowing with satisfaction.

We'd done this with each other—for each other. This perfectly amazing joining of bodies. We were both breathing heavily, and soon I noticed our breaths had synchronized. As we slowed, she began stroking her hand up and down my back. We were both slick with sweat, and I slid my body up and down hers, enjoying the slippery, erotic sensation.

She was lovely. Her entire body was flushed with our love-making. She was ravishing like this.

Ravished.

As I slid free of her and I reached down to remove the condom, I leaned slightly to one side so I could gaze down at her, but I froze.

Something felt different.

Wrong.

I glanced down and was shocked to see the bare head of my penis. No condom covered it, but the remnants of one were still firmly attached to my shaft.

"Lianna, it's—it's the condom."

She shifted back, moving away from me. "What's wrong?

"It broke. I can't believe this. The condom broke." I stared down as I tried to make sense of it.

Lianna stiffened. "How does a condom just break?"

I pushed myself away from her and stood up. "I have no idea. This has never happened to me before."

She looked panic-stricken, but she then took a deep breath. "Stay calm. No need to freak out. I can't get pregnant, so that's not an issue. The only man I've ever had unprotected sex with was my husband. That might not be reassuring since you know he was unfaithful, but the very first thing I did after I found him cheating was to get tested for any diseases he might have given me. I had them redone two months later, just to make sure. I'm clean, thank God, and you're—" she hesitated, her face turning scarlet, "you're the only person I've been with since then."

"Disease risk. Right." I took a deep, calming breath. "I'm in a similar situation. I only had unprotected sex once with my ex-girlfriend. She wanted to—" I stopped myself and shook my head. Did Lianna really want to know that Heather begged me not to use a condom because she hated the feel of them? Of course not. Nor did she want to know the way Heather had clamped her legs around my hips so that I couldn't pull out before I came. "When I broke off the engagement, I was tested too. No diseases."

She nodded slowly. "So, we should be okay."

"I think we're safe."

The tension in her posture eased and she sank into a more comfortable position against the pillows.

I couldn't relax yet though. Not after I'd promised myself I'd never be so careless again. I licked my lips. "But—what if you really *do* get pregnant? Wouldn't it be safer to take a morning-after pill?"

She inhaled sharply and then stilled, her eyes wide. "The possibility never even crossed my mind. There's no way I could get pregnant." She blinked rapidly. "Even so, I—I don't know if I could bring myself to do that."

She sat up in bed, holding tight onto her legs and tucking her knees under her chin. All her calm and ease was gone now. The weight of my question pressing down on her, filling the room like a heavy fog. "There's no hope of me ever becoming pregnant. I've reconciled myself to that, and it's been a painful journey. But, what you're asking feels like an insult to my pain and lived experience."

The desolation in her eyes nearly broke me, but her next words cut even deeper. "I thought you understood how difficult this loss has been, but your suggestion tells me I was wrong. You don't. I understand that you're afraid of being trapped, but you need to understand how much I still yearn to have a child. Perhaps that means I'm not as reconciled to being infertile as I thought I was. But Kincaid, what you're asking me to do would destroy me."

Those words bit deep into my foolish, selfish heart. I might be terrified of an unintended pregnancy, but I should have known better than to make such a suggestion to her. I hadn't taken a moment to think about how she would react. Of course she was upset. She had every right to be.

Her voice was thick with emotion when she spoke again, and tears trailed down her cheeks. "I couldn't possibly bring myself to stomp out a chance—any chance, no matter how unlikely—of something I want more than anything. It would shatter me."

Remorse filled me, softening my voice. "I'm sorry. I didn't mean to reopen such a raw wound. I know how much you've been through. This is difficult for me too, especially with Heather…" My words trailed off as I struggled to find the right way to convey my empathy and support while still letting her know how difficult this was for me. "I have a hard time trusting, but the fact that you're being so straightforward about your wants and needs helps. Forget I ever mentioned that pill."

She unwrapped her arms from around her legs and reached out to me, her eyes imploring. "Please believe me when I say that I trust you and I forgive you for what you said. I'd never want to make you feel trapped or coerced into doing something you don't want to do."

I let out a sigh of relief, feeling tension release from my shoulders. "Neither would I." I ran my hand through my hair, trying to collect my thoughts. "It boils down to trust, doesn't it? I trust you, love, even in this situation."

As I said those words, my heart gave a thud, realizing the depth of my feelings for her. I'd never trusted anyone this much before, not even myself. I felt a wave of gratitude for her openness and vulnerability.

She gave a wobbly smile, tears glistening on her cheeks. "Thank you. That means a lot to me."

I reached out to her, taking her hand in mine. "You don't have to thank me. I meant every word. I trust you, and I always will."

"And I promise you now, if I miraculously end up pregnant because of this, I won't expect anything from you that you aren't ready to give willingly." She leaned in and pressed a tender kiss to my cheek.

I nodded. This was hard for me. Hard for both of us. At least we'd managed to talk it through rather than getting hurt or angry.

I sat next to her and drew her close.

"You know I'm crazy about you, right?"

Since her head was pressed against my chest, I felt her nod. "So am I, so that works."

When I pulled away from her to stand, she raised her eyebrows in surprise. "Are you going somewhere?"

"Downstairs. I'm ready for a second helping of tiramisu."

She groaned and let out a shaky laugh. "I bet you're only with me for my cooking skills." Wiping away her tears, she brushed her hand against her cheek.

"Lianna," I said as I stood and pulled her to her feet, "you have so many exceptional qualities other than your cooking skills that I can't even begin to list them all. Even so, I have to admit, your cooking certainly weighs heavily in your favor." I gave her a wink.

She playfully smacked my shoulder. "I knew it."

"Last one downstairs has to do the breakfast dishes in the morning."

Her eyes widened, and then she darted toward the stairs without bothering to grab her robe.

I followed, loving the sight of her scrambling through the house naked.

Just as we reached the kitchen, a cell phone rang. "That's mine," Lianna said. "Where is it?" She lunged when she spotted it next to her pile of clothes on the floor.

She looked at the caller ID and tensed. "It's my mom," she whispered. "It's like she knows what we were just doing and is calling to reprimand me."

I quirked an eyebrow. "I certainly hope not."

She chuckled as she pressed the phone to her ear. "Hi, Mom."

"Hi, sweetie," I heard a woman's voice say. The volume on Lianna's phone was turned up so loud that I had no trouble hearing both ends of the conversation. "Your dad is dying to have a family pool party, and your sister already agreed to come. Can you make it on Memorial Day?"

Lianna hesitated. "Uh—"

"Why don't you bring over that new man you're seeing?" her mother interrupted.

Lianna glanced at me. "What new man?" She widened her eyes at me and shook her head as though she was confused.

She pressed the mute button on her phone. "I never told her about you."

I grinned at her panicked expression. "Clearly, she knows anyway. Unless there's another new man in your life."

She playfully pushed my shoulder. "Don't be ridiculous."

"The one you were seen kissing on the paddle court," her mother continued. "The one you went out to dinner with at the Not a Yacht Club and who regularly parks out in front of your house."

"Busted," I said, unable to resist.

Lianna poked at the button to unmute the phone. "Are you kidding me? Do you have spies all over Sewickley?"

"Of course not. I don't need them. You know how people gossip. Did you really think you could kiss a man in the middle of the paddle court and not have it get back to me?"

She closed her eyes and shook her head. "I knew that was a mistake."

"Do the rumormongers have it right? Are you really seeing Kincaid Gillette?" her mother asked.

"He's here with me now." She glanced at me. "I suppose you could say we're seeing each other."

"Lots of each other," I added softly, making sure the phone wouldn't pick up my voice.

"Oh, good! Invite him! I'll wait," her mother said.

Lianna rolled her eyes and glanced at me.

"Sure," I said. "Sounds like fun."

"Are you sure?" Lianna asked. "You don't have to."

"I can hear both of you, Lianna," her mother interjected.

"Don't go trying to talk him out of it. If the man said yes, then bring him."

Lianna sighed heavily. "Sure thing. We'll be there."

"That's great news. This Monday, then. Your dad will be thrilled."

23

THE MORNING AFTER

Lianna

The next morning, I woke up in bed, and for the first time in over a year, I wasn't alone.

Kincaid slept beside me; one arm draped across my belly.

I remained still, watching him sleep, feeling content and grateful for last night. It had surpassed my wildest dreams—and considering the intensely erotic nature of my recent fantasies, that was saying a lot. But Kincaid had exceeded even those.

We'd gone through two more condoms last night, and I planned to use more this morning. In a way, they symbolized hope for me. Kincaid and I had both tested negative for STDs, so the only thing those condoms would prevent was pregnancy, the one thing I desperately desired, but also knew would never happen.

Above all, I wanted Kincaid's trust. He'd been candid about his own issues, and I admired that. I refused to make him worry about unintended consequences. It would be selfish and unkind. I wanted to focus on building something special for just the two of us.

To be honest, I was frustrated that one broken condom had brought me back to this place where I once again longed and hoped and dreamed for a baby. It was easier to let go of hope. Holding onto it hurt. There was a reason it was in Pandora's Box in the first place. Hope was a double-edged sword. It could lift you up, but it could also keep you trapped and unable to let go.

I sighed. Dwelling on this was pointless. I'd managed to put this broken dream behind me a year ago, and I needed to do it again. Now. I was supposed to be moving on with my life.

And I would. Starting now. It was time for me. Time for us.

"You're awake," Kincaid said. He nuzzled my neck with his lips, pressing his muscular body against mine and pulling me close, like his own giant teddybear.

"Good morning, love," I replied, borrowing the pet name he'd given me.

"Mmm," he murmured. "I love waking up next to you."

"I can think of something else you'll enjoy," I said, sliding my hand down his belly.

24

MEET THE PARENTS

I brought my truck to a halt in front of Lianna's parents' house on Monday and gaped at the sprawling estate. "You grew up in this place? It's enormous."

The Alversons lived at the top of a small mountain outside the town of Sewickley. Dense foliage shrouded the house, concealing the valley below.

"My mom complains that she's rattling around in there now that Zoey, Nick, and I have moved out. It didn't seem big when we were living here. We always had pool parties, Halloween parties, birthday parties—any excuse to invite friends over."

Lianna took my arm, bypassing the front door in favor of a gate leading to the side of the house. "Mom and Dad will be at the pool, so let's go straight there."

We descended a steep path behind the house, arriving at a secluded area that was both private and expansive. The house overlooked a wooded valley, and the pool was situated on a flat section of land extending from the lowest level. No other houses were visible, only an expanse of treetops. Although I had driven past a few other homes to get here, this oasis was hidden from view.

As we approached the lush pool area, the opening chords of a Jimmy Buffet tune boomed from massive boulder-shaped speakers stationed by the water's edge.

Lianna shot me a wry smile, and I felt a warmth spread through me. "Did I mention my dad's a parrot head?" she asked.

I blinked. "What's that? It sounds painful."

"Only if you live with him." She shot me a grin. "A parrot head is a Jimmy Buffett fan. I probably know every song he's ever written. It was child abuse, I tell you."

I smirked at her, enjoying her playful banter. "I'm so sorry for the torture you endured."

She sighed tragically. "Don't tease. You don't know what it was like, listening to the same music over and over."

"But I do. My dad's a Dave Matthews Band aficionado. I feel your pain."

"Ah. Now I understand. We've suffered the same sort of torture growing up. We'll have to get our fathers together someday so they can duke it out."

I chuckled at the thought. "It could be a match made in heaven. They'd each finally have a friend to drag along to all the concerts."

Lianna shook her head, still smiling. "Oh, the horror. I'm warming up to this idea. A Parrot Head and a... what do you call a Dave Matthews fan?"

"They're just called Dave Matthews fans."

She scrunched up her nose. "That shows a decided lack of imagination. Even so, our dads might be perfect for each other. My mom would be thrilled to miss a concert or two. She refuses to get those open-seating lawn tickets ever again. Years ago, she attended a concert just after a storm passed through Pittsburgh. She was heading off to use the bathroom and she stumbled across a group of guys standing in a circle in the middle of all the concertgoers, peeing in the mud."

I tightened my grip on her hand and let out a hoot of laughter.

"My mom tells a similar story about a Dave Matthews Band concert from when she and dad were first married."

"That's just gross. Guys can be totally disgusting."

A man with graying hair emerged from inside the pool house and strode towards us, beaming broadly. "You're here."

This had to be Lianna's dad. I let go of her hand to shake Mr. Alverson's.

"It's great to meet you, Kincaid." Mr. Alverson's grip was firm and friendly. "I'm Ben. Lianna says good things about you."

"Thank you for inviting me, sir," I replied, handing him the six-pack of beer I had brought. "Where would you like me to put this?"

Ben pointed to a nearby cooler. "Over there is fine. And thanks for bringing cans. I don't allow glass by the pool."

"Good rule," I said, nodding. "The last thing we want is a trip to the emergency room."

As we chatted, the door to the basement level of the house opened, and out stepped a woman with the same wavy brown hair as Lianna. Her face, though more mature, was equally striking, with a distinct character that showed in the subtle lines etched around her eyes and mouth.

"This is my mom, Anne Alverson," Lianna said. "Mom, this is Kincaid."

Anne's face lit up in a broad smile. "Call me Anne. I'm so glad you could both come today. I wish Troy and Felicity could be here, but they live in D.C. You'll get to meet Lianna's younger sister, Zoey, though. She'll be here in about an hour. She has a paper she's finishing up and needs to submit it online before she can join us."

"I look forward to meeting her," I said, smiling.

Ben shook his head. "She's getting an art history degree. Waste of time and money, if you ask me."

Lianna shot her father a disapproving look. "Zoey loves art. It's her passion."

"Passion doesn't pay the bills," Ben replied, his tone dismissive.

Lianna and I dropped our bags beside the poolside lounge chairs and draped our towels over the long cushions. She leaned closer to me and whispered, "They'll stop sooner if they don't have an audience. Dad can get a bit fixated on certain topics, and Zoey's degree is one of them. Mom can usually distract him, though."

A minute later, Ben joined us and dropped down onto a lounge chair, claiming it with an enormous Jimmy Buffett beach towel. "Lianna says you own a construction company. How's business?"

I glanced at Lianna, who kept her face expressionless. She'd already warned me about her father's inquisitions, so I wasn't taken aback. "Things are going great. We always have work to do."

"Do you have a good cash flow? Any issues collecting payments from clients?"

In other words, did I know how to run a business? "Nothing I can't handle. Some clients can be challenging, but they aren't a common occurrence."

Ben nodded. "Any problems with zoning violations?"

Lianna rose to her feet. "Enough, Dad. You're grilling the poor guy." She untied the knot that held her beach cover-up in place, which dramatically fell to the paving stones, revealing a bright red bikini. Then she grabbed my hand and pulled me up. "It's hot out here and we haven't even been in the pool yet."

Ben smiled. "You can't blame a dad for being protective."

"Of course not, sir," I replied, grinning back. "I'd expect nothing less from Lianna's dad." I took off my t-shirt and placed it on the cushion.

Lianna arched an eyebrow. "Last one in's a rotten egg." She headed for the deep end and executed a graceful dive into the water.

I watched as she surfaced, pushing her wet hair out of her face and grinning at me. "You lose!" she yelled at me.

Ben glanced at his watch. "I have a conference call. I'll be busy for about an hour or so. You kids go ahead and have fun."

Lianna frowned as he walked away.

I made my own shallow dive into the pool, breaking the surface next to where Lianna was treading water.

Anne shaded her eyes with her hand. "Are we still on schedule to attend that estate sale next weekend? I hear they'll have jewelry."

"They will?" Lianna grabbed hold of the side of the pool and peered at her mom. "I love estate sale jewelry. You never know what you'll find. This should be fun."

"We'll make a day of it." Anne stood from the lounge chair. "I'm going to finish making dessert now. You two enjoy yourselves." She headed toward the house.

I looked around the now-empty pool area. "Did I do something to drive them away?"

Lianna shook her head. "No. Dad's always busy with work stuff. Phone calls, business trips, dinner meetings. He wasn't around much when we were growing up. Now that we're all out of the house, I think Mom gets lonely. She stays busy volunteering and gardening. I know she enjoys her life, but she's alone a lot."

Lianna swam over and wrapped her arms around me. I pulled her against my chest as I treaded water. She was all slippery and mermaid-like in my grasp, and the water trapped between our bodies quickly grew warmer.

I glanced up at the house and then nuzzled her neck. "Can they see us down here?"

"Not really. Only if they go into my brother's bedroom upstairs, and even from there, it isn't a very good view. I doubt they'd try. Since the house is at the top of a mountain, they couldn't put the pool directly behind it. That spot was too steep. They ended up putting it over here to one side."

As I peered out over the treetops below us, I couldn't help but agree with Lianna. "It's gorgeous up here. Not another house in sight."

Lianna leaned into me, her voice barely above a whisper. "There's a park below us with nature trails, and about five miles in the distance on the other side of the valley is a house, but it's mostly blocked by the trees. It's private up here even though we have neighbors close by."

"I like it."

She planted a soft kiss on my neck before taking hold of my shoulders and wrapping her legs around my waist, pulling me closer. We floated, enjoying each other's company in the secluded pool area.

I grew hard.

She wriggled. "What's that?" She shot me a teasing smile. "Don't tell me you're getting randy."

"'Randy'?" I rolled my eyes as I cupped her bottom with both hands. "Who are you? Austin Powers?" Then I pulled her closer and nibbled at her bottom lip. It was slightly chilled from the water.

"'Oh, behave.'" She wriggled again.

"We're not doing anything about it in your parents' swimming pool. Call me a prude, but that's where I draw the line." I lifted her a bit higher to stop the torture.

"Of course not. What kind of girl do you think I am?" she asked, giving me a coy smile. She then unwound her legs from around me and made her way toward the wide steps leading out of the pool. "In fact, I think I'll go inside and take a quick shower to rinse off the chlorine." She grabbed her towel and draped it over her shoulders, then shot me a playful look. "Care to join me?"

I dove toward the steps, not needing a second invitation, and grabbed my towel to wrap around my hips as I followed her, intrigued by her sudden offer.

We entered the lower level of the house through French doors, and a blast of cool air hit me, raising goosebumps on my arms. Lianna took my hand and pulled me along.

"This way." We crossed the tiled floor, passing by the wet bar, and entered an opulent bathroom, where the floor was softened by a couple of plush rugs.

Lianna let go of my hand, opened the door of the enormous shower, turned on the water, and fiddled with some dials on the wall.

"This bathroom is huge." I examined the dials more closely. "Is that a steam shower? I installed one of these a few months ago."

She moved over to the panel and flipped a switch, turning a dial. "It will take a couple of minutes for the water to heat up, but once it does, we'll have tons of steam. This shower is one of my favorite things about this house." She grabbed hold of the bright red strings holding her bikini top in place and gave them a sharp tug. When the two triangles dropped down to reveal her breasts, I forgot my questions about her steam shower. All I could do was stare.

I'd come to know her body well over the past couple of days, but I was still eager to explore. I loved the way her right breast sat up so pertly. The way her left one drooped ever so slightly because it was a bit larger than its mate. The way her nipples would pucker at the slightest touch. I loved every part of her to distraction.

I did a slow blink. Was I falling in love with Lianna?

This was all happening so fast. I had only known her for six weeks, and I had promised myself that I would take things slow this time. But with Lianna, it felt different. I had never felt this way about a woman before. The last time I had moved this fast, it had ended in disaster. But Lianna was different. There was no comparison to my previous relationships. She made me feel seen, loved, and valued for who I was.

Lianna undid the fastening at her back and let her bikini top fall to the floor, then she reached down and stroked me through my swim trunks.

Every thought fled as I hissed at her touch. I was hereby done with the thinking portion of the afternoon. It was time to move on to the physical part.

"Just relax," Lianna said. She licked her lips. "I've been planning this all day. You have your fantasies, right? Well, I have a few of my own." She smiled up at me. "You might be surprised by this, but I've never done what I'm about to do. At least, not here. Not like this."

"Done this?" I gasped out the words as her hand tightened on my hard length. "What, exactly, are you about to do?"

"I'm about to make your head explode." The gleam in her eyes was downright impish.

My cock pulsed in her hand as though it had a mind of its own. As though it approved of every word she'd just uttered. "Are you trying to give me a heart attack? You want to do this with your parents upstairs?"

She nodded, sinking slowly to her knees on the rug. "This is the perfect opportunity. You have no idea how many years I've fantasized about this. Ever since one of my high school friends told me she and her boyfriend did this very thing in here at one of my parties."

She stared at me and licked her lips again. I let out a groan. "Lianna. You're killing me."

She glanced up at me and grinned wickedly. "Absolutely not. I need you alive for this."

She tried to pull down on my swim trunks, but they were wet and clingy and wouldn't budge.

"Need a hand?" I tugged them down. My cock sprang free, and she immediately wrapped her warm hand around it.

At first, she just stared at the head with concentration. Then, she leaned forward and flicked the tip of her tongue over it.

I let out a hiss. "Lianna."

"Shh. Not too loud. We don't want anyone to hear."

CHEEKY DEVIL

LIANNA

I couldn't believe I was finally doing it. I had fantasized about this for years, ever since Elyse Larkin had confessed to doing the same thing in this very room. Elyse had always been so confident and self-assured, ready to take on anything. That's exactly how I wanted to be, too—living life to the fullest, taking risks, and not looking back.

But now that I was here, certain realities made themselves known. The primary one being that tile floors were really, really hard on the knees.

I reconsidered my position and then folded the towel over on itself for extra padding.

"Do your knees hurt?" Kincaid's voice was rough. "You know you don't have to do this."

I shook my head, determined to see this through. "No, it's fine. I'm good."

I closed my eyes and took a deep breath. This was it. The moment I had been waiting for. When I opened my eyes again, Kincaid was looking at me with concern.

"Are you ready?"

I nodded and then lowered myself down onto my knees, the

towel doing little to cushion the hard floor. But the discomfort was nothing compared to the thrill of finally living out my fantasy.

"I'm fine now." I swirled my tongue around his head.

He let out a soft gasp of pleasure.

Exactly the reaction I was hoping for. I began to stroke him with slow, seductive caresses, my mouth and my hand working in concert. This part was happening exactly the way I'd imagined it.

Bringing this fantasy to life made me feel powerful.

Strong and seductive.

When the steam shower finally clicked on, it startled me, and I released him from my mouth and rocked back on my heels. Mist hissed from the shower nozzles.

The fact that he'd let me do this—here—now—meant the world to me. My own desire began building as I teased and played with him.

Kincaid slid his fingers into my hair as he leaned back against the wall, silently gasping.

I felt in control.

Kincaid was falling apart, and I was the one doing it to him.

Mist drifted out of the shower. "Lianna, I need to touch you." Kincaid's voice was rough and husky with desire.

I lifted my head to glance up at him as tendrils of steam wrapped around us.

"I'm not going to last much longer," he said, panting. "Where…" His words trailed off as if he'd lost the ability to talk.

I didn't let go. A moment later, he released. He threw his head back, the muscles on his neck becoming taut ropes. He froze that way, then let out a gasp of pure, animal pleasure.

He blinked rapidly as he came back to himself, and then grinned down at me with bleary eyes filled with joy and pure pleasure. He helped pull me to my feet.

"That was…amazing. Did the fantasy meet your expectations?" Kincaid slid his hands around my hips, leaned in, and kissed me.

I let out a low chuckle and stroked his chest. "Meet? I'd say it far exceeded them."

"I'm happy to be of service."

I rolled my eyes and nudged him in the ribs. "We should head back outside before we're missed. Everyone will be heading back out to the pool soon."

The mist swirled around us as he pressed a kiss to the top of my head. "Let's rinse the chlorine off first. I don't want to let you out of my arms just yet." He tugged me closer to the shower. I stripped off my swimsuit while he adjusted the knobs until the water cascading from the rainfall-style showerhead was exactly to his liking. Then he took me by the hand and drew me into the tiled enclosure with him.

He lathered soap in his hands, and I did likewise. The languid scent of sandalwood enveloped us, and I reached for Kincaid, needing to touch him again. I couldn't seem to help myself when he was this close and entirely naked. I could barely keep my hands off him. As I slid my palms over his muscled torso, he offered random kisses and caresses of his own.

Lord, but I loved to be touched by this man.

The rainfall showerhead reminded me of the kiss we'd shared during the rainstorm a couple of weeks ago. He'd been so gorgeous. So sexy. If Courtney hadn't shown up, I'm certain we would've ended up in bed within minutes.

"I'm glad you shared your fantasy with me," Kincaid murmured against my lips, sending a shiver down my back. "It was amazing. *You* were amazing. Knowing you'd fantasized about it made it incredibly erotic."

His words made my lingering doubts evaporate. I'd been afraid to tell him I wanted this. Afraid he'd be appalled.

The one time I'd tried to share a fantasy about wearing fishnet stockings with Paul, he'd been repulsed because I'd used the word "fantasy." I'd simply wanted to be open and trusting with him.

It had been a terrible mistake. One I'd never made again.

In Kincaid's eyes, I found only tenderness, pure satisfaction, and deep-seated contentment.

Looking back now, perhaps Paul's rejection had been the first sure sign that there was a fundamental problem in our marriage. The man had always kept secrets. He'd always been afraid to open up and trust people—even me—and perhaps that was because, at heart, he couldn't even be honest with himself. Not even about his own sexual wants and needs.

But Kincaid—he was completely different. He'd trusted me from the very beginning.

He didn't judge me or find me lacking. He liked me. All of me.

It was a novel feeling.

This man was slipping deeper and deeper into my heart. Pretty soon, he'd be so firmly embedded there, I wouldn't ever want him to leave.

I pressed a tender kiss on the corner of his mouth, where he'd missed shaving a small patch of dark stubble that morning. I had a great affection for that spot. It wasn't the first time I'd seen it there, so it must be a difficult spot for him to shave. The patch was rough and masculine, and it proved that he wasn't perfect. He wasn't a fantasy I'd conjured. It made him all the more real to me, flawed and perfect in his own way.

"What was that for?" he asked.

"For being you," I said the words simply, but the sentiment was more than simple. There was more weight to it than I let on. "You're an amazing man, Kincaid Gillette. I'll forever be in Courtney's debt for nagging me into dating you."

He cupped my face and kissed me on the forehead, then pressed his forehead against mine. "And you're an amazing woman, Lianna Alverson, but I draw the line at forever being in my sister's debt." His lips curved into a grin.

I closed my eyes and leaned back, relishing the sensation of the water cascading over my hair and face. With a flick of my hand, I slicked my hair back. "We should head back to the pool."

"You go on ahead. I'll be right there." Kincaid squirted some shampoo into his hand.

I couldn't help but watch the water as it flowed over his sculpted body for one more moment before sighing and opening the shower door and stepping out into the steam-filled room. I quickly toweled dry and pulled on my still-wet bikini. The cold fabric made my nipples stand on end, but fortunately, the cup liners concealed my reaction.

As I glanced back at the steam-filled shower, I could barely make out Kincaid through the mist. "I'll see you outside." I slipped out of the bathroom before I could change my mind.

Arriving at the pool, I found my mom coming down the outside stairs carrying a tray of chips and salsa. "Hi, sweetie." She looked around. "Where's Kincaid?"

"He's rinsing off in the bathroom."

"I like him. He handled your father's interrogation well, which is no easy task."

"Tell me about it. Is he this hard on Zoey's dates too?"

"Definitely." Mom set down the snack tray, and with a few quick moves, arranged everything on the table for a more pleasing display. I admired her talent for making everything look nicer with minimal effort. "I have to admit, I was probably just as hard on Troy's girlfriends… at least, the ones he showed any real interest in. I used to worry he'd never meet a girl. He was always playing around on that computer of his."

"He wasn't playing. He was a hacker, Mom."

"You don't need to tell me that. That boy is lucky he didn't get himself in bigger trouble than he did."

I shifted in my seat, remembering the days when I'd been afraid to answer the phone or check my email, for fear that the FBI was after him and would try to get to him through me. "Ten years ago, I never would have predicted he'd own his own computer security company. After that business with the FBI, I was terrified he'd end up in jail."

"It helped that he didn't have a record and that he didn't

actually do anything once he broke into that financial site. If he'd tried to make changes or download any of their data, everything would have turned out quite differently." Mom adjusted her white Gucci sunglasses, shielding her eyes from the bright sun. "At least he started connecting with real people after that scare."

"And now he's married." I closed my mouth to keep from editorializing.

"That he is." She glanced away. Mom had never been a big fan of Troy's wife, Felicity. Neither had I. We both tried to keep our opinions to ourselves, though.

A moment later, Mom glanced back at me. "Kincaid's a keeper. I have a good feeling about him."

I blushed, hoping Kincaid would appear and save me from this conversation, but there was no sign of him. "We've only been seeing each other for a month. It's early to reach any conclusions."

"Maybe. Sometimes you know right away, though. I just want you to know I like him. He's good for you."

The French doors opened, and my heart gave a little flutter when I spotted Kincaid.

"Definitely a keeper," Mom said. When I glanced at her, I could tell she hadn't missed my reaction to the sight of him. My cheeks warmed.

"I brought snacks," my mom called out to Kincaid. "Chips and salsa okay?"

"Love 'em," he said, scooping up a chip and dipping it into the salsa.

A smile danced in Mom's eyes. "And for dessert, I made tiramisu. I hope you like it."

A broad grin lit up Kincaid's face. "It's my favorite." He shot me a sidelong look, and I felt that faint blush deepen and spread all the way to my toes.

"It's Lianna's favorite, too." Mom's gaze turned to me. "You're looking a bit pink. Have you been in the sun too long?" Mom grabbed a bottle of sunscreen from the counter near the wet bar.

"You haven't even been here very long. I hope you aren't burning."

I reached out to take the bottle, but Kincaid intercepted it. "I'll do your back for you. Your mom's right. You're a bit pink."

Mom reclined on her lounge chair and closed her eyes, a pleased smile tugging up the corners of her mouth.

As his lotion-covered hands slid over my shoulders, the warmth of the sun, the sound of the water lapping against the side of the pool, and Kincaid's touch all combined to create a sense of peace.

He slid his hands past the band holding my bikini in place and down toward my hips with strong, sure movements. I relaxed under his touch. That is, I relaxed until he moved closer and murmured into my ear, "Maybe we can bring home some leftover tiramisu."

His words shivered down my spine. I wanted him. Now. Was it a Pavlovian response to tiramisu? This man was wicked, through and through. And the thoughts he planted in my mind? Quite wicked, indeed.

I turned and plucked the sunscreen from the table where Kincaid had set it. "I can manage the rest," I said primly.

He gave me a mischievous grin. "Too bad," he murmured.

I just shook my head at him. Fortunately, Mom seemed oblivious to his antics—or at least pretended to be—as she focused her attention on her Kindle.

I was surprised when Kincaid suddenly dove into the pool and began swimming laps. I had assumed he was finished for the day after his shower. His strong, smooth strokes sliced through the water, and his splashing created a noisy distraction.

I caught sight of my sister out of the corner of my eye and leaped out of my lounge chair to greet her. "Zoey! How's it going?" She must have snuck up on me under the cover of all that splashing.

"I'm doing great. I submitted my paper online, so now I'm free for the rest of the day."

"That must be a relief not to have it hanging over your head," Mom said with a smile. "Now, you can relax."

"That's the plan," Zoey replied, dropping her pink and black striped beach bag onto the last unclaimed lounge chair. She shaded her eyes and watched Kincaid swim laps. "Is that your new squeeze?" she asked, loud enough for me to hear over the splashing, but not loud enough to carry as far as our mom.

I grinned. "None other."

"He's hot," Zoey said. "What's his name?"

"Kincaid Gillette."

"Really? Courtney's brother?" She peered at him more closely. "He owns that construction company, right? Is he a brainiac like his sister? With those muscles, he's not what I would have expected."

"Not exactly like Courtney. She's in a league all her own, but yeah, he's pretty amazing."

The splashing eased as Kincaid slowed and swam toward us until he was at the edge of the pool. "Hi," he called up. "You must be Zoey."

"And you're Kincaid. Nice to meet you."

He put his hands on the edge of the pool and pushed himself up onto the edge in a single, smooth movement. Water cascaded off him, and he ran his hands over his dark hair, forcing the water to run down his back. He seemed oblivious to Zoey's quick assessment and appreciation of his body, but I wasn't. A smug smile played on my lips as I watched Zoey's reaction.

Zoey stood up, handing Kincaid his towel, and he wiped his face and chest before draping it back on the chair. I shot my sister a warning look when she waggled her eyebrows at Kincaid.

"Good to see you, Dad," I said, trying to refocus her attention as he approached. "You're just in time. I'm starving, too."

Dad grinned. "Well, I'll start the burgers then."

Zoey rubbed her stomach. "About time. I'm famished."

"You always are," I teased.

"That's because I know Mom and Dad won't disappoint me when it comes to food," Zoey said with a grin.

"Speaking of which," Kincaid chimed in, "I hear your mom made tiramisu. Lianna's favorite."

That cheeky man. I felt my cheeks flush at the mention of my favorite dessert. Kincaid's teasing grin only made it worse.

"Exactly," Zoey's eyes lit up. "I love tiramisu, but that's Lianna's favorite, not mine. I prefer something decadently chocolate, like Mom's Killer Brownies."

"Do you all want to come upstairs to the deck with me?" Mom stood and smoothed the front of her sundress. "I thought we could eat out there. One of you can set the table while I finish making the salad."

I quickly grabbed my long sarong from my bag and wrapped it around my body, tying it behind my neck. Kincaid slipped on his t-shirt as we made our way up the staircase, with him trailing right behind me. I could feel his gaze on my backside, so I gave it a playful wiggle. He playfully swatted it, and I couldn't help but grin.

I glanced back at him over my shoulder. "Cheeky devil."

"You know it."

2 6

WHEN LIFE THROWS CURVEBALLS

I stood beside Lianna's dad as he slid burgers onto the grill, the sizzling patties filling the air with the mouthwatering aroma of seared meat. The family gathered at the cast aluminum dining table, its colorful umbrella shading them from the sun's intense heat.

I turned to face the stunning emerald valley, taking in the breathtaking panorama. "You have an amazing view up here, Ben."

"It's why I fell in love with this house," he replied, a smile lighting up his face. "I'm surrounded by people at work all day, so this house is like my own private island."

"It's quite a view." I glanced at Lianna, my gaze catching on her full lips. Mr. Alverson had quite a daughter, too. When she noticed me watching her, she turned pink. Good to know I had that effect on her.

I glanced over and caught Zoey smirking at us.

Busted.

"You'll love Dad's burgers," Zoey said. "He really knows his meat." She gave Lianna a wicked grin. "Lianna's pretty good at picking out a prime cut of beef, too."

Lianna glared at her sister.

"I trained her well." Ben Alverson beamed as though Zoey had given him the best compliment he could imagine.

I considered what I might say, but decided silence was my best option.

"The secret is to start with good quality meat and then add Worcestershire sauce," Ben said as he flipped the burgers on the grill. "Works every time."

"It isn't much of a secret if you tell everyone." Anne cast her husband an indulgent smile.

"It's my sacred duty to improve the world, even when it comes to grilling," Ben intoned, then cracked a grin. "Good grilling is in everyone's best interest. There's nothing sadder than an overcooked, dried-out piece of meat."

"Anything I can do to help?" I asked, eager to contribute to the family gathering.

Ben handed me a plate of fresh buns. "How about buttering the buns and toasting them on the grill?"

I smiled and got to work, appreciating the opportunity to be useful. Growing up, my relationship with my father had been strained. He was always distant and uninvolved, never taking an interest in my life. But Ben was different. Even though this was the first time we'd met, he'd welcomed me into his family and made me feel like I belonged. It was a stark contrast to the way I'd been treated by my own dad.

As I toasted the buns, I couldn't help but feel a sense of appreciation for Ben. He was a good father and seemed interested in his children's lives. I admired him for the way he took care of his family and how he had welcomed me into it. It was a feeling I wasn't used to, but one I hoped to experience more often in the future.

As I finished, a bug dive-bombed my cheek, and I gave it a swat. With so much food on the table, I was surprised we weren't having more trouble with them.

"You don't seem to have many bugs here," I commented as I

sat next to Lianna. "I haven't noticed a single mosquito, which is a pleasant surprise. I'm usually their favorite food. I always carry bug spray in my truck for just that reason."

"We have bats," Ben said, taking a swig from his beer bottle. "They're great at keeping flying insects under control."

I nodded. "That explains it."

Anne placed a bowl of potato salad in the center of the table, and we all eagerly began to serve ourselves. I loaded my plate with a burger, fries, potato salad, and a serving of green salad. As I bit into the burger, the flavors mingled in my mouth, and I couldn't help but moan in delight.

"Everything is delicious," I said. "These burgers are incredible."

"Told you," Ben said, his grin wide.

"Are those pomegranate seeds in the salad?" I asked.

"They are," Anne said. "And I made the pomegranate dressing."

"Love it." I turned to Lianna. "Did your mom teach you to cook?"

She glanced proudly at her mom and nodded. "I've been cooking with her as long as I can remember. I think the first things I helped with were cakes. I remember cracking the eggs for her."

"She's a great cook," I told Anne. "The lasagna she made for me was out of this world."

We all settled into a comfortable conversation, enjoying the warm sunshine and each other's company.

After dinner, Anne and Zoey rose to clear the table, but Anne insisted that I stay seated. "No, you're our guest," she said, patting me on the shoulder. She glanced at Lianna. "You stay here, too. Keep him company. Zoey and I can handle things."

Lianna relaxed back into her chair. "Enjoy it while you can. She'll put you to work next time."

Next time. I liked the sound of that. Lianna and I were getting more comfortable imagining a future together—making plans.

I was grateful that I fit in so well with her family. If everything went as I hoped, we'd be spending a lot of time together. I tried to tell myself to slow down, not to rush things with Lianna, but my heart was on a different timeline than my head. Maybe it was time to stop fighting this thing.

Ben's cell phone chimed from the table.

Anne gathered more dishes. "We almost made it through an entire meal without you taking a call," she quipped as she headed inside.

Ben grinned as he glanced at the screen. "You'll be glad I'm taking this one," he called out to Anne through the screen door. "It's Troy." He answered the call, putting it on speakerphone as Anne hurried back outside.

"Hey, son," Ben said warmly. "The rest of the family is here. We were just finishing up dinner. Perfect timing."

"Hi, everyone," Troy's voice came through the speaker. "Can you hear me okay?"

"Absolutely," Zoey said.

"Hey, Zoey! You're there too? Sorry I couldn't make it for Memorial Day, but it turned out to be for the best. If I'd been there, I would have missed out on my own daughter's birth."

"Today?" Anne let out a squeal of excitement. "She was born today? Are you saying I'm a grandmother?"

Lianna's grip on my hand tightened. Our eyes locked, and she grinned like a kid on Christmas morning.

"You sure are," Troy said. "I'm texting Dad a photo of her as we speak."

Ben opened the photo on his phone and then held it up for us to see. An adorable reddish baby was wrapped in a white blanket and wore a pink and blue striped knit cap. Her hands were balled in tiny fists.

"We're looking at her right now," Ben said. "She's perfect. What's her name?"

"Say hello to Colette Alverson." Troy sounded giddy with happiness.

Lianna's grip on my hand tightened enough to become painful.

Everyone else around the table froze for an instant, and then they turned to stare at Lianna.

She sat completely still, staring at the baby's image, not even breathing. Suddenly, her face contorted, and she snatched her hand from mine, covering her mouth with a napkin before darting toward the door.

Confused and concerned, I tried to stand up, but Anne gently pressed her hand on my shoulder, signaling me to stay put. "Give her a moment," she said. "She needs to process this."

"What just happened?" I asked, looking around the table for answers.

Troy's voice quivered over the phone. "What's going on, guys?"

Zoey's expression turned from surprise to anger as she answered him. "Are you that clueless? Lianna has been talking about naming her baby Colette for years."

Troy sounded confused. "Felicity told me that she and Lianna had talked about it and that Lianna had suggested using the name. I thought we were doing something nice for her…" he trailed off.

Lianna's mom pressed her lips together as though she was trying hard not to say something she'd regret. "I don't think that's true," she finally bit out. "Not based on Lianna's reaction just now. It was obviously a shock."

There was a brief silence, then Troy said, "Shit."

Ben leaned closer to the phone, resting his elbows heavily on the cast aluminum table. "This isn't the first time your wife has lied to you this way," he said bluntly.

Troy's silence confirmed Ben's accusation.

"Maybe you can still fix it," Ben suggested. "Tell the hospital you made a mistake and change the paperwork."

Troy sighed heavily. "It won't be that easy. Felicity's family is here at the hospital. She's telling everyone how much she loves the baby's name. If I try to convince her to change it, not only will I look like an ass, but she'll create a huge scene. I bet she set it up this way on purpose."

I couldn't believe what I was hearing. Zoey seemed to read my thoughts and murmured, "His wife is a piece of work. I think she gets off on causing trouble. Her whole family sees life as a battle. He's right. If her family is at the hospital, they'll make it impossible for him to change the name."

I stood abruptly, anger and frustration roiling inside of me. "This is messed up." I glared at the phone, furious that Lianna was being used as a pawn in some petty game between Troy and his wife.

Anne nodded in agreement. "It is. You should go talk to her now. She'll have had enough time to process it by now."

When I found Lianna coming out of the powder room, I could see that she'd been crying, but had managed to compose herself. She offered me a wobbly smile as she spotted me.

"Hey, babe," I said, opening my arms wide. She immediately stepped into them. "That was a pretty shitty thing for Felicity to do," I said, feeling the anger bubbling up again. "It turns out she told your brother you'd suggested they use the name."

Lianna let out a snort of disbelief. "That sounds like something she'd tell him. You know it's a lie, right?"

"That was pretty obvious based on your reaction," I said, rubbing my hand up and down her spine. "Colette Alverson is a nice name."

She sniffled. "Do you think so?"

"Yeah. It's not a name I would choose for my own kid, though."

Her expression was guarded. "Why not?"

"Colette Gillette?" I said, chuckling. "That name's a lot to hang on a kid."

She relaxed and let out a soft laugh. "Oh, my. That would be a bit too much."

"I'm sensitive to cute-sounding names," I said. "The whole Christopher, Courtney, Conner, Kincaid thing really got to me."

She sniffled again. "You don't think I'm being overly sensitive?"

"Absolutely not. She clearly did it to mess with you and your brother."

She nodded. "She's a real piece of work, that's for sure. I'm just glad they live in D.C. and not down the street. I can't imagine having to see her at every single family gathering. I don't know how Troy puts up with her. We all thought she was nice at first."

"Too many people hide who they really are," I said, reflecting on my own experiences. I'd met plenty of individuals who tried to please others instead of being themselves, or—even worse—manipulated them for their own selfish reasons. People needed to be honest about themselves and live their truth.

Lianna heaved a sigh. "Oh, well. There are plenty of other great baby names out there. At least there's a Colette Alverson in the world now. Maybe it's a good thing after all."

Lianna's mom entered the house and headed straight for the refrigerator. "I'm about to serve the tiramisu," she announced. "Come on out and join us when you're ready. No rush." She pulled the dessert off the shelf and returned outside.

"Mmm. Tiramisu. Want some?"

Lianna blushed. "You've ruined me for life. I'll never be able to say no to tiramisu ever again."

As we sat down for dessert, a heavy silence descended upon us. It was getting uncomfortable.

"How about them Pirates?" Zoey finally said, breaking the silence.

Lianna chuckled. "I heard they won last night."

"That makes it four games in a row," Ben added.

After we finished the tiramisu, Ben's phone rang again.

"You're a popular man tonight," Anne commented. "Maybe you should let it go to voicemail. We've had enough big news for the day.

Ben shook his head. "Sorry, I can't. I need to take it. It's from my CFO. He'd only call on the weekend if there was an emergency." He stood up and walked into the house to answer the call.

Lianna and I exchanged a private smile as we savored the delicious dessert. "This is excellent," I told her, smiling. "Just like yours."

Her eyes flashed with our shared secret, and she gave me such a sweet, flirtatious grin that it made my heart race. "We should take some home with us."

Suddenly, Ben shoved open the door and rushed back outside, his face grim.

"Lianna, something happened," he said, his voice urgent. "You need to check your email."

Lianna's smile faded, and her eyes widened with concern. "What's wrong?" she asked.

Ben's grim reply cut through the night like a bolt of lightning. "Your company just filed for bankruptcy," he said. "I'm afraid you're out of a job."

A HAVEN IN THE STORM

Lianna

An hour later, as Kincaid's truck engine abruptly stopped, I came out of my reverie. I glanced out of his window and saw that we were parked in front of my house. My hands slid down the sides of Mom's bowl of tiramisu, and I was surprised to find them stiff from gripping the cold glass.

My mind raced with worry. All I could think about was my job and my team.

I needed to contact my boss first to find out what had happened. Did he have any information that I could pass along? Once I knew more, I could call my team.

Thankfully, I'd already updated my resume, thanks to Kincaid's advice.

Kincaid came around to my side of the truck, opened my door, and took the tiramisu out of my lap.

"Thanks," I said distractedly. I stumbled slightly as I climbed down from his truck, but Kincaid steadied me.

"Let's get you inside. You look like you could use a drink."

I waved away the suggestion. "No alcohol. I have too much to do right now. I'll have a drink with you later tonight, but right now, I have a bunch of phone calls I need to make."

As I approached the front door, I realized I didn't have my purse or my pool bag. Which meant I didn't have my door key either. I realized I hadn't grabbed them when we'd left.

I slumped, suddenly overwhelmed. Today had been a supremely bad day. "I left my purse and my keys at my parents' house."

Kincaid lifted his arm, showing me my purse and pool bag. "I grabbed them on the way out." He handed me my purse.

A wave of gratitude hit me hard. "Thanks," I managed to say. "You're the best boyfriend ever."

I located my keys. Should I call Kevin, or Pam? Kevin would know more, but I bet his assistant Pam would be more forthcoming now that the news was out. I'd start with her and then use whatever she told me to wheedle more details out of Kevin... but Kevin could be a hard ass. What if he figured out what I was up to and stonewalled me?43

I gazed down at my keys, lost in thought as I pondered the situation at hand. Kincaid took them from me and unlocked the front door. "Why don't you make your phone calls? I'll put away the tiramisu and bring you something to drink." He gently tucked a strand of hair behind my ear. "Water or juice?"

"Water," I replied.

Moments later, I was settled in my living room with my feet up on the coffee table and my laptop open in front of me. Kincaid placed a glass of ice water on a coaster and headed back into the kitchen, returning with a scented candle. He lit it and a pleasant fragrance filled the air, providing a soothing atmosphere.

"Lavender," Kincaid said. "It's supposed to be calming. Is it helping?"

I chuckled softly. "It might take a minute. But thank you; it's thoughtful."

"No problem," he replied. "You've had a rough day. I'll stay out of your way, but will be here if you need me."

As I made phone calls, Kincaid kept himself busy with some

much-needed yardwork. It wasn't until I finished my calls that I looked outside and noticed all his hard work.

After talking to Pam and Kevin, I didn't have all the information I was hoping for. However, I managed to piece together enough to email my team with what I knew and to offer them job references. I then contacted my business contacts, asking if anyone knew of a job opening. I even sent an updated resume.

I searched through local job postings and applied for a few that piqued my interest.

Finally, I closed my laptop. A weight lifted off my shoulders. Losing my job was a blow, but with eight weeks of paid severance, I had time to find a new one. If not, I could dip into my savings for a while.

"I'm done for now," I said, turning to Kincaid who sat next to me, engrossed in an e-book.

"Glad to hear it," he replied, powering off his screen. "You seem calmer, less stressed."

"I found some job leads," I told him, glancing toward the kitchen. "But what do you think about the addition? Should we scale things back to save some money?"

He took a moment to think before shaking his head. "We're in the homestretch now. If we cancel, there will be a penalty for the orders I've already placed. Don't worry about it. I'll cover the rest of the renovation if cashflow is an issue."

I chewed my lip. "I can't let you do that. I don't want to put you in a bind."

He dismissed my concerns with a wave of his hand. "I'll be fine. Let me worry about it."

"I'll see how the job hunt goes first before we worry about the addition. With some luck, I'll find something I like quickly," I said, feeling grateful for his unwavering support.

He picked up a bottle of wine from the end table and poured two glasses, then handed me one. "This is for you."

His thoughtfulness filled me with warmth. "Were you a boy scout when you were younger? Always prepared?" I took a sip, closed my eyes, and let out a heavy sigh. When I opened them, Kincaid leaned toward me, holding out a spoonful of tiramisu.

I smiled as the tension in my chest melted away. Even though I'd just lost my job, I felt content in this instant. "What is this?"

"Me taking care of you. Open."

I obliged. "Mmm. Delicious."

"I like seeing you smile like this. Feeling better?"

"I am. In a way, it's a relief to have found out today. I knew something strange was going on at work. Now I know what it was."

"That makes sense. I always feel better once I know exactly what I'm dealing with." He fed me another bite.

"Do you plan to keep feeding me, or are you going to let me have the spoon?" I licked a bit of the dessert off my upper lip.

His blue eyes crinkled around the corners as he smiled. "I think I'll keep feeding you for now. I'm enjoying myself."

Kincaid surprised me at every turn. Who would have thought a man who looked the way he did—so masculine and rugged— could be so thoughtful and supportive?

Maybe… just maybe… we had something real here.

Growing up, my father was rarely at home, and my husband was always traveling for work. I realized I wanted more than a part-time partner in life. I wanted someone committed to me. Someone I could count on. Someone who would be there through both the good times and the bad.

Someone like Kincaid?

The thought sent a chill cascading down my spine. Maybe I was rushing things. Asking for too much. Being too needy. My mom had stood on her own two feet and dealt with every family crisis because my dad worked such long hours. She'd been a great mom, too. A model parent. It was just…

Did I really want to face all my problems alone? Independence was well and good, but having someone by your side when things went wrong… that was pretty amazing.

"Thank you. For everything. You're making this entire day

more bearable." I leaned closer to him, and he met me in the middle. I planted a kiss on that little patch of razor stubble next to his mouth.

My imagination was running away with me again. But this time, I was envisioning a future Kincaid and I could share.

All it would take would be a leap of faith.

He certainly seemed worth the risk.

2 8

THE EX FACTOR

Kincaid

Lianna losing her job hit me harder than I let on. I tried to be strong for her, but it was difficult not to feel the weight of it all. I couldn't help but be reminded of when Heather lost both her job and her apartment not long after we started dating. I'd taken pity on her and asked her to move in, but things hadn't ended well.

But Lianna was nothing like Heather. She handled the job loss with grace and determination, diving headfirst into the job market like a kid jumping into a pool. It was paying off, too. Recruiters were already reaching out to her, and she had a promising in-person interview today as well as a couple of video interviews scheduled for later in the week.

I had spent the night at her place again and was making her breakfast while she got ready. I cooked up an omelet with diced ham, eggs, cheese, and milk, and brewed some coffee. When she walked into the kitchen, dressed in a conservative gray dress and striking red pumps, I couldn't help but admire her.

"Damn, but I love those shoes," I said, giving her an appreciative once-over. "I'd hire you on the spot."

She grinned at me. "Thanks," she said, sitting down on a barstool as I served her breakfast. "This smells delicious."

"Anything for you. Good luck today."

She sat up straight and tucked a strand of glossy brown hair behind her ear. "Thanks. I'm feeling good about this. What about you? What's on your schedule for the day?"

"I'm meeting your building inspector this afternoon. Once the final inspection is done, my crew can start the finish work," I said.

She smiled at me. "That's great news."

After she finished eating, she grabbed her keys and purse. "Wish me luck," she said, giving me a quick peck on the cheek.

"Knock 'em dead," I replied as she headed for the basement garage.

Later that afternoon I peered through Lianna's front window, searching for the building inspector's car, but there was no sign of him. He was already late, and I was starting to worry. Just as I was about to give him a call, my phone buzzed.

I hoped it wasn't the inspector canceling on me. When I saw Heather's name on the caller ID, my heart sank. Why would she be contacting me? Did I even want to answer?

I hesitated, debating whether to take the call. But with Heather, it was always better to deal with her problems right away. She was nothing if not persistent. If I didn't pick up, she'd just keep pestering me.

"Hello?"

"Hi 'Caid. It's Heather."

"Hi." I kept my tone distant and cool. That was the safest approach with Heather.

"I hope I'm not catching you at a bad time."

"I'm waiting for the building inspector to arrive at a job site. I'll have to hang up when he gets here."

"At the Murphy house?"

My irritation percolated. "How did you know I was working on that job?"

"Small town. Gossip. You know how it is. Plus, the guy I've been seeing lost the bid to you."

I sighed inwardly. Hadn't Conner mentioned something about

her new boyfriend at cooking class? I'd promptly put it out of my mind. Now, I sifted through people who might have put in a bid. "Adam Buckner?"

"None other."

I felt a pang of discomfort. What should I say? Good luck? Glad you're with him and not me? Then again, she'd just called me. That could be a bad sign.

I settled on something non-confrontational. "I didn't know you two were together."

"Uh—that's kind of why I'm calling. I need your help, 'Caid. I think I rushed into things by moving in with Adam. I've decided to move out. I want to sublet an apartment in town."

My shoulders tensed. I wasn't inclined to offer the woman any sort of help. Not even a reference for a landlord, if that's why she was calling. "What kind of help do you need?"

"I know it's a lot to ask, but since I just moved in with Adam, I don't want to get my same friends to help me move out again. It's been less than a month. I don't have much stuff. I bet we could fit it all in your truck and move it in a single trip."

Through Lianna's front window, I saw the building inspector pull up to the curb. "That's not a good idea. I have to go, Heather. The building inspector's here."

She let out an irritated sigh. "You're always busy. You have to take a day off sometimes, though. Use one to help me move."

I huffed out a laugh. "I don't think helping you move counts as a day off."

"It does—if I make sure you have fun."

I recoiled at the innuendo in her tone. "Not interested. Besides, I'm seeing someone. You'll need to ask one of your friends for help."

Heather let out a beleaguered sigh. "Is she that Lianna person I've heard about?"

My stomach clenched. I didn't like hearing her speak Lianna's name. If felt too familiar, as if she was intruding into our lives. "She's my girlfriend." The familiar warm glow that always filled my chest whenever I said those words pushed away some of my stress.

Heather didn't speak for a long moment. "Are things serious between you two?" Her voice seemed a bit distant, as though she'd moved away from the phone.

"They are."

She sniffed, loudly. It sounded forced, like she was trying to manipulate me. But she was usually better at lying than this. Or maybe I was just too jaded now.

"I can't believe it," she said with another sniff. "I thought you and I could still have a future together. You know, once you cooled off a bit."

"'Cooled off?'" I pulled the phone from my face to stare at it in disbelief before returning it to my ear. "Heather, you lied to me about being pregnant. That isn't a minor misunderstanding. It's a huge betrayal. I'm done with you. Period. We have no future together."

The doorbell rang, interrupting us.

"I have to go. The building inspector's at the door, and I need to let him in. I can't help you."

"Yeah, whatever," she snapped, dropping the pretense of being upset. "It's not like I did something a million other women haven't done. I don't see why you have to get all pissy about it. Have fun playing house with your girlfriend." The connection went dead.

I closed my eyes and sighed, feeling exhausted. Heather was seriously delusional if she thought we'd ever get back together. But then again, it took someone a little off her rocker to lie about being pregnant in the first place. The woman had made me feel like a fool. It had taken me months to move beyond her betrayal and trust a woman enough to date her.

And then came Lianna. She had finally broken through to me.

I'd wasted enough time and energy on Heather. I mentally composed myself as I opened Lianna's front door.

"Hi, Charlie." I slid my phone into my pocket. "I already

checked everything out and it looks good. With any luck, this will go smoothly."

As soon as I walked in my front door at home that evening, Mick raced toward me. I felt guilty for leaving him alone for over twenty-four hours. Sure, he had plenty of dry food, but the poor cat was lonely and needed companionship.

Lianna was due to arrive soon. If I asked, she might agree to let me bring Mick over to her place for a visit.

As always, Mick followed his routine and jumped onto the newel post, then onto my shoulders, where he draped himself around my neck like a fur stole. His motor ran incessantly.

I put a pot of water on the stove and started prepping to make shrimp linguine. Lianna arrived a few minutes later wearing a pink and white summer dress and pink low-heeled shoes, looking as radiant as a summer day.

I pulled her in for a kiss. "How was the interview?" I asked, eager to hear her news.

"Good, I think. They liked me, but I'm not certain it's the right fit." She shrugged like she was trying to shake off a bad feeling. "I didn't get a good vibe. Everyone there seemed unhappy."

"That sounds like a terrible work environment," I said, frowning. I took a bottle of red wine from the shelf and pulled the cork.

"My thoughts exactly, but that was only the first company I interviewed with. I'll keep looking. Lots of places in Pittsburgh are hiring."

"How about a glass of wine?" I asked.

"Sure."

I poured. "I have something I need to tell you."

"Something that requires wine?" She raised one eyebrow and the corner of her mouth curved up.

"I hadn't thought of it that way, but maybe." I swallowed. "Heather called me. She wanted me to help her move."

Lianna went still. "Your ex?" There was a sharp tang of irritation in her voice.

"I told her no."

"Well, that's something, at least." She took a long swallow of wine.

"Are you pissed at me?"

"No." She sighed. "Not with you. I'm irritated at Heather for asking you, and at Paul for making me suspicious." She inhaled deeply, and when she released it, she seemed calmer. "Sorry about that. I shouldn't get annoyed simply because Heather has boundary issues and Paul was a cheating asshat."

I smiled. How could I not? "No problem. I wanted to be open with you. No secrets."

"Fair enough. I'm glad you told me."

"You're sure about that?" I asked, peering into her eyes.

She leaned her hip against the kitchen counter. "Absolutely. Don't keep stuff like that from me. That would be even worse."

"Good. I feel exactly the same way."

Mick came tearing through the kitchen. He careened off the door of the stainless-steel refrigerator and then went tearing back in the direction he came.

"What the heck just happened?" Lianna asked, laughing.

"Crazy cat. I've been leaving him alone too much lately. Do you mind if I bring him over to your place with me sometimes? I think it would help."

She shot me a dubious look and then narrowed her eyes. "He won't climb my curtains, will he?"

I winced, knowing Mick's tendencies. "I don't think so," I said, hesitantly. "But he's been a bit unpredictable lately, so no promises."

She cocked her head to one side as she thought, then she shrugged. "Sure. Let's give it a shot. After all, it's my fault he's been alone so much. I've been monopolizing you."

The pot of water on the stove started bubbling. I opened the refrigerator and pulled out the shrimp. "Can you boil the linguine while I start cooking this?"

As we ate dinner, we talked about Lianna's upcoming interviews. She was particularly excited about her interview with Rainforest, a company that she was passionate about.

"They're my dream job," she said, her eyes shining. "I'd love to work there."

I raised my glass for a toast. "Here's to Rainforest."

She clinked her glass against mine. "Cheers."

A CELEBRATION

LIANNA

"Did I mention how gorgeous you look in that black dress?" Kincaid's low, delicious voice rumbled through me.

I felt a blush creeping up my cheeks. "Only twice now." Our eyes met briefly before I turned back to the road, and that playful gleam in his eyes made my heart flip over with happiness. "I'm looking forward to tonight. This should be fun. It's been ages since I've spent time with Mara other than at book club."

As we ascended the steep road toward the summit of Mount Washington, the tall trees that lined the roadside whipped past, momentarily blocking our view of the surrounding hillside. Yet, with every bend we took, I felt my excitement growing. I knew that once we reached the top, we would be rewarded with a breathtaking view. With a sense of anticipation, I navigated a sharp hairpin turn and as the trees cleared, an expansive panorama unfolded before us. The Ohio River stretched out below, its serene waters dotted with boats, and I delighted in the sheer beauty of it all.

"I'm just relieved we were finally able to set something up," Kincaid said. "Ford and I have been trying to find a date that works ever since you told Mara you'd accepted the job with Rainforest, and you've already been working there for a week now."

"Life's been crazy. Between Ford and Mara's travel schedule and my new job, I'm surprised we found a day when we're all free." I pulled to a stop outside of the restaurant and climbed out of my car. The valet handed me a claim ticket, and as I looked up, I spotted two people kissing near the restaurant's entrance. Mara's blue-tipped hair was a dead giveaway.

I snuck up behind them. "Knock it off, you two."

Mara whirled to face me. Her eyes went wide, and she grinned. "Sorry. Too much PDA? This man's hard to resist."

Ford waved as he tightened his arm around Mara's waist and pulled her close. "Let's go inside."

"I've always wanted to come to this restaurant," I told them.

"You'll love this place. Mount Washington has the best views in the city." Ford pulled open the door and held it for us.

As I stepped inside, I was struck by the luxurious interior, gleaming marble, and the warm glow of the lighting. But the view through the huge windows overlooking the city far below took my breath away.

"Ford and I had our first date here," Mara said, her eyes shining.

"That's so romantic." Those two were adorable together. "And this place is stunning. No wonder you fell for him."

"Didn't you mention something about filming a scene for your movie up here?" Kincaid asked.

"Yeah. It'll be just down the road." Ford gave his name to the hostess, and we were immediately led to a table with a stupendous view.

I gazed out the expansive plate glass window at the breathtaking view of the city and the three rivers far below. "This view is breathtaking," I whispered in awe.

"I know, right?" Mara said. "I had the same reaction the first time I came here. We're planning to watch the Fourth of July fireworks up here next week at Sin's place. Want to come?"

I glanced over at Kincaid, but his attention was focused on the menu. "We can't," I said regretfully. "My parents invited us over to their place. Dad wants to shoot off fireworks with Kincaid. I think it's supposed to be a male-bonding experience. Maybe we can join you next year."

Kincaid shot me a wink. "Making things go 'boom' is manly. It'll be a night filled with testosterone. Your dad and I will have a blast."

The waitstaff, dressed in black and white, moved gracefully through the room, attending to guests with professional precision. We placed our drink orders as our server left us with menus.

"How's the movie coming along?" Kincaid asked.

"Some of the filming has started," Ford said. "Pretty soon, we'll get to the part where Max earns his keep. He'll be busy promoting."

"Not that you won't be busy, too," Mara grumbled. "I thought that once you were done filming, I'd see you more. I was wrong. Max sent over the schedule. He has you traveling for interviews and events all over the freaking world."

"Will you get to go with him?" I asked.

"Not as often as I'd like," Mara said. "The good part about running a video game startup is that, as long as I have a good internet connection and phone service, I can work from just about anywhere. The bad part is, I still have tons of work to do, and a tight schedule. Traveling will eat into my time."

I leaned in, loving all these details. "The two of you just came back from Paris though, right? You were at an event? Was the trip worth the time you had to take off work?"

Mara's eyes lit up. "Absolutely! I finally found the perfect wedding dress."

"Pictures!" I demanded, holding out my hand and wiggling my fingers in a 'gimme' motion.

Mara rummaged through her purse and pulled out her phone. "Got 'em," she said, glancing at Ford before scooting closer to me.

"No peeking," she warned him. "You're not allowed to see it until the wedding."

Ford held his hands up in surrender. "Wouldn't dream of it."

Mara leaned in, revealing a photo of her and Sonya standing next to each other, each in a different style of wedding gown. Mara's was sleek and form-fitting, while Sonya's was beaded and had a full skirt. Both beamed radiantly at the camera.

"Sonya went too?" The pure joy on their faces warmed my heart.

"We had a blast," Mara said. "Max and Ford did work stuff while Sonya and I tore up Paris."

"I've never been to a double wedding," Kincaid said. "Or is it weddings?"

"Beats me," Mara told him. "I'm just happy Sonya and Max agreed to share their day with us."

"I can hardly believe your wedding is just a little over a month away," I said. "You must be freaking out."

Mara shrugged. "Actually, the wedding venue in Turks and Caicos is handling all the details. All we have to do is show up. Easy-peasy."

"I have the dates blocked off on my work calendar. When I signed my employment contract with Rainforest, I made them give me the time off. Normally, I wouldn't have any vacation until I'd been there for a year, but they're letting me borrow days."

Kincaid winced. "I guess that means I won't be whisking you away for a beach vacation over Christmas."

I turned to face him, touched by his thoughtfulness. "Really? You were going to do that?"

He shrugged as if it didn't matter, but I could tell he was disappointed. "I was working on it."

I tugged on my earring, disappointed. "Maybe next year. I'll be working over Christmas this year."

"How do you like working for Rainforest?" Ford asked.

"It's amazing. It's my dream job. The interview process was

fierce, but fast. I was thrilled when they made the offer so quickly."

"I'm really happy for you," Mara said. "Tell me, what's it like to work there?"

I considered. "Invigorating. A little intimidating, too. Everyone there is exceptionally talented and has excellent credentials."

"That says a lot about you that they hired you," Mara pointed out.

"I need to hit the ground running if I want to stand out in this crowd. Now that I have my dream job, I want to shine. If things go as planned, they'll make me lead program manager soon. But first, I need to get up to speed on how they do things there. They offer so many opportunities for growth. I'd be foolish not to pursue them."

"Good for you," Mara said. "I know you can do it."

I was pretty sure I could too, but it'd take long hours and hard work.

After dinner, our server offered coffee and dessert.

"We're still going out dancing, right?" Mara asked, her excitement palpable.

"That's the plan," Kincaid confirmed.

"Then coffee all around, and dessert too," Mara added.

The server presented our options, and Kincaid's grin was electrifying. "Tiramisu, please."

I playfully poked him under the table. "You're incorrigible," I murmured.

"I try."

As we sipped our coffee, I couldn't help but think about the work I'd brought home with me. I needed to put in a few hours tomorrow, but if we stayed out too late, I'd fall behind. However, dancing until midnight before heading home seemed like a good compromise.

Suddenly, my stomach started feeling queasy from the coffee. It was my early-warning stress barometer, and it signaled that I was pushing myself too hard. I'd have to do a better job juggling my new responsibilities. If I wanted to keep putting in long hours at Rainforest, I'd need to figure out better ways of handling the stress. I decided that I would start hitting the gym more than once a week; exercise always made me feel better, and I hadn't gone at all this week. If I didn't get this under control, my stomach would progressively get worse.

But... dancing with Kincaid would qualify as exercise, wouldn't it? Plus, bedroom shenanigans would make for an excellent stress reliever.

My gaze softened as I looked at my sexy boyfriend, and my mood brightened again.

Spending the night de-stressing with Kincaid was exactly what I needed.

COMPLAINTS

Kincaid

It was Friday, a week since our dinner with Mara and Ford. Between hanging out with them and spending the Fourth of July with Lianna's family, the entire weekend had been a blast. But I'd barely seen Lianna since then. She'd been putting in long hours at work, and so had I.

Today had been a long one for both of us, and even though it was past eight, it still wasn't over. As I pulled up the driveway leading to the Murphys' sprawling mansion, the sun was dropping low in the sky, and it nearly blinded me.

Their place was located up in Sewickley Heights, near the country club. It was newer than many of the other estates up here, but it still needed updates. The Murphys' renovation was coming along nicely. We had already finished the master bathroom and moved on to the kitchen, main living area, and sunroom addition.

I'd already been here earlier today to meet with Brunner, my electrician. I hadn't expected I'd need to come back again, but Chrissy Murphy had called a few minutes ago and had insisted I needed to meet her right away.

I hoped this wouldn't take long. A pan of Dante's Gourmet Mac and Cheese and Grits needed to come out of my oven soon.

When I was done here, I'd swing by my place to pick it up along with Mick before going to Lianna's.

I knocked on the front door, and Chrissy opened it. "That's another thing that doesn't work," she said, referring to the doorbell.

I pointed toward a small cardboard box in the foyer. "Your new door chime is in that box. It arrived this morning, and the electrician plans to install it tomorrow when he's here."

She eyed the box suspiciously. "Good."

As I followed Chrissy to the kitchen, I couldn't shake off the feeling that she didn't like me. Maybe she was just stressed out from overseeing the renovation, or maybe there was something else bothering her.

I tried to focus on the task at hand and asked, "Can you show me the problem?"

Chrissy scowled and replied, "I hate being the one who has to oversee all this work. I wish John could do this instead of me, but he's in China right now."

I sympathized with her and said, "Business?"

"He's touring his plants," she said, her face brightening slightly. "He's doing a worldwide upgrade to them, and the timing has to be perfect."

She tugged at her yoga pants and made a face. "I don't know how much longer I'll be able to wear these. Yoga pants are the only things I can still fit into. They're pretty forgiving, but these are getting too tight. I wonder if Lululemon makes maternity clothes. Maybe I should ask the other moms in my Yoga Moms class."

I tried to keep a straight face and said, "How many months until your due date?"

"Four," she said, pausing for a moment before frowning at me as if she'd just remembered that she didn't like me. She waved her hand dismissively and said, "Follow me, and I'll show you what I was telling you on the phone."

As we walked into the gutted kitchen, Chrissy pointed to an

outlet box with electrical wiring protruding out. "Look at that," she said. "Wires just poking out into the room. That's a fire hazard, isn't it? What if someone were to brush up against that and electrocute herself? They're all like that."

I nodded again, acknowledging her concern. Chrissy seemed to be in a foul mood, and I couldn't help but wonder if it had something to do with me. Did she simply resent managing the renovation, or was it something more?

I walked over to the outlet box and examined the wires. "First, I want to reassure you that the power isn't turned on in here, so you're perfectly safe. The outlets and switches would already have been connected, but you changed your mind and decided you wanted smart switches. Brunner ordered them, and they'll arrive tomorrow. He plans to install them right away."

Chrissy narrowed her eyes suspiciously. "Are you sure about that? The electricity works in the rest of the house."

"But not in here. It's on a separate circuit." Frustrated with all her second-guessing, I reached out and brushed my hand against the dead wires. "See?"

Chrissy let out a frightened shriek and jumped back. I realized too late that my actions were ill-considered. "Sorry. I didn't mean to startle you. I was here this morning with Brunner. I already confirmed the circuit isn't live," I tried to reassure her. Besides, I should never assume the circuit was still off. What if someone had turned it on after I left?

Chrissy huffed indignantly. "Fine. Tell me about this inspector person. Why is he checking up on you? Did you do something wrong?"

I tamped down my irritation and forced out a tight smile. "Not at all. Every house with significant renovations is required to undergo a series of inspections. Once the electrical, plumbing, and mechanical systems are in place, an inspector comes out to ensure that the work was done to code. We've already passed all the inspections on the master bathroom. The roof inspection was today, and you'll have an inspection for the kitchen soon as well.

The county and city require them to make sure houses are safe. Every reputable contractor does them. They're for your safety."

Chrissy still looked suspicious. "I heard they were only done if the contractor has had problems in the past."

I raised an eyebrow in surprise. Seriously? Who was she talking to? "That's completely untrue. Your source must have been mistaken."

She scrunched her forehead in thought. "I suppose that's possible."

"Is there anything else that's been bothering you?" I asked, trying to keep the conversation on track.

She sighed, clearly disappointed. "The plumbers are coming tomorrow, right?"

"Yes, they're scheduled to add plumbing for your new center island, mudroom, and the hot tub in the new sunroom."

"My hot tub," she said with a mournful sigh. "I can't use it until after the baby is born. It's bad for her."

"You're having a girl?"

She scowled at me. "Not that it's any of your business, but yes." She stroked her belly gently. "She's my little princess."

"We'll have everything done well before she arrives," I reassured her. "You and John should be able to move in here in around two months."

Chrissy looked at me sternly. "You better be right. I'll be checking in every day to make sure the work is progressing."

I tried to keep my frustration in check. "Is there anything else that we need to discuss today?"

"No. You seem to have an answer for everything."

I LOADED dinner into the car, then went back inside and scooped up Mick, depositing him into a cat carrier, and headed for the front door.

His "Meow," sounded like a complaint.

"You'll like it at Lianna's. It's better than spending the night here alone."

Just as I opened the passenger door of my truck to load Mick's carrier, my phone began to ring. Lianna's name flashed across the screen, and I quickly answered.

"Hi, love."

"Hi." She sounded preoccupied, like she was eating something. Strange, since we'd be having dinner together shortly.

"How was your day?"

"Long. Frustrating." She let out a heavy sigh. "I've been having trouble getting access to data on the secure servers. I finally figured out the problem twenty minutes ago. It was a clerical error on my part."

"At least you sorted it out," I offered.

"Not fast enough. I'm just frustrated it took me most of the day to figure out what was wrong. I've only been working here two weeks, and I feel like I'm falling behind. The other new hire is already way ahead of me. She got access to the data yesterday. I've lost nearly two full days of work sorting out my own mistakes."

"But you have access to it now?"

"I'm waiting for it to come through—a-a-any moment now."

"And then you'll be heading home? I picked up everything to surprise you with Dante's Gourmet Mac and Cheese and Grits."

She moaned. "You're killing me. That stuff is to die for. Don't hate me, though; I have to cancel on you. I need to stay a couple of hours and try to catch up. It'll be quiet here and I'll be able to make a lot of progress."

My heart sank. "I can't say I'm not disappointed. I haven't seen you since we left your parents' place on the Fourth."

"I know. I'm sorry. You've been incredibly patient with me. I promise it won't always be like this. I just really want to make a good impression, and I'm afraid I'm failing at it."

I nodded, even though she couldn't see me. "It's okay. I get it.

I'll drop off leftovers in your fridge so you can eat when you get home."

"You, Kincaid Gillette, are the very best boyfriend on the planet."

I smiled at that. "I am. I'm glad you noticed. Did you know last Sunday was our three-month anniversary?"

"Was it?" she asked. "Three months from when?"

"From the day you signed the contract and had dinner with me. Officially our first date."

"Does that mean we're calling that night a date now?" she teased. I was relieved to hear the playful note in her voice. "That's sweet. I'm sorry we didn't celebrate it."

"We'll do something special for our four-month anniversary instead." I picked up Mick's carrier and headed back to my house. "Miss you."

"Miss you, too."

After we hung up, I opened Mick's carrier and let him out. Mick scowled at me, affronted, and immediately licked his ruffled fur to smooth it back in place.

"It looks like it's just you and me tonight, buddy."

Mick stuck his tail straight up in the air and stalked off.

WHAT DOESN'T KILL US... MAKES US FALL IN LOVE?

Lianna

As I made my way to Kincaid's apartment on Thursday evening, exhaustion weighed heavily on me. I hadn't been sleeping well, and the long hours at work were taking their toll. Plus, the thought of coffee still turned my stomach, which only made my whole lack of energy situation even worse.

I needed this to end soon. I couldn't keep going like this.

A quick knock on Kincaid's door, and I let myself in, the tantalizing aroma of garlic and curry hitting me. He was cooking again, and the sight of him in the kitchen filled me with warmth and happiness. Kincaid was amazing. I couldn't have invented a better boyfriend if someone had let me design him from scratch.

I gave a soft sigh of satisfaction. Coming home to this man made me feel perfectly at peace. This was where I belonged, with him by my side.

And I'd even managed to make it here on time for a change.

Just then, Mick sauntered into the room, his blue eyes fixed on me. He rubbed against my legs.

I reached down to rub him under the chin, but he backed away.

"Still not sure about me, huh?" I asked him. "I'll win you over, yet." Kincaid had cat treats in the kitchen. I bet those would help.

"Hi, honey," I called out. "I'm home."

I heard Kincaid padding down the stairs barefoot, his hair damp from the shower. He reached the front entryway and wrapped his arms around me, kissing me senseless. "You're a sight for sore eyes."

I blinked at him, taking in his delicious scent. "That's an excellent way to greet a woman."

"Then you're really going to love this." He opened the door to his hall closet and pulled out a pair of pink slippers that looked similar to the ones I had in my closet at home.

I stared at them, then at him. "You have an interesting choice in footwear."

He dropped to one knee, removed one of my heels, and slid a slipper in its place. "For you. I know how much you love kicking off those shoes at the end of the day." He repeated it with my other shoe.

When he stood back up, I grabbed the front of his shirt and pulled him close. "You know I'm crazy about you, right?"

His gaze was steady as he looked into my eyes. "Me, too. Crazy in love."

My breath caught. Had he just said what I thought he'd said? "Kincaid?"

He touched his forehead to mine. "I've been thinking it for a while, but I was afraid to say it. Afraid it was too soon. But love doesn't work on a timetable. It happens when it happens."

A weight fell away from me. He was right. Love happened when it happened. "I love you too. I was afraid to say it too, but you're right.

"I hope you don't think I've been taking you for granted, because I haven't. I appreciate everything you've been doing for me. You've been so patient. I know I've been working crazy hours, but it won't last much longer." I let out a laugh. "I don't think I could handle it if it did."

"I believe you. Remember, I was with you before you started working at Rainforest. I know this isn't typical. You'll get through this. And I want you to know, you're worth the wait."

My eyes filled with tears. Happy ones. "I love you, Kincaid. I love you like crazy."

Mick bumped his head against my ankles, and I looked down to find him eyeing the pink bow atop my slipper as if he wanted to attack it.

"Oh, no you don't." Kincaid scooped up his cat, cradling him in his arms, and turned to face me. "Come with me to the kitchen, love. Dinner's almost ready. And when we're done, I have a few ideas to help you relieve some stress." He grinned, a mischievous glint in his eye that could make me follow him anywhere.

In the kitchen, I located Mick's cat treats in the cabinet and set a few on the floor for him. He sauntered over, gave them a sniff, and started purring as he gobbled them up.

Success.

Kincaid took the lid off his chicken curry, releasing a burst of steam.

I hummed in satisfaction. "That smells delicious."

He spooned rice onto the plates and then added the curry. "Sit. Let's eat." He set the plates on the kitchen island.

I moved my food around on my plate, waiting for it to cool. "Before I forget, can you help me drop off my car on Tuesday morning? I need to take it in for its 20,000-mile maintenance."

Kincaid checked his phone calendar and shook his head. "Can we drop it off Monday night instead? I have a concrete pour scheduled early on Tuesday at a new job site, and I need to be there."

I shook my head. "We can't. I'm having dinner with Mom and Dad on Monday, and you have your cooking class. I'll ask Mom to help. It's no big deal."

"Can I make it up to you?" Kincaid wiggled his eyebrows at me in a comically suggestive way. "You know I'll do anything to make my woman happy."

I giggled. "I might be able to come up with one or two ideas."

Mick meowed, and we turned to find him looking up at us in that judgmental way only a Siamese cat can pull off, as if to say, "I hope this isn't the start of another one of those 'ideas.'"

32

ORGANIZATION IN THE FACE OF CHAOS

KINCAID

I carefully secured the final shelf support into Lianna's custom closet system and reached for the last shelf, but paused when I noticed Mick eyeing the open shelf above him. With a graceful leap, he landed soundlessly on the shelf, level with my face. I scratched him under the chin, admiring his agility.

As I finished snapping the shelf into place, I couldn't help but feel a sense of satisfaction. This closet system was a labor of love, a surprise for Lianna that I'd been planning for weeks. The all-white shelving system brightened her new walk-in closet, complete with hanging space, shelves for shoes, and drawers for her lingerie. It looked perfect

Mick purred approvingly, so I let him climb onto my shoulders. "You like it, don't you?" I asked him.

He responded by rubbing his face against my ear before draping himself over my shoulders.

After closing the closet door, I attached the red bow that I'd brought with me. I couldn't wait to see Lianna's expression when she saw it.

After I headed downstairs, I preheated the oven and switched on the television. Tonight was supposed to have been a special date night for us, but work emergencies had forced us to change our plans. Even so, I was looking forward to spending time with her, even if it was just the two of us and Mick.

As I settled onto the couch with my cat by my side, my thoughts drifted back to last night. I'd finally told Lianna I loved her. I'd held off long enough. My feelings weren't going to disappear. This was real. Even better, she'd told me the same thing.

The rumble of the garage door opening beneath me caught my attention. Lianna was home, and earlier than expected. Why hadn't she texted me?

I shifted Mick off my lap and headed into the kitchen. The room was warm and cozy, the scent of spices filling the air. I slid a tray of French fries into the preheated oven and turned my attention to Lianna's slow tread on the basement staircase.

When she entered the room, I couldn't help but smile. She looked exhausted, but her eyes lit up when she saw me. It was like the weight of the day had been lifted from her shoulders.

"You're a sight for sore eyes," she said, smiling. She hung her purse on a hook next to the door and then slid into my arms. It felt good to hold her close.

"Hi, love. Hungry?"

"Famished."

"Then I need to feed you, pronto. I have fries in the oven. Let me start the burgers, and then I'm all yours."

As she snuggled closer, she murmured, "I have clothes in the dryer I need to fold. Is it okay if I do that while you're cooking, or do you need my help?"

"That works perfectly. Take your time." I planted a quick kiss on her forehead before heading back to the stove.

She disappeared into her new laundry room and emerged a few moments later, holding a basket of fresh laundry which she proceeded to fold as we chatted.

After about fifteen minutes, I served the burgers on our plates. Lianna's laundry basket was filled with neatly stacked clothes as she frowned down at her phone.

"Work?" I asked.

"I was just making sure there aren't any more problems. It looks like my team's fix went through and everything is back on track."

"Sit. Put your phone away and eat." I directed her into her dining room, and she almost collapsed into her chair.

She inhaled deeply, staring hungrily at her plate. "Those burgers smell delicious."

"The secret is the Worcestershire sauce. Your dad told me about it."

She took a bite and let out a moan of happiness. "Thank god he did. These are perfect. I'm glad the two of you get along."

I winked at her and shot her a devilish grin. "Of course we do. We have something important in common. *You.*"

Lianna grinned at me, her eyes sparkling with amusement. "That's really sweet. Weird, but sweet," she teased, taking a sip of her drink. "Well, I'm not complaining. If this is the kind of food I get to enjoy, I don't mind being the glue that holds you two together."

As we ate, the kitchen felt cozy and intimate. The soft lighting from the pendant lights above the island cast a warm glow over us.

As soon as she finished helping me clean up the kitchen, she let out a big yawn. "I'm sorry. That was rude."

"Are you tired?" I asked.

"A bit. Maybe it's because I stopped drinking coffee."

I raised an eyebrow. "Or maybe it's because you're working such long hours. You need more rest."

She chuckled. "Could be." She yawned again. "But things are getting better. I've made it home at a reasonable hour the last couple of days."

"I noticed. It's a nice change. Come on. Let's head upstairs." I took her hands and led her to her lavender-gray bedroom. She stopped in her tracks as soon as she saw the enormous red bow on her closet door.

"For me? Does this mean my closet is done?" she asked, grinning.

"Go ahead and take a look," I said, motioning toward the door.

She glanced sideways at me as she edged toward it. When she flung it open, her jaw dropped. "Kincaid, what have you done? This is gorgeous! Look at all these shelves for my shoes. I'm in love with it." Lianna turned to me and hugged me tightly. "Now I just have to figure out when I can move all my clothes in here. I'll need to buy more hangers since you gave me so much space."

She opened her phone's calendar. "I have to work the weekend because my team is on call at the help center, so I don't think I'll have time to make it to the store. You have your cooking class on Monday, and I'm having dinner with my parents. Then I'm dropping off my car. It looks like we'll have to wait until Wednesday. I'll buy the hangers after work and spend the evening setting up my closet."

As soon as she finished, my mood soured. "I wanted the closet organizer to make you happy. It seems like it's just adding to your workload."

Her expression fell. "Oh, no, I didn't mean to sound ungrateful. I'm thrilled, really. I was just trying to find time on my calendar to set everything up. I love that you did this for me. It's incredibly thoughtful. You're too good to me."

I let out a heavy sigh. "I hope things will be less stressful for you soon."

"Me too." Lianna yawned, exhaustion etched into her face. "Just when I started getting the hang of things, my team got stuck running the help desk for the weekend. At least we only have to cover it once every six weeks."

Mick jumped onto her bed and batted at her hand, demanding her attention. Startled, she yanked it away and whirled to see what had just touched her. When she spotted my cat, she grinned.

"Well, hello Mick. Are you here for a sleepover, too?"

She scratched the top of his head, and he pushed his head into her hand, purring lustily. Her eyes widened and she gave a triumphant smile. "I think he's finally starting to like me."

"It's okay that he's here, right?"

"Of course. He was so quiet, I forgot about him." She kicked off her shoes, pulled a pink nightshirt from her drawer, kissed me on the cheek, and headed for the bathroom.

I went downstairs to turn off the lights and lock up. By the time I came back upstairs, Lianna was under the covers and had already fallen into a deep sleep.

Mick was curled up next to her feet. He opened drowsy eyes, curled up a bit tighter, and then promptly ignored me.

"Traitor. All you want is a warm body to curl up next to."

But the cat did have an excellent idea.

I stripped out of my clothes and climbed into bed with her. She roused briefly and snuggled closer to me. "I love you. Thank you for tonight," she murmured. "For everything."

"I love you too." I kissed her nose.

Her breathing gradually slowed, and she surrendered to a peaceful night of sleep in my arms. In that serene moment, as our breaths intertwined in perfect harmony, I couldn't ignore the longing that tugged at my heart. The truth was, her demanding work schedule had created a void in our togetherness—a void I yearned to fill. I imagined a future where our nights would no longer be dictated by separation and missed opportunities. Instead, they'd be filled with shared moments like these, falling asleep together as we held each other close, finding comfort and solace in the warmth of our love.

The weight of this realization settled upon me, mingling with the tranquility of this peaceful moment. It beckoned me to take action, to change our circumstances and mold a future where our time together triumphed above the constraints of daily life. A future where we started and ended each day together. With every gentle rise and fall of her breath, my determination grew. Choosing her, embracing her, and having her by my side—these were the choices that would lead to true happiness. I knew this deep in my soul.

Merging our lives was the only path worth pursuing, and I vowed to make it a reality. As I drifted off to sleep, a relaxed, confident smile on my lips, I knew in my heart that choosing her, embracing her, having her by my side, was the only decision that made sense.

33

DINNER WITH THE PARENTS

Lianna

I didn't bother to knock on my parents' front door on Monday evening. This was home, after all, where I grew up. Since Kincaid was at his class at the Not a Yacht Club, I had decided to spend the evening here.

"Lianna, you're here!" My mom's voice carried from the kitchen. "Come give me a hand with dinner."

I dropped my overnight bag by the door and followed her to the kitchen. The delectable smell of fresh baked bread filled the air, and I saw the steaming pot of mashed potatoes on the stove.

Dad came in from the living room and gave me a big bear hug. "Glad you could make it. You're one busy lady."

"What can I say? I'm kicking ass and taking names at work. They love me," I replied, trying to keep my tone upbeat.

Mom pointed to the salad supplies on the counter. "Can you put together your famous salad, sweetie? We always love it when you do."

"Sure," I said, pulling a large mixing bowl from the cabinet and finding the ingredients for a tasty dressing.

As I started preparing the salad, I took a deep breath and tried to relax. It felt good to be back in my childhood home, but the last few weeks had been hectic at work, and I was exhausted. The warm and familiar surroundings of the kitchen reminded me of simpler times, but I couldn't let my guard down just yet.

Dad leaned in and smiled. "I should have known you'd throw yourself into your new job. You're a chip off the old block."

"Are you sure that's a good thing?" Mom shot him a pointed look. "She needs to take care of herself too, dear. Work-life balance is important."

"You make a good point, Mom. I can't keep working all these extra hours long term." Besides, I wanted to spend more time with Kincaid and actually enjoy my life—not just work all the time." Dad never appreciated everything Mom did for him while he threw himself into his work. He accepted everything she did to make his life easier without ever being grateful. That was something I'd always disliked about my dad—those blinders he wore when it came to Mom.

"I'll make more time for Kincaid," I vowed. "He's been amazing these past few weeks, so supportive."

My mom's face brightened. "I really like him. Your dad had a blast with him on the Fourth, setting off all those fireworks. You should bring him over again soon."

"Sure; I'll see what we can work out. I have a business trip next week, so maybe we can meet up after that. I've been burning the midnight oil, trying to make a good impression. It's taking a toll on me, though. I've been struggling with insomnia and feeling run down."

"I'm glad you're here so I can take care of you," Mom said. "Take a seat, and we'll have dinner."

Her freshly baked bread and Italian wedding soup smelled delicious. My mouth watered as she set the bowls on the table.

"Cheers to your new job," Dad said, raising his wine glass.

I clinked my glass against his. "You know, when I found out my company went bankrupt, I was devastated. But in the end, it was a blessing in disguise. I wasn't being challenged there anymore, and now I'm in a perfect place. Great job, adorable house, and an amazing boyfriend. Life's good."

"I'm so happy to hear that, kiddo. Makes a dad proud to see his little girl happy in life."

As my parents beamed at me, I basked in their approval.

I offered to help clean up, but Mom shooed me away. As she tidied up in the kitchen, Dad and I made our way to the living room. We scrolled through Netflix, debating which movie to watch. This was a typical back-and-forth with my dad; he could never make up his mind.

Mom came in a few minutes later carrying a tray with three mugs. "Decaf," she said as she set it on the coffee table.

The scent of it turned my stomach. A Pavlovian response from all the stomachaches it had been giving me lately. "No thanks," I declined. "Lately, it gives me an upset stomach. It's just stress from my new job. No big deal. It happens every time I'm under a lot of pressure."

Mom looked worried, and I inwardly groaned.

"Don't worry," I reassured her. "Rainforest is my dream job, and everything is going perfectly. I even get to spend the entire night with you. Work is easing up, and my stomach will return to normal soon."

"I'm glad to hear that," Mom replied, glancing at the TV. The screensaver was on, and she asked, "Did you two choose a movie?"

"We're thinking about a classic," Dad said. "How about Gaslight?"

"The black and white one where the woman thinks she's going crazy?" Mom asked as she sat down beside me.

"That's the one," I said.

"That sounds great," Mom said. "I haven't seen it in ages."

Mom took a sip of her coffee, and the smell made me cringe. I scooted away from her and grabbed a blanket from the basket beside the couch, snuggling up with it under my nose to block out the scent.

It was soothing to spend a peaceful evening with my parents. I felt like a child again, with my parents caring for me and complimenting me. Kincaid was always supportive, but there was something special about having my parents dote on me.

I opened my eyes, thinking only a few minutes had passed. The credits were rolling on the TV, and my mom was standing over me clutching a brown paper bag.

I sat up, rubbing my eyes. "I'm sorry. I must have dozed off."

"I need you to do me a favor," Mom said, a worried frown tugging at the corners of her mouth, her eyes searching mine.

I hesitated, unsure of what was coming next. She held out the bag, her hands shaking slightly.

I reached for it and peeked inside, my heart pounding in my chest. A small rectangular box stared back at me. I pulled it out, and my mouth went dry as I read the label.

"A pregnancy test? Are you kidding me?" I blurted out, my mind racing.

"I know you're tired of me asking questions and raising your hopes, but hear me out," she said, her voice low and urgent. "When I was pregnant, I couldn't stand the taste of coffee. Not even the smell of it. Take the test. Please. For me."

It hit me all at once, and my eyes went wide. I stared up at her in shock as I suddenly realized my period was late...by at least a couple of weeks.

She might be right. I could actually be pregnant.

Hands shaking, I snatched the bag from her and scurried upstairs to the bathroom off my old bedroom—my place of refuge—and I took the test.

I'd been through this routine so many times over the years while I'd kept trying to get pregnant. I'd peed on that stick so many times that I should have bought stock in the company.

Each time with the same result.

Except for today.

Because when I stared down at the stick five minutes later, a pink plus sign stared back at me.

I sat on the edge of the tub, staring at the test in my trembling hand. I was pregnant. After all these years, I was finally going to have a baby.

34

A BOURBON KIND OF NIGHT

KINCAID

The first one to arrive at the Not a Yacht Club, I was greeted by Dante as I walked into his gleaming kitchen.

"Hi," he said as he popped a cork on a bottle of white wine. "Tonight's recipe is a pretty simple one. Shrimp scampi."

"I've made that one on my own already," I replied.

Dante looked surprised but proud. He handed me a glass of wine, which I sipped and found to be cold and dry.

"This tastes good after a long day. It's been a rough one," I said.

"I'm sorry to hear that," Dante said, clapping me on the shoulder. "Just put it out of your mind for now and enjoy the moment."

Just then, Max and Ford Ross walked in with someone I didn't recognize, a tall, dark-haired morose-looking man. Max introduced him. "This is our brother-in-law, Sin Bachar. We brought him along tonight to try the class."

Sin must be their niece Emma's uncle. She was half-Turkish, and I could see the family resemblance in the brooding man.

Conner came in from the bar.

"Welcome," Dante said, stepping forward and shaking Sin's

238

hand. "Glad you could join us. I'm Dante, and I'll be your chef tonight." He grinned at his own joke.

Max joined the conversation. "He lives up on Mt. Washington with an amazing view of the city, the lucky bastard. We were there for the Fourth and watched the fireworks over the river."

Sin scratched his jaw. "You could live up there too, you know. It's not like we put up a fence to keep people out."

Max shot him an easy grin. "Or I could just invade your place whenever I'm feeling deprived."

Sin gestured grandly. "*Mi casa es su casa.* Just make sure you bring the munchkin along."

Max shook his head in mock despair. "Emma's got you wrapped around her little finger, doesn't she? Me too. That kid's a charmer. I worry about her teenage years. She's going to put gray hairs on my head."

I held out my hand. "I'm Kincaid Gillette. Glad you're joining us tonight. If you want to learn to cook, Dante's your man."

I noticed the tired lines around Sin's eyes and the way he held himself, as if carrying a heavy weight on his shoulders. His dark hair was slightly tousled, and his eyes looked as if he hadn't slept much.

Sin gestured toward Max and Ford. "My brothers-in-law convinced me to come. They thought a night out learning something new would get my mind off some problems," Sin explained.

Max rubbed the back of his neck. "Just the one problem."

Ford furrowed his brow. "I assume Miranda's facing some serious consequences."

Sin gave a dismal shrug. "Probably." He looked down at his hands, rubbing a spot on his palm. "They informed her this morning they're pulling her medical license. She won't be able to practice medicine."

"What does she plan to do?" Max asked.

Sin's mouth tightened, and his voice cracked slightly as he replied. He was trying to hide his reaction, but the man looked broken. "According to her, it's none of my business. She packed her bags and bought a one-way ticket to Chicago. As of this afternoon, she's out of my life."

As Sin revealed his heartbreaking news, a heavy silence filled the room. Ford's face was stricken with worry as he asked, "Does that mean the wedding's off?"

Sin's response was a nod and a heavy sigh. "She gave me back her engagement ring," he said.

Curiosity got the best of me, and I asked, "I take it Miranda was your fiancée. She lost her medical license?"

Sin met my gaze, and I could see the sadness etched into his eyes. "She's an anesthesiologist at the hospital and got caught helping a drug ring that was stealing meds from the hospital."

I was stunned. "Well, shit. That's serious."

Sin nodded in agreement. "Serious as a heart attack. Hospitals don't tolerate that sort of thing. She won't be able to practice anywhere."

Max chimed in, "All those years of hard work. What a waste."

Sin scratched at his cheek, looking lost. "I asked her what happened, but she wouldn't talk to me about it. She said the less I knew, the better off we both were."

Dante, ever the gracious host, tried to lighten the mood by gesturing toward the wine glasses and bottle. "You need a drink. If anyone could use one tonight, it's you."

The room fell into a contemplative silence, and I couldn't help but feel grateful for my own comparatively small problems. While I might have some difficulties to deal with, they paled in comparison to what Sin was going through.

As we went to our cooking stations, Conner and I started prepping the ingredients for the Shrimp Linguine. Suddenly, my phone rang, displaying Chrissy Murphy's name on the screen. Was she calling to make more changes, or did she want to complain about something? Either one was bad.

I took the call. "Kincaid here."

"I'm calling to let you know your services are no longer wanted," Chrissy snapped, anger rolling off her. "In fact, if you step foot on my property again, I'll have you arrested for trespassing."

I went cold, and my stomach twisted as I struggled to figure out why she was being so hostile. "I'm sorry, Mrs. Murphy, but I have no idea what's going on here. What happened? Why would you want to fire me?"

Conner overheard and snapped to face me, blatantly eavesdropping.

"Because you disgust me!" She said it so loudly I had to move the phone away from my ear to avoid the sheer volume of her voice.

Conner's eyes went wide, matching mine.

"I don't want you anywhere near me, my unborn baby, or my house." Her words hit me like a freight train, leaving me confused and disoriented.

I shook my head, still trying to comprehend what was going on. "Please, Mrs. Murphy, I have no idea what you're talking about—"

"Don't give me that." Pure loathing dripped from her words. "You know exactly what you did. Don't come to my house. Don't call me. Don't even think about me. If you do, I'll sic my lawyer on you so fast, you won't know what hit you. When I'm through with you, you'll never work in this town again."

My heart thudded painfully in my chest. "This is insane," I protested, trying to keep my voice steady. "You can't just fire me and threaten me without giving me an explanation. Whatever the problem is, I'm sure we can fix it."

The room fell silent as everyone turned to look at me. The air crackled with tension.

"What's wrong is you," she spat, her voice thick with fury. "Stay away from me."

The line went dead, leaving me staring at my phone in disbelief.

Dante's expression mirrored my own shock. "That woman is beyond angry."

Conner's mouth hung open. "What the hell did you do to piss her off?"

I slumped onto my stool. "I have no idea." My mind raced. How could I fix this? I couldn't simply walk away from the project I'd poured six figures into. Maybe I should call John, but was he even in town?

As I sat there, the future of my business flashed before my eyes. I couldn't afford for her to refuse to pay for the supplies and work I'd already completed.

Their next payment was looming, and I had subcontractors to pay. Dread filled me as I considered the worst-case scenario: what if I had to take the Murphys to court to get paid? How long would that take, and how much money would I have to spend on lawyers? And what if Chrissy followed through on her threat and spread nasty rumors about me, damaging my reputation and preventing me from landing any new contracts?

Conner pushed open the door from the bar, startling me. I was so lost in thought that I hadn't even noticed he'd left. He held out a glass of liquid the color of dark honey and shoved it into my hand.

"Bourbon," he said. "Your favorite. Knob Creek."

I stared at it, feeling both grateful and apprehensive. "And you think this will help?"

"At least it'll make you pleasantly numb," he replied. "I'll drive you home."

As I took a sip, the warm liquid spreading through me, my phone rang again. I grabbed for it. Maybe it was Chrissy, finally coming to her senses.

No such luck. It was Heather.

I tossed my phone on the counter without answering it. The last person I wanted to talk to right now was Heather. She and Chrissy were both crazy, and I could only handle one of them at a time.

In Dante's sparkling clean kitchen, the only sounds the hum of the air conditioning and the clink of glasses. The bourbon tasted strong and smooth, burning a trail down my throat. I tried to relax, to let the alcohol soothe me, but my mind kept racing.

I rubbed the back of my neck, feeling the tension knotting my muscles. "I need to think this through," I muttered, unable to stand still. I started pacing, desperate for a solution to my problems. "There has to be a way for me to fix this."

Conner's voice interrupted my thoughts. "I'll finish cooking," he said, already adding chopped shallots to the sizzling pan of olive oil and butter.

"Thanks." I downed the bourbon in my glass, feeling its warmth spread through me.

I racked my brain, trying to come up with a plan. Maybe I could call Chrissy's husband, John. I checked my watch, trying to calculate the time difference between here and China. John was traveling there for business, and I had no idea what city he was in. China was enormous, but I guessed it would be somewhere around an eleven-hour time difference. So, it was around six in the morning there? I decided to wait until it was mid-morning in China before trying to call.

As I paced, Conner added the shrimp to the pan, then disappeared to the bar. When he returned, he had a whole bottle of Knob Creek bourbon and six glasses. He poured me another drink and put it in my hand.

I barely noticed I was drinking my second one. Or was it my third? This was a night to lose count.

Conner took my arm and guided me into the bar. I stumbled a little, the bourbon making me unsteady on my feet. A table was set up for us, and the others were already seated around it. I hadn't even noticed when they'd all left the kitchen.

As we settled down to eat shrimp scampi, Conner lifted his glass in a toast. "Here's to good food and good friends."

Sin nodded in agreement, his dark eyes gleaming. "And here's to Uber."

We downed our shots, the smooth liquor burning its way down my throat. Despite my worries, it felt good to be among friends, even if only for a little while.

A SOLUTION

Lianna

My heart raced as I descended the stairs from my bedroom. I could feel my mom's anticipation building as she waited for me in the foyer. As soon as my feet touched the ground, she let out a loud exhale and clutched the newel post.

"Well?" She was practically breathless.

I held up the pee-stick so she could see it.

"A plus sign? Does that mean you're pregnant?"

A huge grin spread across my face.

"You're pregnant!" Mom shrieked, tears filling her eyes.

Dad burst into the room, looking just as stunned as Mom. "You're pregnant?" he echoed.

I nodded, confirming the news.

Mom wrapped me in a tight hug, and I felt tears pricking at the corners of my eyes. When I finally broke free, laughing with joy, she grabbed my hand and led me into the kitchen.

"Sit here," she said, pushing me into a chair at the kitchen table. "I knew it. I just knew it. This is the best news in the world."

Dad stood to one side, staring at me speechlessly.

Mom rummaged around in the pantry, then quickly wrote something with a Sharpie. A moment later, she was standing in front of me, holding open a Ziplock bag that read, "Proof Positive - July 18th", on it along with a couple of hearts.

Pure, unadulterated joy and satisfaction flooded me as I dropped the pregnancy test into the bag.

Mom sealed it shut and handed it back to me. "Now, you can keep it forever." She wiped happy tears from her cheeks with the back of her hand.

Over the years, I'd thrown dozens of these tests away, but this one was a keeper.

I looked down at the pregnancy test, and although I was happy, I was still stunned and struggling to process the news. "I don't get it. How can I be pregnant?" I said it mostly to myself.

Mom burst out laughing. "You had sex. That's how. I know we've had the birds and the bees talk."

Her teasing broke through my dazed state, and I narrowed my eyes at her. "This is serious, Mom. Stop cracking jokes."

I looked down at my flat stomach and smoothed my hand over it. A baby. I was having a baby?

"This is insane." I shook my head in disbelief. "After all those years of trying, I get pregnant now that I'm single? I've only been seeing Kincaid for just under four months." My chest tightened as the reality hit me hard.

Looking up at my mom, panic began to well inside me. "I just started the most demanding job of my life. I work long hours and leave on the first of many business trips next Monday. I took this job to dedicate myself to my career, knowing it would be a challenge. And I love it. How can I balance work and taking care of a baby?" Tears pricked my eyes. "Maybe I should quit Rainforest and find a less demanding job."

The thought of leaving my job, which I had worked so hard for, twisted my heart.

Mom frowned. "Don't be so dramatic. Plenty of single women manage just fine. Besides, you aren't alone in this. I'm here for you. There's nothing I'd love more than to help raise my grandbaby. And Kincaid will be involved, too. I'm certain of it."

Mom scooted her chair closer to mine, cradling my hands in hers. "I'll come to your house every day and take care of my grandbaby. And when you have to travel, your baby can stay with us."

I stared at her, hardly believing what she was offering. "Are you sure, Mom? That's a lot to ask."

"I want to. Having my only grandchild live all the way in Washington has been heartbreaking. I want to see her every day. Besides, I'd rather take care of your baby than have you hire someone else. You know I love being a mom. Being a grand-mother will be even better."

Hope lifted my heart, loosening the tight band around my chest. The thought of being a single mom and having Kincaid in the picture was exhilarating. It felt like Mom had given me a way to have my cake and eat it too.

And Kincaid. Mom was right. He'd be in the picture; I was certain of it. That was just the kind of man he was.

But that brought me right back around to my original ques-tion: how did I get pregnant so easily after years of infertility? It had to have happened the night the condom broke. We'd used protection every other time, but fate seemed to have had other plans.

Before I disappeared down that rabbit-hole of a question and tried to figure out how this miracle had occurred, there was some-thing important I needed to do.

Tell Kincaid.

I glanced at my watch. It wasn't that late yet. He was probably still at the Not a Yacht Club. Should I wait until he was home?

Maybe, but I didn't think I could wait that long.

I needed to see him.

Now.

36

THE TRUTH WILL OUT

Kincaid

My phone chimed with a text. I fumbled to unlock it and then I tried to focus on the screen. Maybe I'd had a bit too much to drink. I closed one eye to turn my double-vision into a single image. It was a text.

"Lianna," I said aloud.

"Your woman misses you," Sin said, his words slightly slurred. "Thas nice."

"Sure is." I grinned down at my phone.

> Lianna: I need to tell you something. Are you still at NAYC?

> Me: Sur am. Call me?

My phone rang a second later.

I stood, almost knocking over my chair, but managed to keep it upright. I stumbled a few steps away from the guys.

"Hey, love. I mis-s-s you," I slurred into the phone.

"Hey yourself," a woman's sultry-sounding voice replied. "I miss you too."

I pulled the phone away from my ear and blinked at the caller ID. Damn. It was Heather. I put the phone back to my ear. "Sorry. Thought you were—never mind. Wha-do-you need, Heather?"

The guys at the table fell silent, and I glared at them. Nosy bastards.

"Heather?" Conner looked up while pouring another round of drinks and splashed some on the table. "What the hell, dude!"

"I wanted to check in," Heather cooed in my ear. "See how things are going with you."

"Everything's fine," I lied. There was no way I'd share my problems with her.

Heather paused. "I heard the building inspector wants you to make changes to the roof you installed on the Murphy house. Chrissy was upset about it."

Her words hit me like a face full of cold water, momentarily cutting through my brain fog. A rock of cold dread dropped into my stomach. "You know Chrissy Murphy?"

The guys openly eavesdropped. Not that I could blame them. Watching me had to be like watching a slow-motion train wreck.

"Sure. We take yoga classes together."

"The Yoga Moms class?" I asked incredulously, locking eyes with my friends. This wasn't good.

"That's the one. We met last fall when I was pregnant, and she was still trying." Heather's chirpy voice grated on my nerves.

"You were never pregnant," I said in a growl.

"Whatever. Anyway, that's how I got to know her. She mentioned how upset she was that the inspector found something wrong. It freaked her out."

I let out a tired sigh and rubbed my eyes, feeling drained by this conversation. "It was a minor issue. The inspector just wanted an additional piece of roof flashing."

Heather's voice was overly sweet when she replied, and I could practically hear the underlying malice in her words. "Is that it?"

"What do you want, Heather? You broke up with your boyfriend. Are you trying to get back in his good graces by digging up information about me to share?" As if I was that stupid. But—I was pretty damned drunk. Maybe I shouldn't be talking to her right now.

"No," Heather insisted. "Not that. It's just that I thought—I wondered—Kincaid—I think I may have made a mistake."

I struggled to follow her train of thought. "A mistake? What kind of mistake?"

She let out a sigh. "Adam and I are still together. When I found out you were seeing someone, I decided to give it another try with him. You made me really angry when you refused to help me move out. I still can't believe you'd push me aside for some other woman."

I rubbed my forehead. The woman drove me crazy. "Heather, you and I aren't together anymore. We broke up over a year ago."

"But we had something real, didn't we?" Heather's voice was pleading now. "Otherwise, you never would have asked me to marry you."

Say what? The woman didn't make sense. "What we had was based on lies, even—"

"Just listen," Heather cut me off, her desperation evident. "I think I said something to Chrissy that she took the wrong way. I need to make things right."

A burst of clarity cut through my brain fog, and a knot of dread tightened in my belly. Heather was the mastermind behind this entire fiasco. "What did you tell Chrissy Murphy?" I asked, my voice taut.

"Please don't be angry, 'Caid. Back when we first broke up, I told Chrissy my boyfriend left me because I lost our baby. I never mentioned your name, but she took it really hard. It made her angry as hell. She had just miscarried a few months earlier and was still grieving. When she mentioned today that you were renovating her house, I might have told her you were my ex-boyfriend."

I felt like I'd been punched in the gut. "And now she thinks I dumped you because you lost a baby? The one you made up that never even existed?"

"I know! I'm sorry!" Heather's voice grated on my nerves. "It's not my fault. It's just that I hate the idea of you dating anyone else."

"Seriously, Heather?" I closed my eyes. "Anything else?" As if that wasn't bad enough.

"I, uh, might have said some things about your business… about you not being very trustworthy."

I slammed the phone against my forehead a few times, trying to retroactively knock some sense into myself. Why had I ever dated this woman? Did she have any idea what she'd done to me? "Are you trying to destroy my business? Ruin me?"

"No, at least that wasn't what I meant to do. I was just jealous."

I pressed my fingers to my sore forehead. Just great. "Heather—"

"I want you back. I know I lied, but any woman would do what I did if she was afraid of losing you," she pleaded, her voice taking on a wailing tone. "I fell in love with you, Kincaid. I still love you. Don't you still love me, too? Deep down?"

"No, I don't," I said, my voice cold. "I cared for the person you pretended to be, not the liar and manipulator you really were. They aren't the same person. She was a phantom. A figment of your imagination."

Heather let out a sigh. "I know I can make you love me again. I'd do anything to get you back."

Hot anger burned through me. "Including lie? Including ruining my business?"

"No!" She paused. "Well," she added in that pouty tone I hated so much, "maybe I can see how it might look that way. I suppose I didn't think that part through."

"That seems to be a recurring pattern with you, Heather. You don't think things through." I paused, feeling a knot form in my stomach. How was I going to fix this? "You need to tell Chrissy the truth. That you were never really pregnant."

Heather's voice trembled as she replied, "I can't do that! She's my friend. If she knew I lied to her about being pregnant, she'd never speak to me again."

"You've got to be kidding me? Why is it you can understand that a friend would be angry with you for lying, but you can't understand why I would be?" I asked, trying to keep my voice level.

"That's different. You love me." Heather's voice turned wheedling.

"No. I don't."

"You did. You could again," she continued, her voice hopeful. "We could be together, like before. I could fix the problem with Chrissy."

I let out a deep sigh. "I'm not doing this with you. I'm not negotiating. Tell Chrissy the truth."

"And then we can be together?" Heather's voice perked up as she sensed an opening. "I'd do that for you, Kincaid. I'd ruin my friendship with Chrissy if I knew we'd be together again."

I felt my body tense up. "Are you blackmailing me?"

"What?" Heather's voice squeaked with affront. "No! Of course not."

"Either I take you back, or you keep lying to Chrissy, do I have that right?" I pressed.

"I—I—I suppose?"

"You suppose?" I needed a drink to deal with this. "I'm done talking to you. All you ever do is lie and manipulate. That isn't love. It's sick."

"But I do love you." Heather's voice was filled with tears. "I'll do anything to get you back. Doesn't that prove how much I care? How much I need you? Any woman in my shoes would do the same thing."

"Goodbye, Heather." I ended the call, feeling drained and defeated.

Conner stopped in front of me, holding out a glass. "Is it as bad as it sounded on this end?"

I nodded as I took it. "Maybe even worse." I downed the drink in one gulp, feeling the alcohol burn down my throat.

37

BOOZY BOMBSHELLS AND BREAKDOWNS

Lianna

As I pushed open the heavy oak door of the Not a Yacht Club, the sounds of clinking glasses and muffled chatter fell silent. I strode into the bar, my eyes adjusting to the dim lighting. The place was deserted, except for Kincaid's cooking class, huddled around a table near the stage. The only light came from the large, garage-door-sized windows that overlocked the Ohio River, casting an orange glow across the room.

I strode into the Not a Yacht Club, brimming with excitement and joy. Of course, Kincaid would be shocked to learn that I was pregnant after the whole "I can never have babies" talk, but I knew he'd be supportive. He was Kincaid, after all.

I approached the group, the clacking of my heels echoing through the empty space. The smell of bourbon hung heavy in the air, and I could see that Kincaid and his friends had already polished off most of the bottle.

"They're closed. No women allowed," one of the men said, slurring his words.

"That's Lianna," Dante said, motioning toward me. "Kincaid's girlfriend. Lianna, this is Sin."

I gave a little wave, my gaze focused on Kincaid. He was

slumped in his chair, his face flushed, and his hair mussed. I had never seen him like this before.

"What're yer doing here? I thought you were going to call," he said, his voice thick with alcohol—as well as a slight Pittsburgh accent I'd never heard him use before.

"I texted you I was coming over," I said, my concern mounting as I took in the state of the men around the table.

He glanced at his phone, squinting as if he could hardly focus. "Shit. I musta missed it."

"Is something wrong?" I asked, my eyes flicking over the empty bottle of bourbon and the disheveled appearance of Kincaid and his friends.

"Long story." Kincaid stood up, his movements unsteady as he dragged his fingers through his hair. "I thought you were spending the evening with your parents."

I ignored his comment and moved closer to him, searching his face for any signs of distress. The silence of the empty bar hung heavy between us, and I could hear the gentle lapping of the river outside.

I ended up taking a small step back to avoid the stench of alcohol, which made my stomach roil. "Something came up, and I thought you'd want to know about it right away." I lifted my chin, trying to project confidence despite my nervousness. "I see you've all been drinking."

Kincaid shrugged, his words slurring slightly. "Only a couple. Or three. I've lost count."

My stomach flipped. This wasn't turning into the touching moment I'd envisioned. The last thing I wanted to do was tell a drunk guy he was going to be a dad. "Maybe we should talk tomorrow."

He squinted at me, his forehead furrowing with concern. "No. You drove all the way here. Tell me."

The sound of the river lapping against the shore coming through the open windows was soothing, but it did little to quell the anxiety bubbling up inside me.

I eyed the men listening to us, feeling uneasy about having an audience. I didn't want to do this in front of them. Glancing back toward the hostess stand through the doorway in the waiting area, I asked, "Can I speak to you in private?"

Kincaid followed me toward the entrance, unsteady on his feet. I'd never seen him even slightly drunk before today.

We positioned ourselves so his back was to his friends, but I could see them watching us. When they noticed me staring back at them, they looked away.

Taking in Kincaid's appearance, I could tell something was off. He looked like he was reeling from bad news. What I was about to tell him probably wouldn't help.

I hesitated, knowing my timing couldn't be much worse.

He set his feet wider and gestured for me to continue. "Whatever it is, just tell me," he urged.

I sighed, recognizing he was right. I needed to tell him.

"I told you about my insomnia and my problems with coffee, remember?" I tugged at the sleeves of my hoodie and pulled them down over my hands. "My mom said the same thing happened to her."

He blinked a couple of times and stared at me blankly. I could feel my nerves getting the best of me.

Should I ease into the subject, or just blurt it out? "I got to thinking, and I realized I'm over two weeks late."

"Late?" His expression was blank.

"My period."

He stared at me, clearly confused. "What are you saying?"

I licked my lips, feeling more uncertain by the second. "My mom made me take a home pregnancy test."

"You're pregnant." His voice was flat, but his face became a rigid mask.

"I'm pregnant."

"Jesus, Lianna." He dragged his hand down his face and ran his fingers through his hair. "I thought you couldn't get pregnant."

Not the reaction I'd hoped for. "That's what I thought, too. Like I told you before, my doctor couldn't find anything wrong that he could treat. Paul's sperm analysis said the problem wasn't on his end. It had to be me." Suddenly, I recalled that Paul had refused to take a post-coital test because he said it was "too gross." Was that a clue?

"Your doctor couldn't find anything wrong." Sarcasm rang in his voice. "Really?" His look made me feel like he didn't believe me, like I was lying to him.

I froze, not knowing how to react. I'd expected shock, of course. An adjustment period—but sarcasm and disbelief?

"That's what I said." I stepped away from him. "I really don't like the belligerent tone you're using." My belly tightened, turning to iron, as if it was trying to protect the life growing inside me. "I can see that talking to you now is a mistake. You're drunk. I've never seen you this way before, and I don't like it."

He shook his head in disbelief. "Are you serious? It's like I hardly know you anymore, and now you drop this bombshell on me. You're telling me you're pregnant, just like Heather did. And what, you expect me to propose? Like some clueless jagoff? I can't deal with this right now. It's insane."

There was a moment of silence as his words resonated in the room. His friends, who had been pretending not to eavesdrop, dropped all pretense.

Conner's jaw dropped.

Dante spoke up. "What the fuck, Kincaid? Dude. Not cool."

Conner pushed his chair back with a screech, but then he checked himself and remained where he was.

I clenched my jaw and locked eyes with Kincaid. "Clearly, this isn't a good time. I don't know what your problem is, but I think it's bigger than me. Bigger than this baby. I don't want to continue talking to you right now." I spun around and grabbed the front door handle. I paused and faced him. "You aren't the man I thought you were."

The look of dawning comprehension on his face told me he

was starting to realize how much he'd just screwed up, but it was too late. I yanked open the door and stormed outside.

Kincaid ran after me and caught up halfway across the parking lot. "Jesus, Lianna. I didn't mean—" He reached out to take my hand, but I snatched it back.

His friends gathered in the doorway, watching in horror.

"Stay away from me," I said over my shoulder as I kept walking. "I don't want to see your face. I can't talk to you. You're drunk, and I don't like you very much right now. I was full of joy, and you just broke my heart." I yanked the car door shut, and he quickly pulled his hand away to avoid getting it caught.

38

THE NOT-SO-SOBER ROAD TO REDEMPTION

Kincaid

I stalked back toward the door of the Not a Yacht Club feeling a hot flush of shame and anger in my cheeks. How could I have accused Lianna of lying to me? Of manipulating me? That had been my fear talking, not my brain.

I knew exactly what I needed to do. I'd find my keys, drive to Lianna's place, tell her I was a complete jagoff, and beg her forgiveness.

I'd fucked up royally. What the hell was wrong with me?

Conner's voice startled me as I burst back into the restaurant. "Dude. What the fuck was that? I know you've had a rough day, but are you seriously so wasted that you'd accuse Lianna of lying to you?"

I ignored him and stalked over to the table, where I fumbled for my keys and cell phone. I reached for them, but my aim was off, and I knocked over a shot of bourbon in the process.

"Easy there, man." Dante stood up and blocked me. "You can't drive. You're too drunk."

Max plucked my keys out of the spreading puddle on the table and tossed them to Conner, who promptly disappeared into the kitchen.

A groan escaped my lips. "Seriously?" I doubted I would ever find my keys now that Conner had them. "Yinz're pissin me off. Give me back my goddamned keys!" I yelled, my voice echoing through the empty bar.

Dante crossed his arms and scowled at me. "Why? So, you can follow her? And do what? Apologize? Tell her you screwed up?"

"Yeah, 'zactly. I need tuh fix this." I pressed my head between my hands as if I could squeeze the alcohol out of my brain. Why the hell had I done this to myself? I never got drunk like this. Sure, I'd have a drink from time to time, but get drunk? Never.

Except for today.

I loved Lianna. She was everything to me. Had I just ruined it all with her? Was this the proof I was always secretly searching for —that I wasn't worthy of her love? I could hardly believe I'd been lucky enough to have found her in the first place, let alone to have her love me in return. And what did I do with that good fortune? I shattered it. Tossed it in the trash. Stomped all over it. I destroyed what we had built like a kid knocking over a tower of blocks—or like a drunk opening his own stupid mouth.

She needed to know how I felt about her. I had to tell her. She was everything I wanted. For now and always. Pregnant, not pregnant, infertile, or constantly having babies—none of that mattered. What mattered was us being together, for now and for always.

"You already tried that," Conner said, bursting back into the room through the swinging door. "It didn't work. And in case you haven't noticed, your ass is drunk. You won't be getting behind the wheel of a car until you've sobered up."

"Don't you get it?" I shouted at Conner. "She's pregnant, and I all but accused her of tricking me and doing it on purpose."

I can't believe how stupid I was. How the hell was I going to fix this?

"We know," Dante said. "We were right here."

"Kind of hard not to overhear," Sin muttered.

"But we tried," Max added.

Ford nodded like a drunken sage offering pearls of wisdom. "When someone's drunk, it's hard for them to control the volume of their voice."

I flipped him off as I dropped back into my chair and reached for my phone. "I'll get an Uber."

Suddenly, my phone disappeared too. I stared at my palm, confused. It took me a moment to figure out Conner had snatched it from my hand.

"Do we have to spell it out for you? Do. Not. Go. See. Her. When. You. Are. Drunk." Conner enunciated each word slowly. "You'll just make things worse."

I stared at him blearily. This didn't make sense. "Don't see her?"

"He's right. You need a plan," Ford said. He glanced at Dante. "My advice is that you eat humble pie."

Dante smirked. "My advice? Cook for her. Food can be a shortcut to forgiveness."

"Pie?" This sounded complicated. I groaned and dropped my head into my hands, running my fingers through my hair in frustration. Were they right? Maybe. Probably. But my thoughts were all jumbled up, making it hard to think straight.

How was I supposed to make this right?

39

UNPACKING THE LIES

LIANNA

What just happened? I'd been so excited to share my news that I never paused to consider that Kincaid would react this way. Even if I had considered it, I could never have predicted this. He'd all but accused me of lying to him. Did I even know him? Because he clearly didn't know me if that's what he believed.

Tears streamed down my face as I pulled my car to the side of the road, the sound of gravel crunching beneath the tires. I needed to compose myself, to breathe. The air was thick with the scent of freshly cut grass, and the sun was low in the sky, casting a golden glow over everything.

Was I really that terrible at judging people? First, Paul cheated on me, and now Kincaid believed... what? That I had tricked him? That I was as deceitful as his ex-girlfriend Heather? As dishonest as Paul?

Men. I really could pick 'em.

And now, I was pregnant—and beginning to feel all those pregnancy hormones, considering my current emotional state. But even with my world crumbling around me, I couldn't help but marvel over that particular miracle. No matter what else happened, that was a good thing.

But how did it happen? I wasn't one to believe in miracles. I preferred science and facts.

Paul. He had already proven himself to be a liar and a cheater. Had he been telling me even bigger lies? It was easier to believe that than to think that I'd miraculously become fertile since leaving him.

My ex-husband had some serious explaining to do. Like, how was it that the very first time I had unprotected sex with someone other than him, I got pregnant?

Ten minutes later, I parked in front of my former house and stared at it, trying to figure out what I wanted to say. The family room lights facing the street were on, and I caught a glimpse of Paul moving behind the sheer curtains I'd chosen, along with the drapes. I wondered if Gloria resented the fact that I'd decorated the entire house.

I hoped so.

I jammed my finger into the doorbell. And held it.

Paul opened the door. "We need to talk," I said, pushing past him into the house.

Gloria was on the sofa, looking tense and upset. Had I interrupted something? I gave a mental shrug. Not my problem. I had enough on my plate right now.

"This isn't a good time," Paul said, glancing at Gloria.

Gloria narrowed her eyes, but waved me in. "It's fine," she snapped. She stood and approached me. "You look angry. I want to hear what you have to say."

Paul's eyes flicked between us before settling on me. "What is it?"

I smiled tightly. "I got some news that came as an enormous surprise, and I'm hoping you can explain how something I thought was impossible is, in fact, completely possible. Very much so."

"I—don't follow you." Paul crossed his arms in that irritating way he had when he was digging in and preparing to be stubborn, like a recalcitrant five-year-old.

I watched him closely, not wanting to miss his reaction. "I'm pregnant. What do you have to say for yourself about that?"

Paul looked stymied. "You aren't suggesting I'm the father, are you?"

"Wait. I have two enormous problems with this." Gloria interrupted, clearly angry. "First of all, you told me you had a vasectomy, and second of all, your divorce was final six months ago. Have you two been hooking up behind my back?"

My jaw hung open. I couldn't be hearing that right. I gave my head a sharp shake. "What vasectomy?"

Gloria looked from me back to Paul, obviously confused. "You told me you had a vasectomy over ten years ago. Did you lie about that, too? You know how I feel about getting pregnant. I refuse to let that happen."

Paul held his hands up to placate Gloria. "Of course, I didn't lie. I had the surgery after my dad was diagnosed with Huntington's and I found out I had it too. I already told you that."

Gloria crossed her arms and raised one skeptical eyebrow. "Did you tell your ex-wife?"

I gaped at him. "You told me you'd been tested and you *didn't* have Huntington's. Why would you lie about that?"

Paul avoided my gaze, looking guilty. "You wanted a baby so much. You would have left me if you knew I couldn't give you one."

My knees turned wobbly. I was afraid they might buckle. I dropped onto the arm of the sofa as I stared at him in shock. How had this happened? How had he tricked me? Tricked my doctor? "But you showed me your sperm analysis that proved you were fertile."

He pressed his lips together in a tight frown. "I doctored someone else's sperm analysis. Replaced his name with mine."

The air left my lungs as if I'd been punched. "That's why you always refused to do the post-coital test. It wasn't because you were creeped out. It was because you knew the doctor would figure it out."

Paul's eyes widened beseechingly. "I couldn't let you know I'd had a vasectomy. I knew you'd either leave me or try to get me to have it surgically reversed."

"Not if you had Huntington's! What kind of a person do you think I am? And I wouldn't have left you, either. Certainly not for that." I shook my head, barely able to process what I was hearing. "How could you do that to me? How could you let me believe I was infertile? Don't you know what that did to me? All those tests? All those months hoping I'd get pregnant and then failing again and again?"

He jutted out his chin in a pout. "What can I say? I want to live life on my own terms."

"What the hell, Paul!" Gloria snapped. "By lying to her, you stole her choice to live her life on *her* own terms. I knew you were a cheater, but I didn't realize you were such a complete asshat. You stole her choices."

Paul looked stunned. "Gloria don't be like this. I've been completely honest with you."

She held up her hand for him to stop. "Wait. Just wait. That's a lie. Just like the lie about the text you just received from that bimbo and then deleted."

"I didn't delete a text. I swear."

"I know what I saw. You read it. You chuckled. You replied, and then you deleted it. I watched you."

"It was nothing. I swear. That's why I deleted it."

Gloria shook her head. "So, now you admit you deleted it? You know what? I don't care. I'm done. We're done. I'm out of here." She turned her back on him, flung the front door wide, and stormed into the night, her shoulders rigid with fury.

I stared blankly at the empty doorway, my mind still processing everything that had just happened. The only sounds were the soft chirping of crickets in the background. It was as if the world had paused just for a moment.

I turned to Paul and made no effort to disguise the icy contempt in my voice. "I guess my work here is done."

Once outside, I saw Gloria pacing frantically in front of the house, her phone held up at odd angles as she cursed under her breath. When she noticed me, she immediately asked, "Does your phone have a signal? Can you call me an Uber? I don't want to ask him for help."

I hesitated, then said, "I'll give you a ride into Sewickley."

Gloria stood still. "Are you sure? I don't want to put you out."

"It's fine," I said, shaking my head. "I wouldn't want to walk back inside that house, either."

We climbed into my car. "Where do you want me to drop you off?"

"Loco Mocha is fine. My apartment's next door."

As we drove, the tension in the air was palpable. "I might grab a chamomile tea while I'm there. My mom said it would help me sleep."

Gloria just nodded silently, staring out of the window. It was clear we both had a lot to think about.

40

DARK CHOCOLATE

Kincaid

Dante asked, "You're sure she likes chocolate?"

I looked at him incredulously, "Of course, I'm sure." The memory of the chocolate-dipped strawberries we'd had last month flooded my mind. "Dark chocolate is her favorite."

Dante turned to Ford. "Dark Chocolate Ganache Cake?"

"Absolutely," Ford replied. "It worked for me. I highly recommend it."

"What are you two talking about?" I asked, confused.

"We're talking about making the perfect dessert to get you back in Lianna's good graces." Dante said.

"I nearly blew it with Mara last summer," Ford chimed in. "This cake helped convince her to give me another chance."

I dropped my chin and considered the suggestion. "Don't you think a heartfelt apology is a better idea?"

"Sure, that part's key, but you can never go wrong with a dessert you make yourself," Dante insisted. "It's physical proof that you're remorseful—plus, it tastes great."

"Verily, methinks of whence he speaks, he knoweth," Max declared, placing his hand over his heart and striking a Shakespearian pose. "His counsel hath aided Ford and Mara's reunion, and soon they shall be wed."

I blinked a few times, trying to parse what he'd said. Sounded like a damned good endorsement. "Yinz're getting all fancy on me. But I'll try anything. Tell me what to do."

"Step one, drink water," Dante said. "Time to wash all that alcohol out of your system."

With Dante as the commander-in-chief, we all began to work in a haphazard manner. Ford and Max took over the task of baking the cake, since they were the least intoxicated among us. Dante and Sin handled the chocolate ganache, while Conner and I started making the buttercream frosting.

After a while, the cake was ready for assembly, and I had sobered up enough to get started. My friends stood behind me, giving me tips and suggestions as I worked. Finally, it was done, and I took a step back to admire our handiwork. The cake looked incredible, but— "It's missing something."

"You're right," Dante agreed. "You need to decorate it."

"Curls," I said, nodding thoughtfully. "It needs curls."

"Chocolate curls?" Dante asked, already reaching for blocks of white and milk chocolate. "Perfect." He quickly got to work, shaving off curls with a potato peeler.

I carefully arranged the curls on the sides of the cake and around the top, leaving the center clear. It looked stunning.

"I've always believed that cooking is an art," Dante remarked. "But baking is more like chemistry. You have to get the proportions of the ingredients just right, so they work together to create magic. And that's what you and Lianna have: chemistry."

"Artful chemistry," Sin chimed in.

"I like that," Dante said, nodding. "Getting the proportions right is crucial, but there's a certain degree of creativity involved if you want to take a dessert from great to amazing. Like those chocolate curls you added."

The atmosphere was filled with a sense of camaraderie as we

admired the cake's perfection. The delicious aroma of chocolate mingled with the other scents of the kitchen.

"What should he write on top?" Ford asked.

"I'm sorry?" Dante suggested.

"But she's pregnant," Max pointed out. "It shouldn't sound like he's apologizing for getting her pregnant."

"Good point," Conner said.

"Shouldn't he, though?" Sin asked. "It wasn't planned."

"Making a baby takes two," Max said. "Besides, she seemed thrilled about it at first."

"She is," I said, rubbing the back of my neck. "She's been longing for a baby. I think it should say something like 'Congratulations.'"

"Maybe," Ford said. "How about 'I couldn't be happier?'"

"Too long," Dante said. "It won't fit."

"A simple 'I love you' is best," Sin said.

I peered at the center of the cake surrounded by chocolate curls, envisioning how the words would fit. "I guess that would do."

"There is no 'guess,' only 'do,'" Dante said in a terrible Yoda impersonation.

Conner glared at me, his brow furrowed. "You do love her, right?"

I met his gaze. "Without a doubt."

The kitchen fell silent at my declaration, and my friends all turned to me, expressions dead serious. It was a brief moment that made me realize how much they all had my back. I felt grateful for their support and friendship, and I knew I could always count on them.

Dante broke the silence. "Well then, let's get that message on the cake."

41

THE ZEN OF CHAMOMILE

Lianna

As we waited at a stop light, I turned to Gloria and said, "You figured out Paul was lying a lot faster than I did."

Gloria shrugged. "Only because I knew he cheated on you. The guy is sneaky. If I hadn't been watching for it, I never would have caught him at it."

Gloria's words made me feel a little bit less naive. "I suppose."

Gloria faced me in her seat. "Don't let the assholes bring you down. You're a nice person. Stay that way. Just get better at identifying the shitheels in the first place so you can avoid them."

I furrowed my brows. Was Kincaid one of those shitheels? I'd thought he was one of the good ones.

As I parked in front of Loco Mocha, Gloria spoke up. "Let me buy you that cup of chamomile tea. It's the least I can do after you drove me home and saved me from going back inside to use his phone."

We ordered our drinks and sat at a small table. The aroma of the tea was pleasant. It was a different experience from my usual coffee, but I had to get used to it for the next nine—no, seven-and-a-half months. I needed to see my obstetrician to figure out my due date. The thought made me anxious.

The environment of the café was calming. Soft music played in the background, and the muted chatter of other customers filled the air. I took a deep breath, trying to relax. With Gloria by my side, I felt stronger, but the unknowns of my future loomed over me.

The chime of the door announced the arrival of a young couple. The woman, around five or six months pregnant, beamed at Gloria and walked over to our table. "Gloria, it's great to see you!"

The woman's husband went to order their drinks.

Gloria stood up and hugged her. "Chrissy, this is my friend Lianna. Lianna, meet Chrissy. Her husband John is over there at the counter."

My heart sank as I realized this was Kincaid's client, the one who had been calling him almost every day. "Nice to meet you," I said, trying to keep my voice steady.

"How are the renovations going?" Gloria asked. "Will everything be done before the baby comes?"

Chrissy rolled her eyes. "It isn't looking good. I fired my contractor today. Found out he's a complete lowlife."

I tightened my grip on the handle of my tea mug but kept my face carefully neutral. "That's terrible. What happened?"

Chrissy dragged a chair over to our table and sat down. "It has to do with Heather. From class?"

Gloria nodded, and I realized Chrissy and Heather were both students in the class Gloria taught.

"Heather told me the most shockingly horrible story about Kincaid Gillette," Chrissy said, her tone serious.

My frown deepened. This couldn't be good. The cozy café seemed less welcoming as the buzz of the other customers faded into the background.

Gloria's glaze flicked briefly toward me. "What did she say?"

"You know she was pregnant last fall and lost her baby, right? Well, I just found out Kincaid Gillette was the father. When she lost her baby, he just dumped her like a bag of trash and kicked her out of his house! The poor woman was devastated. I can't believe he'd be such a complete piece of you-know-what."

"Oh, Chrissy. No," Gloria said, her brow furrowing. "That's not what happened."

Chrissy frowned. "No? What do you mean, 'no?'"

Gloria reached out and patted Chrissy's hand. "Heather's feeding you a pile of bullcrap. She probably made the entire thing up."

Chrissy snatched her hand away and looked at Gloria as though she was affronted. "How can you say that about her? I thought she was your friend?"

"Because it's true," Gloria said.

"Heather has a reputation for being less than honest," I interjected. The more people who told Chrissy the truth, the better.

Doubt started to seep in, and Chrissy looked confused. John walked up just then and set a cup of tea in front of her.

"Heather is a liar," Gloria said baldly. "Ask anyone. The woman can't seem to help herself."

"I hate to be the one to tell you," I said, "but Heather lied to you about being pregnant. She never was. She lied to a lot of people about it, including Kincaid. She even tricked him into proposing because he believed she was carrying their child."

Chrissy's face twisted in disbelief. She glanced at her husband, who placed a calming hand on her shoulder. She reached up and held on tight as she jutted out her chin. "No," she said firmly. "That can't be true. I don't believe it. Heather wouldn't lie to me that way." She shifted in her chair as she prepared to stand.

"Wait," John said. "Let's hear them out. I want to know what they have to say."

Reluctantly, Chrissy settled back into her chair. Clearly, she didn't want to hear us say anything negative about Heather, but at least she was staying.

"As rumor has it," Gloria said, "Heather was caught when she went out drinking with some friends. The bartender refused to serve her because she was pregnant, so she told him she wasn't and never had been. She was pretty wasted by then. Apparently, her drinking friends already knew about the lie because they confirmed it."

John set his jaw. The man's eyes bugged out and he looked like he was about to burst a blood vessel.

"That's insane." Chrissy shook her head as tears welled in her eyes. She clearly didn't want to believe what she was hearing. "Are you absolutely certain? Why would she do something like that?"

A woman sitting at a nearby table stood and came over. "I'm sorry for eavesdropping and butting my nose in, but I overheard everything you were saying."

Chrissy scowled at her.

The woman hesitated, but then said, "It's just—I wanted to confirm what they're telling you. I was at the bar that night, too. The night Heather got wasted and blabbed about how she'd tricked Kincaid. That whole story was pretty messed up, if you ask me. Heather's a pathological liar. I don't know how she lives with herself. It's why we're no longer friends."

Chrissy's face suddenly crumpled, and tears streamed down her cheeks. "I can't believe she would lie to me like that. She had me totally fooled."

John squeezed her shoulder gently. "It seems like she fooled a lot of people."

"But I already fired Kincaid," Chrissy wailed. "That poor man. I told him I'd ruin him."

My eyes went wide. Is that why Kincaid had been drunk tonight?

"It's not too late to make amends with him," John said, stroking her back soothingly. "I'll call him first thing in the morning to apologize and ask him to come back. This isn't the end of the world."

"You could sweeten the pot by offering him a bonus," Gloria suggested.

"That's an excellent idea," John said, nodding. "I'll do it."

Gloria shot me a sly wink, and I managed a small smile despite my exhaustion. Tonight had taken a lot out of me, and I was ready for some much-needed rest.

As I covered my mouth to stifle a huge yawn, I apologized, "Sorry about that. I guess I should head home."

I stood, then stopped and frowned. "Wait, no, not home. I'm spending the night at my parents' place." Geez. Mom would have freaked if I'd hadn't shown back up at their place and slept through her phone calls.

Gloria stood and hugged me. "Bye, Lianna. And congratulations," she said softly so the others wouldn't hear.

I let out a short laugh. "Thanks. I really appreciate all your help tonight."

"Come to my yoga class for expectant moms. I have a morning one and an evening one." She tipped her head toward Chrissy. "I'd suggest the evening one if you want to avoid Heather and all the drama that's about to unfold."

As I drove to my parents' house, thoughts of Kincaid consumed me. His drunken behavior, Heather's lies, and Chrissy's hasty decision to fire him all left a sour taste in my mouth. I couldn't help but wonder how many others had been hurt by Heather's deceit.

It struck me that Paul's lies had hurt me in similar ways, but unlike Kincaid's drunken response, I'd buried my feelings under a facade of calm and turned to chamomile tea.

Pulling into my parents' driveway, the events of the evening left me feeling raw, vulnerable, and emotionally exhausted. Kincaid's situation had hit a little too close to home, and I struggled to process it all.

But then I thought of Gloria and the unexpected bond that had formed between us. Despite everything that had happened, I felt grateful for the new friendship that had emerged from the chaos. She had a remarkable talent for cutting through drama and telling it like it is.

As I contemplated the possibility of fixing what was broken between Kincaid and me, I couldn't help but feel hopeful. After all, if Gloria and I could form an alliance amidst the turmoil, maybe there was a chance for Kincaid and me to do the same.

42

BITTER AND SWEET

Kincaid

Making the chocolate ganache cake took longer than I'd expected, but that was probably for the best since I was sober now. Well, mostly sober. At least I'd been able to drop my yinzer accent, so that was a good sign. I wished I hadn't gotten drunk tonight. My throat felt parched, and my friends' voices echoed in my ears.

I was thirsty as hell, too, and my stomach felt like I'd drunk a vat of acid.

Dante shot me an assessing look and then handed me a bottle of Gatorade. "This will help. A little. Electrolytes."

I downed about half of it and then screwed the lid back on. Scrubbing my hand over my face, my palm rasped against my stubble.

I needed to do this. Face the consequences. Kiss up. Make amends. Eat crow. Whatever it took, I had to do it as soon as possible. I hated being in this state and hurting Lianna.

Dante grabbed a sheet of white cardboard and assembled it into a cake box that he handed me. I slid the perfect cake inside. The cake I hoped would be the "in" I needed for the apology she deserved.

I carried the box to my truck, placed it on the passenger side floor, and drove up the hill to Lianna's place. Her lights were off. Was she asleep? Checking my watch, I saw that it was almost eleven. Normally, she'd be getting ready for bed by now, but maybe she'd gone to sleep early.

Should I wait until morning or knock on her door now?

I stepped out of my truck and walked up her driveway, peeking through the garage door window to check if her car was there. It wasn't. Where the hell was she?

I called her, and it rang a few times before going to voicemail. At least she hadn't blocked my calls, which was a good sign. But why hadn't she answered?

I didn't leave a message. I needed to talk to her, see her, and beg for her forgiveness. I stared at my phone, willing it to ring, but it remained silent.

I wracked my brain, trying to remember where she'd said she would be. Oh, that's right. She went to her parents' place for dinner. Maybe they knew where she was now.

Fortunately, Lianna had given me her mom's number a while ago. Checking the time, I saw it was almost midnight. Late, sure, but Mrs. Alverson might still be up. Besides, this was an emergency.

I called her number and heard Anne Alverson's tentative voice on the other end. "Hello?"

"Hi. This is Kincaid. I hope I didn't wake you. I'm calling because I stopped by Lianna's house, and she isn't there. I'm worried about her."

"Oh, honey. Don't worry. She's fine. She's spending the night here." She let out a yawn. "We're helping her drop her car off at the shop in the morning. I thought she told you."

Damn. "I completely forgot. Can I talk to her? I sort of screwed things up between us tonight."

"I don't think that's a good idea right now," Anne said. "She's exhausted, and she has a long day tomorrow. Besides, I don't want to get in the middle of whatever's going on between the two of you."

This meant Lianna had told her *something* about what had happened between us tonight, but not everything; otherwise, Anne wouldn't be talking to me. I thought for a moment. "What about tomorrow morning? Would it be okay if I stop by before she leaves for work?"

"You'd have to be here early," she said doubtfully. "Lianna needs to leave no later than seven."

"I'll be there at six."

Anne chuckled. "Make it six-thirty. You can join us for breakfast."

We ended the call, and I stared down at my phone. If I wanted to get this right, there was one more thing I still needed to do. I made another call.

AFTER COMPLETING ONE FINAL ERRAND, I arrived home, but I tossed and turned all night.

Mick attempted to sleep beside me, but my restlessness prompted him to nip my arm and leave the room in a huff.

The following morning, I woke up early, showered, shaved, and dressed in jeans and a collared shirt. By six-fifteen, I stood on the Alversons' doorstep with a cake box in hand. I rang the bell and waited five minutes before anyone answered.

Anne Alverson answered the door in a pink fluffy bathrobe. "You're early. You didn't even give me a chance to dress." Her gaze flicked to the cake box, but she didn't inquire about it.

"I'm sorry, Anne. May I speak with Lianna?"

"No, but you can come in and wait for her in the kitchen while she finishes getting ready for work."

Anne led the way, her white slippers scuffing against the hardwood floors, and I followed meekly.

"Have a seat," she instructed. "Coffee?"

"Yes, please," I said, pulling out a chair.

"Not that one, that's Ben's seat. Sit here," she directed, pointing to the one with its back to the door.

I did as I was told, and a moment later, she placed a cup of coffee in front of me.

Heavy footsteps approached from behind. "Kincaid? What are you doing here?" Ben Alverson, dressed in a neat gray suit, strode into the kitchen. He cast a cautious glance at me. Anne handed him a cup of coffee, and he sat down across from me.

I cleared my throat, then looked him in the eye. "I'm here to ask your daughter for her hand in marriage… if she'll have me."

Ben looked stunned. He glanced at his wife, who merely shrugged. He took a sip of coffee. "Now?"

I nodded resolutely. "That's the plan."

Ben sat silently staring down at the table as he sipped his coffee.

"What's in the box?" Anne asked, gesturing toward the white cake box I'd set on the table.

"A peace offering," I replied.

"Is it chocolate?" Ben asked, sniffing the air. "Smells like chocolate. Dark chocolate? Lianna loves dark chocolate."

I smiled. "It's dark chocolate."

"Perfect." Ben nodded decisively. "Lianna says dark chocolate is the perfect combination of bitter and sweet. She'll love it."

High heels clicked on the hardwood floor, and I swiveled to watch Lianna approach. She wore a slim gray skirt and a pink blouse paired with gray high heels. She looked stunning.

Her eyes were glued to her phone, and she didn't even notice me at first. "Kincaid called me last night, but I slept through it. That chamomile tea really did the trick."

I braced myself for the worst, but her frown softened when she spotted me. "What are you doing here?" she asked, her tone less accusatory than I'd expected.

"I screwed up last night, and I came to ask you to forgive me."

Lianna's eyes flicked between me and her parents, but then

she turned back to me, her expression serious. "I happened to run into Chrissy Murphy last night. She told me that she fired you because of something Heather told her about you."

I winced. "Yeah."

"Fired?" Ben's voice cracked on the word.

I nodded, feeling the weight of Heather's lies. "That's why I took your news so badly last night. First, Chrissy threatened to ruin me, and then Heather called and tried to blackmail me. She said she'd tell Chrissy the truth if I agreed to take her back. Of course, I refused."

Lianna's expression turned to one of disgust. "Heather is loathsome," she said, shaking her head.

I couldn't help but grin at Lianna's swift support. "That, she is."

"I was at Loco Mocha with Gloria when we ran into Chrissy," Lianna said, a hint of satisfaction in her voice.

Surprised, I raised my eyebrows at that.

"She set Chrissy straight about Heather and told her Heather lied about you. John was there too, so they both know the truth now."

I gave my head a hard shake, shocked by the news. "They do?"

Lianna nodded. "John plans to call you this morning to apologize and ask you to come back. Gloria suggested he give you a bonus, so don't accept the first offer."

I stared at her, stunned. "You're amazing. Did you know that?"

She gave me an impish grin. "I know."

I glanced down at the table and my gaze caught on the cake box. I'd gotten sidetracked. I was here for something more important than my business, and I needed to stay focused.

"I brought you something," I said, pushing the cake box closer to her.

"A peace offering?" She opened it, and the words 'I Love You' in icing stared back at her. Her face softened, and I felt a spark of hope.

"You didn't seem quite so certain about that last night," she said.

My chest tightened. This was it. The moment for me to bare my soul and tell her everything that was in my heart.

I took a breath. "What you heard last night was my fear talking," I admitted. "I was afraid of trusting someone completely. Afraid of being deceived. It was a mistake. I regret every word I said. Please don't let one screw-up ruin what we have."

She blinked a few times and hesitated. "I've been hurt, too. Lied to. Deceived. It's hard for me to trust."

"I know. But we can work on that together."

Lianna took a deep breath. "I'm willing to try."

My heart lifted, but it sank again as she spoke the next words. "But there's something else. I went to confront Paul last night."

My stomach turned. Where was she going with this? "And?"

"Gloria was there, and I found out the truth. Paul had a vasectomy before we even met and hid it from me."

I was stunned. "What the hell?"

Ben cursed.

Anne shot to her feet. "What a complete asshole." Her eyes narrowed. "Maybe I should go over there and leave a flaming bag of dog poop on his front porch."

"Mom!"

Anne frowned. "I wouldn't actually do it, but wouldn't that be a sight? Paul with flaming dog crap all over those five-hundred-dollar shoes of his?"

I turned back to Lianna. "That man is a complete lowlife."

Lianna nodded. "I know. It's over between us, but his lies keep coming back to hurt me." She met my gaze. "Like the way Heather's lies keep hurting you."

I reached for her hand. "I'm sorry."

She looked at me, and her expression softened. "Thank you."

I shifted forward on the edge of my chair, determined to get us back on track. Lianna's forgiveness was crucial, and I had to make sure she knew how much I loved her.

"There's one moment of my life I wish I could go back and change, and it's how I reacted when you told me you were pregnant last night. I love you, Lianna. Please believe me.

"We've both been hurt. Both have been deceived. But that makes us who we are now. We're better when we're together. Stronger. It's like we're the two broken halves that make an invincible whole. Like the Japanese art Kintsugi, where they put broken pieces of pottery back together with lacquer and powdered gold. The bonds make it stronger, and beautifully unique. Like us."

"Kincaid, that's beautiful," Lianna said, swaying closer to me, but then pulling back as if remembering herself. She glanced at her mother. "What do you think?"

"He seems sincere," Anne said, her eyes twinkling as she smiled. "Plus, he baked you a cake."

"Can we eat it even if she says no?" Ben quipped.

Lianna furrowed her brow. "What do you mean, 'if I say no?'"

I had to act fast before Ben spilled the beans. "Do you love me?" I blurted out.

Lianna sighed, her eyes softening as she smiled at me. "Unfortunately, yes," she teased. "But it's against my better judgment."

Those words were like music. Light. Joy. Perfection.

I grinned and dropped to one knee, taking her hand. "Lianna Alverson, will you do me the honor of becoming my wife?"

She froze, staring at me for a moment, then broke into a wide grin. "Seriously, Kincaid? You're asking me to marry you while kneeling on the floor in my parents' kitchen? Do you have any idea how adorable that is?"

I raised my eyebrows, waiting for her answer. "Adorable enough for you to say yes?"

She abruptly sat in the chair and faced me. Our eyes locked, and she asked me the question weighing on her mind. "Tell me the truth. This isn't just because I'm pregnant, is it?"

I shook my head. "That fact might be speeding up the process, but I realized a month ago that I want to marry you. I love you, Lianna. I want to spend the rest of my life with you."

Lianna's smile widened, and she leaned in closer to me.

"Do you love him?" Ben asked. "That's what I want to know."

She didn't glance away from me. She simply kept smiling. "Absolutely and completely."

"That's all I needed to hear. You both have my blessing." Ben leaned back and smiled, looking extremely satisfied.

Anne was beaming. When Lianna glanced at her, Anne nodded aggressively. "What he said."

Lianna smirked at them. "Then I guess it's official. We're getting married."

I took out the ring box from my pocket and opened it. The square-cut diamond sparkled under the kitchen lights, and Lianna gasped when she saw it.

"Kincaid—it's perfect. Where did you get it?" she asked, taking it from me.

I saw the brief hesitation in her eyes, and I quickly reassured her. "No, no. Baby—like I said, I've been thinking about this for the past month. I spotted this ring at the jewelry store in Sewickley and called in a favor last night so I could pick it up this morning. This is yours. No one else's."

Lianna threw her arms around me, enveloping me in a warm embrace. As she pulled away, she extended her left hand, and I carefully slipped the ring on her finger. It fit perfectly, as if it had been made for her.

She looked up at me with a smile that could light up the whole room. "Well, Kincaid, you knocked me up. I guess you're stuck with me now."

I chuckled. "Hey, it's not like I had a choice. You were just too irresistible."

Lianna let out a laugh, the sound making my heart sing. "There's no getting away from me now."

We shared another kiss, the kind that makes you feel like you're floating on air. And in that moment, I knew that we were both in this for the long haul.

"I love you, Kincaid Gillette," she whispered against my lips.

43

HAPPY BIRTHDAY!

Lianna

February - Seven months later

I let out a deep moan, feeling the tension in my lower back finally release under Kincaid's strong hands.

"Am I pushing too hard?" he asked, his beard tickling my neck.

"Not at all. In fact, you could push harder," I said, leaning forward to give him better access to my aching muscles.

We sat cozied up in my living room, surrounded by plush cushions and warm blankets. The vibrant flowers Kincaid had gifted me for Valentine's Day adorned the coffee table, adding a touch of beauty to the dreary February day outside. When he'd handed me the bouquet, he'd playfully announced he'd "removed the jaggers" so I wouldn't get pricked by any thorns. I'd stifled a grin, secretly delighted by his use of the Pittsburgh slang word. Now as I gazed out the large picture window, the bare trees swaying in the wind, I couldn't help but feel grateful for this unexpected romance in my life.

Kincaid's strong hands worked their magic, massaging the base of my spine with just the right amount of pressure. I felt my muscles slowly begin to unwind.

"Oh, that's perfect," I moaned, my eyes closing in pleasure.

The baby was one day overdue, and I had been counting down the days until my due date for what felt like an eternity. It's the program manager in me. I tend to fixate on deadlines. Going past my due date had left me feeling restless and anxious.

But in that moment, with Kincaid's hands working wonders on my aching body, I felt a sense of contentment wash over me.

"Ah." I let out a satisfied sigh. "Even better." I arched my back and my fingers brushed against the chain I wore around my neck as my engagement ring and wedding band slipped out of my shirt. My swollen fingers had grown too big for them.

"I hope my poor hands will shrink back down to normal size after the baby comes," I sighed.

Just then, my phone chimed with a notification. I picked it up off the coffee table and read the message.

"Who is it?"

"Zoey." I sighed. "She wants to know if I'm in labor yet. She's about to get in the bathtub and she's convinced I'll call her the moment she leans back and relaxes."

> Me: Not yet. Enjoy your bath.

"I need to lean back." I was having trouble getting comfortable.

Kincaid moved his hands away, and I sat back against the sofa, but my lower back immediately started to ache again. I let out a frustrated sigh.

I so wanted to be done with this.

With my large belly poking out—completely unobstructed—Mick saw his opportunity. He jumped onto the back of the sofa and crept over my shoulder to perch on my belly. For some reason, this was his new favorite spot.

He began purring contentedly, staring me in the eyes and giving me one of his slow blinks.

I let out a soft chuckle. "What will he do after the baby's born and my belly shrinks?"

Kincaid scratched Mick under the chin. "He'll adapt. My guess is that he'll switch to standing on your shoulders." He relaxed into the sofa next to me.

My back still hurt.

I shifted uncomfortably, and Mick stopped purring.

The cat tensed—or was that my belly?

I caressed my baby bump, noticing how firm it was. "Kincaid?"

"Lianna?" he mimicked in a teasing tone as he stared at his phone screen.

"I'm pretty sure I just had a contraction. In fact, I'm beginning to think my back hurts because I'm in labor."

Kincaid faced me, his entire body going tense in almost exactly the same way Mick's just had. He stared at my belly. "Are you sure?"

"As sure as I can be since this is the first time I've ever had a baby."

Kincaid bolted to his feet.

As the next contraction hit, I took deep breaths, trying to focus on the sensation and the breathing techniques I'd learned in childbirth class. Mick meowed in concern and nudged his head under my hand.

"Thanks, buddy," I whispered, scratching behind his ears.

Kincaid met my eyes, his mouth tense. "How far apart are they?"

"The contractions? This is the first one I've counted, so I'm not sure."

He sat back down abruptly, then stood again. "This could take a while, right?"

"I believe so. You seem agitated." My program manager skills kicked in, and I decided to find a task to occupy him. "Why don't you go check the list on the refrigerator and make sure we have everything ready."

"Good idea." He tugged at his beard and then headed for the kitchen.

Another contraction hit. I fumbled for my phone to check the time. Four minutes since the last one.

Kincaid walked back in staring at the list. "This says we should head to the hospital when the contractions are five minutes apart."

Kincaid walked back in, staring at the list. "This says we should head to the hospital when the contractions are five minutes apart."

"Four?" His eyes went wide.

"It's time for you to warm up the car and then send that group text letting everyone know. I guess Zoey won't get her bubble bath after all."

THREE HOURS LATER, I collapsed back in the delivery chair utterly exhausted, but unable to stop smiling as I was rewarded by the glorious sound of a soft, mewling whimper.

"Is that her?" I asked, my voice hoarse.

Dr. Walker—the same doctor who had delivered me thirty years ago—cradled my daughter in his arms, holding her up high enough for me to see. "It is. She looks great. We'll get her into your arms in just a moment."

Kincaid's face was wet with tears as he smiled at me and squeezed my hand. "She's perfect. Just perfect."

Someone—a nurse—placed my swaddled baby in my arms. She was lighter than I'd expected. Our cat Mick weighed more than this tiny bundle. Joy surged through me like a freight train as the miracle of this moment overwhelmed me. All I could do was stare at this perfect being Kincaid and I had created.

I sniffled back tears. Maybe I did believe in miracles after all.

I looked up and met Kincaid's gorgeous green eyes. Eyes that were filled with so much joy and love that I could drown in them.

Our baby moved, and my attention snapped back to her as she blinked up at me with her gorgeous, deep blue eyes. "She's perfect."

Dr. Walker appeared next to me. "Congratulations. Have you chosen a name yet?"

"Harper," I said. "Her name's Harper Gillette."

"Happy birthday, Harper Gillette," Dr. Walker said, stroking a hand down her swaddled back. "We're glad you could join us."

As I looked down at Harper, I knew that our lives would never be the same. But I was excited for the journey ahead and couldn't wait to see what adventures lay in store for our new family.

EPILOGUE

Kincaid

It was a breathtaking May evening, and the warm sun had dipped below the horizon, painting the sky with a vivid array of pink and orange hues. The grill was sizzling, filling the air with a mouthwatering aroma.

Life was good.

I carefully lifted the burgers off the grate, their juices sizzling and popping as they made contact with the plate. I turned to hand it to Courtney.

Behind her, Lianna removed Harper's rosebud mouth from her nipple and adjusted her shirt. As she lifted the sleeping baby to her shoulder and gently patted her back, I couldn't help but take a moment to appreciate the perfect image my wife made against the stunning sunset. The sun's last rays cast long shadows across the backyard, where the pink azaleas I'd planted next to the back porch I'd built last fall were in bloom.

"I'm famished. Those burgers smell heavenly," Lianna said, breaking my reverie as she placed Harper in the bassinet I'd set up.

While Lianna's back was turned, Courtney quickly snatched a

burger and set it on Lianna's plate, and I served her some crispy French fries, arranging everything perfectly before Lianna turned back to the table.

Lianna's eyes lit up when she saw the full plate of food. "You two are so good about keeping me fed." She patted her belly. "Nursing gives me an enormous appetite." She grabbed the bottle of Heinz ketchup and squirted some next to her fries.

"That's because we know how hangry you can get," Courtney said, tossing her hair back, the diamond on her finger glittering in the fading light.

I grabbed a beer from the cooler, enjoying the chill of the can against my palm. "I have a surprise for you, love," I said, taking a seat across from Lianna. "We have an anniversary of sorts. It's been one year since our paddle match. I booked a court for tomorrow. I might even win this time. You haven't played since Harper was born, so that should level the playing field." Of course, I'd lose. Lianna was a killer on the court. But the point wasn't to win. It was to spend time with the woman I loved.

Lianna raised an eyebrow. "I'm undefeated. Are you sure your ego can handle another crushing loss?"

Mick meowed at me through the screen door, his soft meow adding to the peaceful evening's sounds.

Lianna shot me a confident grin. "Even Mick agrees with me."

"The two of you need to have more faith in both my paddle skills and my self-esteem. I can handle losing. The question is, can you?"

"Ooh, those sound like fighting words," Courtney said. "Lianna, are you going to let him talk to you like that?"

Lianna narrowed her eyes at me. "Let's make this interesting. Let's raise the stakes. If I win, you finally have to make that Bittersweet Chocolate Soufflé you keep promising me."

I considered it. "That, I can do. And if I win, you have to come home by six every evening next week."

"High stakes," she said, narrowing her eyes. "But I love that we both win, no matter what."

"Deal?"
"Deal."

———

291

AFTERWORD

(Recipes are included and follow this section)

Paul and Heather's Lies

The storyline of From Bitter to Sweet revolves around two lies that had significant consequences for my characters, Lianna and Kincaid. Both lies were self-serving to the individuals who told them and caused long-lasting emotional and psychological damage to those affected.

Since the entire premise of the book may seem far-fetched, I wanted to provide some context.

Regrettably, these storylines are inspired by real events. A friend similar to Lianna struggled for years to have a baby. Her doctor couldn't find any significant reasons why she wasn't conceiving. Their marriage ended in divorce, and a few months later she unexpectedly and miraculously found herself pregnant. This situation left her with many questions and few answers.

Her ex-husband was a skilled liar and gaslighter, which is why I referenced the movie "Gaslight" in the book. He subtly undermined her confidence and made her doubt herself and her choices. Given his devious mind and his experience in computer security and risk management, I have no doubt that he manipulated the lab results. I'm not suggesting he hacked medical data, but he may have found other ways to circumvent it, such as doctoring a report before the doctor received it.

Similar to Lianna in my story, my friend had given up on the possibility of becoming a mother and decided to focus on other aspects of her life. The unexpected pregnancy brought joy but it also forced her to reexamine her former marriage and the ways her ex-husband had undermined her confidence. Even now, she is uncertain about what was true and what was a lie. She still struggles to overcome the emotional toll of her ex-husband's lies and manipulations, but she's making wonderful progress.

Kincaid's storyline came from merging two stories together. One involved a friend whose story is complex and cannot be easily summarized, but it is enough to say that the loss of his daughter (who was later discovered not to be his biological child) following his divorce left him struggling with depression and trust issues.

The other half of Kincaid's story came from overhearing a woman at a bar tell her friends she'd lied to her boyfriend about being pregnant. I was happy to see that at least one of her friends was outraged. That moment stuck in my mind, and I felt compelled to include it in my book.

YINZER GLOSSARY

Although I hear the Pittsburgh accent fairly frequently, I'm not very good at channeling it. Thank you so much for Pittsburgh native Tom Roberts of his help in getting dialogue to sound right. He surveyed his neighbors as well, so thank you to everyone living on Spring Hill. I tried to be careful and portray this unique accent as accurately as possible. Any errors are mine n'at.

As a general note of interest, although I only occasionally hear a heavy Pittsburgh accent, I frequently hear certain Pittsburgh slang words such as nebby, jagoff, buggy, jaggers, gum bans, yinz, and Kennywood's open.

Speak Like a Yinzer: A Guide to Pittsburgh Phonetics and Pronunciation

Yinzer English - Standard English
    'er - there
    aht d'air - out there
    a'yor - of your

aht - out
ahta - out of
at - that
at'll - that'll
bafwoor - before
basemen' - basement
buggy - grocery cart/shopping cart
cahmin - coming
caht - cut
corntine - quarentine
thuh - the
dahn - down
dahntahn - downtown
dohrk - dark
dawr - door
dem - them
dems - them
der's - there's
dere - there
dey're - they're
dis - this
dohwn't - don't
durway - doorway
duwr - door
existin' - existing
fuhters - footers
fur - for
gahta - got to/gotta
gawn - going
gawt - got
gimme - Give me
git - get
git ridda - get rid of
grinny (grinnies) - ground squirrel (Eastern Chipmunk)

gumbans - rubber bands

haus - house

heer - hair

inta - into

jag-wire - jaguar

jaggers - thorns

jagoff - jerk (rarely used affectionately)

jus' - just

keller - color

n'at - And that/and all that

nebby - nosey/intrusive

neighborhoot - neighborhood

awtah - ought to

pourin' - pouring

projec' - project

red up (sometime redd up) - Clean

rhul - Real/really

rhul good - Really good/Very well

serio - stereo

shauer - shower

shoor - sure

skirls - squirrels

still mills - steel mills

stoohrm - storm

stoor - store

summon - someone

tuh - to

tahl - towel or tile (use your context clues!)

tahrs - towers or tires

warsh - wash

watter - water

worsh - wash

woll - we'll

woof - wolf

y'inz or yinz - You (singluar/plural) or Y'all

yeh - yeah

yer - your (first person singular)

yins can wedge a chair n'at - you can wedge a chair under it (the doorknob)

yinz're - you're

RECIPES

Thank you for joining Kincaid on his culinary adventures throughout the novel. Whether he was whipping up a delectable dessert or crafting a savory main course, his passion for food was palpable on every page. For those who have been following the series, you may recognize a few of the recipes that were mentioned. For your enjoyment, the following are the exclusive recipes that first made their appearance in From Bitter to Sweet. Get your aprons ready and prepare to indulge in some delicious dishes!

CHEESE SOUFFLÉ

Level: Moderate
    Prep Time: 20 min.
    Cooking Time: 35 min
    Total Time: 55 minutes
    Serves: 6

Special requirements 1 1/2 quart soufflé dish (On a soufflé dish, the sides of the dish are smooth and perfectly vertical so the soufflé can rise properly)

Ingredients:

- 1/4 cup plus 2 tablespoons freshly grated Parmigiano-Reggiano cheese
- 3 tablespoons unsalted butter
- 3 tablespoons all-purpose flour
- 1 1/4 cups heavy cream
- 4 large eggs, separated, plus 3 large egg whites
- 3 tablespoons dry sherry

- 6 ounces Gruyère cheese, shredded (2 packed cups)
- 2 tablespoons sour cream
- 1 1/4 teaspoons kosher salt
- 1 teaspoon Dijon-style mustard
- 1/2 teaspoon dry mustard
- 1/4 teaspoon cayenne pepper
- 1/4 teaspoon cream of tartar

Directions:

1. Preheat the oven to 375°F. Butter a 1 1/2-quart soufflé dish and coat it with 2 tablespoons of the Parmigiano-Reggiano.
2. Pat the chicken dry with a paper towel. Salt and pepper it to taste. Dredge chicken in flour and shake off any excess.
3. In a medium saucepan, melt the butter. Stir in the flour to make a roux or paste. Gradually whisk in the cream and bring it to a boil over medium heat, whisking. Reduce the heat to low and cook for about 3 minutes, constantly whisking it. It should be very thick when it is done.
4. Transfer to a large bowl and let it cool enough so that it won't immediately curdle the eggs when you add them. Stir in the egg yolks (not the whites), sherry, sour cream, salt, Dijon mustard, dry mustard, cayenne, Gruyère, and the remaining 1/4 cup of Parmigiano-Reggiano.
5. Put the 7 egg whites into a large, room temperature, stainless steel bowl. Add the cream of tartar. Use an electric mixer to beat the whites until firm peaks form. Use a rubber spatula to fold one-third of the whites into the soufflé base, then gently fold in the remaining whites until no streaks remain.

6. Scrape the mixture into the prepared soufflé dish. Run your thumb around the inside rim of the dish to wipe away any drips. Bake for about 35 minutes, until the soufflé is golden brown and puffed. Serve right away.

Note: This dish does not keep well. All the puffy bits flatten out.

BITTERSWEET CHOCOLATE SOUFFLÉ

Level: Moderate
Prep Time: 20 min
Cooking Time: 35 min
Total Time: 55 minutes
Serves: 6

Special requirements: 8 4-ounce ramekins. (Use ones with smooth vertical sides so the the soufflé can rise properly)

Ingredients:

- ½ cup (114 grams) unsalted butter (1 stick), softened, plus more for coating the ramekins
- 4 tablespoons (50 grams) granulated sugar, plus more for coating the ramekins
- 8 ounces (225 grams) bittersweet chocolate (60 to 65 percent cacao), finely chopped
- 6 eggs, separated, at room temperature
- Pinch fine sea salt

- ½ teaspoon cream of tartar

Directions:

1. Heat oven to 350 degrees. Coat 8 (4-ounce) ramekins with butter and sprinkle it with 2 tablespoons granulated sugar, then tap out the excess. Make sure sugar covers all the butter on the sides of the dish. Place the ramekins on a baking sheet.
2. In a medium bowl, melt chocolate and butter over a pot of simmering water. Remove from heat and let it stand for three minutes, then whisk in egg yolks and salt while it is still warm.
3. Using an electric mixer, beat egg whites and cream of tartar at medium speed until the mixture is fluffy and holds very soft peaks. Gradually add the sugar, beating until the whites hold stiff peaks and look glossy.
4. Gently stir one-fourth of egg white mixture into chocolate mixture. Gently fold in the remaining whites, then transfer batter to the ramekins. Rub your thumb around the inside edge of the dish to create about a ¼-inch space between the dish and the soufflé mixture. Slide the baking sheet with the ramekins into the oven.
5. Bake at 350° for 15 minutes or until puffy and set. (Do not open oven door while the bake.) You can adjust the cooking time… less time for a runnier soufflé and more for a firmer soufflé. Remove from oven and sprinkle with powdered sugar. Serve immediately or within 30 minutes of removing it from the oven.
6. Note: This dish does not keep well. All the puffy bits flatten out.

DANTE'S GOURMET MAC AND CHEESE AND GRITS

Level: Easy to Moderate
Prep Time: 20 min
Cooking Time: 40 min
Total Time: 60 minutes
Serves: 8

Ingredients:

- Kosher salt
- 1-1/2 cups dry orecchiette pasta (small, flat, round pasta)
- 1 tsp olive oil
- 1/3 cup plus 3 Tbsp butter, divided
- 1/3 cup (1.7 ounces) all-purpose flour
- 1/2 teaspoon nutmeg
- 1 teaspoon onion powder
- 1/2 teaspoon salt
- 1/4 teaspoon dried mustard
- 1/4 cup long-cooking grits
- 4 medium garlic cloves, finely minced, (or 4 Tbsp minced garlic packed in oil)

•6 cups milk, divided

•3⁄4 lb sharp cheddar cheese, shredded (I used an aged 5-year-old variety)

•1⁄2 lb gruyere cheese, shredded 1⁄2 cup asiago cheese, shredded

•1⁄2 cup Fontina cheese, shredded

•1 teaspoon black pepper

•2 to 3 cups fresh breadcrumbs (or use 1 Cup Panko breadcrumbs

Directions:

1. Adjust oven rack to middle position and preheat oven to 350°F. Bring 2 quarts water with 2 tablespoons salt to a rolling boil in a large saucepan over high heat. Add orecchiette and cook until barely al dente (follow package instructions for timing). Drain and toss with olive oil. Set aside.

2. 2.Meanwhile, mix all the shredded cheeses together in a large bowl, set aside.

3. 3.Melt 1/3 cup butter in a large heavy saucepan or Dutch oven over medium-high heat. Add flour, onion powder, salt, nutmeg, dried mustard. Cook, stirring constantly with wooden spoon, until light blond, about 3 minutes. Stir in the grits and minced garlic. Cook until fragrant—about 3 minutes.

4. 4.Slowly add 3 cups of milk in steady stream, whisking constantly. Bring it to a simmer and cook, whisking occasionally, until slightly thickened, about 7 minutes.

5. 5.Add the remaining 3 cups of milk and some of the cheese to the mixture, reserving 1-1/2 cups of the cheese for later. Whisk until smooth. Season to taste with salt and pepper. Stir in the cooked orecchiette.

6. 6.Pour half the mixture into a greased 9 by 13 baking dish. Layer with 1 cup of the remaining cheese, them put the remaining Mac and cheese mixture in the pan. Put the final 1/2 cup of cheese on top. Sprinkle the breadcrumbs over the cheese and dot with the remaining 3 Tbsp of butter.
7. 7.Bake until it is golden brown on top and bubbling, about 40 minutes. Allow to cool 10 minutes before serving.

SHRIMP SCAMPI

Level: Easy
    Prep Time: 15 min
    Cooking Time: 20 min
    Total Time: 35 minutes
    Serves: 4 to 6

Ingredients:

- 1 pound linguine
- 5 Tbsp butter, divided
- 4 Tbsp olive oil, divided, plus more for drizzling
- 2 shallots, finely diced (can substitute onions)
- 2 cloves garlic, finely minced, or 2 Tbsps minced garlic in oil
- 1 pound shrimp, peeled, de-tailed, and deveined
- Kosher salt and freshly ground black pepper
- 1/2 cup dry vermouth or 1/2 cup dry white wine (I prefer the vermouth, but either one works)
- Zest from 1 lemon

- Juice from 1 lemon (zest it first)
- 1/4 cup chopped parsley

Note: Prep all your ingredients before cooking, because this cooks fast.

Directions:

1.Boil water for the pasta. Add salt and 2 Tbsp oil. Cook the past according to the directions on the package. Drain and keep warm.

Meanwhile, in a large skillet, melt 3 tablespoons butter over medium-high heat. As soon as it foams, it is ready. Add shallots and garlic sauce until the shallots are translucent, about 3 to 4 minutes.

Season the shrimp with salt and pepper and add them to the pan and cook until they are no longer translucent, about 2 to 3 minutes.

Remove the shrimp from the pan; set aside and keep warm. Add the vermouth (or wine) and lemon juice and bring to a boil. Add lemon zest, 2 tablespoons butter, and 2 tablespoons oil. When the butter has melted, return the shrimp to the pan along with the parsley and cooked pasta. Stir well and season with salt and pepper. Drizzle over a bit more olive oil and serve immediately.

ABOUT THE AUTHOR

I'm Sheridan Jeane, and I write the **Way to a Woman's Heart** series of romcoms set in Sewickley, a small town near Pittsburgh. These books all feature my favorite things: food, books, family, and friends.
You can also check out my exciting Victorian-era romances from my **Secrets and Seduction** series. They're filled with spies, intrigue, and tender, sensual moments.

More about me?
I'm the daughter of an artist / art-therapist / professor mother and an opera-loving / computer engineer / do-it-yourself father. Growing up, I assumed parents routinely converted their garages into well-stocked art studios complete with potter's wheels, kilns, and every color of paint under the sun. Didn't every second-grader learn how to weld or nail shingles on the roof of the 2-car garage their dad built? And what about all those after-opera cast parties? Weren't they run-of-the-mill too?
No?
Go figure!
That probably explains my quirky outlook on life.

Sheridan Jeane

BOOKS BY SHERIDAN JEANE

Contemporary Romances

The Way to a Woman's Heart series - the **Coming Home** trilogy

Slow Simmer

Here's the Scoop

From Bitter to Sweet

Coming in 2024

The Way to a Woman's Heart series - the **Destination Wedding** trilogy

Too Much On My Plate

Say Cheese!

Turkish Delight

Historical Romances

Gambling On a Scoundrel

§

Secrets and Seduction series:

Lady Cecilia Is Cordially Disinvited for Christmas

(A prequel only available through my VIP club)

It Takes a Spy…

Lady Catherine's Secret

Once Upon a Spy

My Lady, My Spy

Along Came a Spy